For Aunt Diane:

Our family has been blessed to know you. You're a treasure 😊

Love
Colleen

Psalm 33:11

Dedication

For David ... so thankful to be going

through this life with you.

Misconceptions

A Suspense Novel

by

Colleen Scott

First in the Missteps Series

Castle Gate Press

Misconceptions by Colleen Scott
Published by Castle Gate Press
244 E Glendale Rd
Saint Louis, Missouri 63119
www.CastleGatePress.com

Copyright © 2016 by Colleen Scott
All rights reserved

This book or parts thereof may not be reproduced in any form, stored in a retrieval system, or transmitted in any form by any means—electronic, mechanical, photocopy, recording, or otherwise—without prior written permission of the publisher, except as provided by United States of America copyright law.

This is a work of fiction. Any similarity to actual people, organizations, and/or events is purely coincidental.

Cover Designer: Andrea Orlic, Artrocity
Watermark Designer: Nicolas Raymond, www.freestock.ca

ISBN 978-0-9904399-2-9

Chapter One

Dominique Sherwood had her instructions: get the story, then get out. She stared at the solid oak door. Did she have the guts to open it and start living a lie?

Her boss's words still rang fresh in her mind, but Stew hadn't pulled any punches when he gave her the assignment. *This is the opportunity you've been waiting for, Dominique. But you only have one chance. Your angle on the story is to find out why southern Ohio has a higher birth rate. Why are these women able to conceive when others around the country can't? If you can't handle it, I'll find someone who can.*

She hated lying, always had. Maybe the life of an undercover TV news reporter wasn't for her. No. This was the career she chose, and it included undercover work. She had to do this. She *would* do this. She grasped the brass doorknob, opened the door, and walked into the consultation room of Valley Memorial Hospital.

A dusty fake plant sat in the corner, and the small room smelled of burnt coffee. Two people sat at a brown Formica table. A bulky woman with a head of thin, dull, brown hair wore an expression that reminded Dominique of a withered grape. The attractive man across from her wore a knee-length, bleached white coat and possessed an incredible smile.

"You must be Dominique Sherwood," the caustic woman said.

"Yes, I am."

"You're late."

"Please accept my apology." No sense arguing with a bitter woman. Dominique settled in a chair and took a deep breath to organize her thoughts. She tucked a stray hair behind her ear. "Well, we all know who I am. Would it be too much trouble if you two introduced yourselves?"

The harsh woman cleared her throat. "I'm Penelope Nordstrom, Clinical Manager, and your acting supervisor. We spoke briefly on the phone after your interview."

"Of course." The polite smile she offered Penelope was met with a disapproving glare.

"I'm Dr. Joseph Armstrong. My friends call me Dr. Joe. It's nice to meet you, Dominique. Welcome to Valley Hospital." He flashed her a million dollar smile that sent a tingle all the way to her toes.

Her lips curved in response to Dr. Joe's gentle tone. From the kind expression radiating from his dark brown eyes to the appealing dimples that appeared on either side of his mouth when he smiled, his presence had a calming effect on her. Her shoulders relaxed, and she settled back into her seat.

"Thank you, Dr. Armstrong... Dr. Joe." She pulled a thin blue file from her attaché case. "If you don't mind, I'd like to spend a few minutes reading over this case file."

"First you're late, and now you're not prepared," Penelope said. "The administrator was impressed with your credentials, but you weren't my first choice. I hope the hospital doesn't come to regret hiring you."

Dominique bit down on her tongue. "Rest assured, that won't happen. I'm more than qualified."

"There's plenty of time for her to get acclimated." Dr. Joe pushed his chair away from the table and crossed the room to the coffee maker on the countertop. "Can I get anyone a cup of coffee or refill?"

Dominique sighed. She needed an ally, and Dr. Joe fit the bill. The fact he was attractive and kind only sweetened the deal. She opened the file with the name Emily Sanderson printed at the top of the first page. Scanning the document only added to her confusion. So much had changed in the years since she'd received her degree. Her social work minor combined with her communications major was pivotal in earning this assignment. Plus she had limited on-camera exposure and was less likely to be recognized.

After studying the file more thoroughly, a few concerns became apparent. First of all, how did a twenty-eight-year-old woman end up in a coma? Secondly, what in the world was EOT?

As if reading her mind, Dr. Joe leaned in toward her and asked, "Do you have any questions?"

He smelled so inviting—like warm sunshine after a long week of cloudy, rainy days. His deep voice held an engaging tone. She glanced at his left hand. *No ring.*

But it didn't matter. Regardless of how attractive the man, it was never a good idea to pursue a relationship while undercover.

Penelope slammed her hand on the table. "Dr. Armstrong. As per the hospital and healthcare regulations, you're not permitted to unduly influence any member of the EOT committee."

He took in a deep breath and let it out slowly. "We wouldn't want to break procedure, now, would we?"

Dominique tore her eyes away from the file, but only for a moment. "Please bear with me. This is my first day on the job." She searched the file for the patient's name. "I'm aware of all regulations, and I know I'm permitted to ask questions. Can someone please explain how Emily came to be in a coma? I didn't see this information mentioned."

Dr. Joe turned in his seat, and his eyes met Dominique's. "Emily was attacked when she was eight months pregnant," he said in a quiet and somber tone. "The perpetrators were only interested in the baby. They performed a barbaric C-section and left her for dead."

Dominique gasped.

Penelope retrieved the pen lodged behind her ear. "That's not pertinent to our meeting today. The sole purpose of this meeting is to determine what treatment, if any, will be offered."

EOT. Their meaning became clear. End of treatment. The purpose of this meeting was to decide Emily's fate. Dominique hadn't agreed to this. Her undercover assignment directed her to investigate why this county was not affected by the declining birthrate as much as the vast majority of the country, not make life and death decisions.

She pushed her chair back and stood. "I need to make a phone call."

"Sit down. We've delayed this decision far too long." Penelope removed her glasses and laid them on the table. "While the hospital sympathizes with the family, we cannot justify the expense of keeping the patient on the ventilator."

Dr. Joe sat up in his chair and leaned forward. "I acknowledge Emily's condition hasn't changed in the past seventy-two hours, but she is stable, and once her body has recovered from the trauma, she has a great chance of making a full recovery."

"You have no proof to back up your prediction. In the interim, the hospital and national health care programs are losing money. As the clinical manager,

I can't continue to warrant utilizing the hospital's funds to sustain a comatose patient. The ventilator should be disconnected immediately."

Silence hung in the room.

The woman had to be kidding! Why had she been included in this meeting? Dominique's stomach clenched, and she swallowed the lump lodged in her throat. "You're talking about ending a woman's life. Shouldn't we at least discuss the situation first?"

"It's in her file. I assumed we would all be familiar with the facts, so all we needed to do was make the decision. I have other work that requires my attention." Her disapproving gaze drifted from Dominique to Dr. Joe and back.

"As Emily's physician, I recommend we continue the current treatment plan." Dr. Joe picked up his pen and clicked it several times. "All of Emily's major organs and systems are functioning normally. It's only been five days since the attack, and while we haven't seen any drastic improvements, her condition has remained stable for the last seventy-two hours. If we remove her from the ventilator too soon, she'll die."

Dominique's opinion would make the final decision. That shouldn't be; she wasn't a doctor. "What about Emily's family? Don't they have a say?"

Penelope glared at her. "I'm going to pretend you didn't ask that question. Health care laws may have changed significantly, but there's no excuse for any licensed social worker not to be aware of the fact that the doctor in charge *is* representing the family. I would think you'd be aware of that."

Heat rushed to Dominique's cheeks. She wiped away the perspiration on her upper lip. What should she do? If she agreed that the ventilator should be turned off, Penelope would be off her back. The last thing she needed was someone checking into her credentials. But she couldn't be involved with terminating a life … not a second time.

After several long minutes of uncomfortable silence, Dominique made her decision. "I agree with Dr. Joe. Hospital administrators and government officials shouldn't be making life and death decisions, doctors should. Isn't this clear in the oath doctors take?"

Dr. Joe nodded. "First do no harm. It's the most well-known part of the Hippocratic Oath."

Penelope stood and glared at Dominique. "Your rejection of the law does not change it. This meeting is over. Ms. Sherwood, I'll see you in my office. Immediately." She grabbed her belongings and stormed out of the room.

Dominique released a long, slow breath. She had just made her first enemy. Unfortunately, the woman could annihilate her undercover assignment.

Dr. Joe grabbed his phone from his coat pocket. "I'd love to talk with you further about this case, but I need to check my messages first. I silenced my phone for this meeting. The secretary gets upset if I don't check my messages regularly." He punched several buttons, then scrolled down. "That's strange."

Dominique leaned forward. "Is everything okay?"

"I'm not sure. My brother Houston left me three messages. They're all marked urgent." He paced while he made the phone call, and soon the color drained from his face. He clicked off his cell and started picking up his things from the table, his eyes dark with worry.

"What's happened?"

He shook his head. "My brother-in-law Travis is at the police station. My nephew's been kidnapped."

Chapter Two

Travis stared at his reflection in the large two-way mirror that covered one wall of the interrogation room. The smell of stale coffee filtered in through the opened door, and the remaining three walls were in need of a fresh coat of paint. Why had they put him here? Did they think he was somehow involved in his own son's kidnapping?

He swallowed the bile in his throat and turned back to the missing person's form the investigator left on the table. He only made it to the second question before his eyes blurred.

Age of child?

Two.

Two years old. How in the world were they going to find Max? The little guy could tell people his first name, but he couldn't quite pronounce their last name yet. Instead of Montgomery, it came out as *Gomrey*.

The door swung open, and a large policewoman trudged into the room. "Do you have a current photo of Max?"

He pulled out his phone and opened the photo gallery. "You can use a digital picture, right? The only one I've got in my wallet is an old one of me, Cindy, and the girls taken six months before the boys were born." That and four maxed-out credit cards.

"Absolutely."

Travis scrolled through the photos on his phone. "Do you need one of Max by himself? Most of them have Justin in them too. They're identical twins." At her frown, he resumed his search.

He stopped at an image of Max holding up his favorite car and grinning from ear to ear. "Here. Will this work?" His hand shook as he passed his cell phone to the officer.

"Perfect." She gave him a half smile. "I'll email this to the lab. You're lucky to have such a good shot. Getting a photo out there as soon as possible is crucial."

Lucky. That was one word Travis wouldn't use to describe his life. He picked up Justin from the chair on the other side of the table. "Have you had any word on the security footage from the mall?"

"Not yet, but from what I understand, Detective Armstrong is working on it."

Houston. What would he have done without his brother-in-law? Since this nightmare had begun, Houston was the one who took control and convinced the security people at the mall to cooperate.

His brother-in-law walked through the door carrying a laptop and placed it on the wooden table next to Travis. "Are you ready to watch this?" He dropped into the chair by Travis and pecked at a few keys, then loaded the DVD.

Justin pulled on Travis's shirt. "Movie … watch movie." Travis settled him in a chair with a few quiet words. "Is that the security camera recording from the mall?" he asked Houston. "Is there anything on it we can use?"

"Let's take a look."

Travis distracted Justin with a toy car he had stashed in his pocket. His heart ached as he recalled Max playing with it on the way to the mall. Life without Max would leave a huge hole in their lives that could never be filled.

But what if the security footage was a dead end? It had to reveal something—anything. "What are the chances the camera caught anything?"

Houston swiped his hand through his hair. "Let's see what we have here." He hit the play button.

Seven minutes into the recording, Travis shot up, his heart racing. "Stop! Rewind it! I think I saw something." His abrupt movements caused Justin to start crying. Travis rubbed his back and kissed his head. "Sorry, buddy."

"Is this far enough?"

"Yeah, that's good." Travis sank back into his chair and focused on the screen like a half-starved coyote stalking its prey. People passed by, some just strolling, some rushing by, others with shopping bags dangling from their hands.

Then a man dressed in khaki shorts and a black shirt walked by the camera. He carried a small girl.

"That's it!" Travis leaned forward to get a closer look. "Dear God ... it's him."

Houston leaned in. "Where?" Skepticism tinged Houston's tone.

"Look closely. That's not a little girl. It's Max." He pointed at the stilled image.

"The woman at the mall said she saw a man in an overcoat carrying off a *boy*. One who matched Max's description."

"The guy must have taken off the overcoat and changed Max's clothes." Travis's hand slid over his son's image on the screen. "I know my son. That's Max." He tapped his son's ankles on the screen. "It's Max's socks. I would recognize them anywhere. They're blue with race cars on the side. You know how much Max loves cars." He stammered the last few words.

Houston leaned forward and squinted. "He could have easily left the overcoat somewhere. I'll have the guards look for it."

Travis grabbed onto the hope Houston offered. "He could have changed Max's clothes too. He knew everyone would be looking for a little boy."

Houston nodded. "And he dressed Max as a girl so no one would give him a second glance."

The truth slapped Travis in the face. Some monster had his little boy. The image on the screen didn't lie. Someone had kidnapped his son.

He stumbled back. "What are we going to do? He could be miles from here." *God, please protect him.* He wiped his sweaty palms on his khaki pants. Why was the room so blasted hot?

"I'll get a copy of this to the captain." Houston released the DVD from the laptop. "We'll get him back. That was a good catch, Travis."

As hope ignited, his wife rushed past the officers huddled just outside the door, talking in low tones, and she made a beeline for Justin. Cindy glared at Travis, and a scowl etched her face as she snatched Justin from the chair and placed a kiss on his temple.

She glowered at Travis with puffy, red eyes. "I don't understand, Travis. Are you such a coward you couldn't even give me the courtesy of a phone call to tell me about Max? Instead, you pawn it off on my brother. You had no right to keep this from me! How could you have let this happen?" She didn't wait for him to answer but paced the floor in front of the two-way mirror.

Houston looked up from the monitor. "Hold on, sis. We're all under a lot of stress. I volunteered to call. Travis has taken this pretty hard."

Travis stood and held his arms out to her. How he longed for the familiarity of her touch.

Instead, she backed away. "Walk me through it, Travis. How could our son just disappear?"

"I-I-I don't know. Things happened so fast. One minute he was playing on the rocket launch pad, the next minute he was gone."

"Weren't you playing with them?"

"No. I was … " His thoughts drifted back. He *hadn't* been paying attention. He had been too busy on his cell phone, trying to juggle their overdue bills.

"You were what?"

"Justin came over and asked me to play. I told him Max would play with him." He fought against the urge to start sobbing again as he relived the frantic search, the overwhelming fear, the twist in his gut when he knew Max was gone.

Cindy shot him a look that sliced to his core. She must have been biting her tongue, keeping inside the accusations she probably longed to hurl at him: *Why weren't you paying more attention? I warned you before you left that the kidnappings had been increasing. This pregnancy crisis has people going crazy. Why didn't you listen?* All questions he'd asked himself a million times since this nightmare began. He was a failure … as a husband and a father. Now Max might be lost to them forever because of his failings. With each minute that ticked by, it became more unlikely Max would be found. Their fragile marriage would shatter.

Another policewoman entered the room. "Channel WSBC is here. Do you want to give an interview?"

"No," Travis and Cindy said in unison.

Travis cleared his throat. "We're not prepared for that yet."

"Tell them to put Max's picture up and let them know he's probably dressed as a little girl," Houston said.

"What?" Cindy grabbed Travis's arm.

He filled her in on the details. As long as he lived, he would never forget her empty stare and pale complexion. He held out his arms to her. This time she didn't refuse him. He lifted Justin and eased her into the chair. "Can someone get her a glass of water?"

Beyond her, his other brother-in-law, Joe, walked in with an unfamiliar woman trailing behind him. *I hope she's not a reporter.*

* * *

At the sight of the family huddled at the table, the reporter in Dominique wanted to start asking questions and formulating theories as to what could have happened, while the compassionate side wanted to sit with the family and take care of their needs.

If the phone call she placed to her boss at the TV station before they left the hospital panned out, maybe she could do both. Their affiliate in Cincinnati had sources. Maybe one of them could help. It was worth the few extra minutes she'd taken to return to her office to place the call in private before she drove Joe here.

As Joe introduced her to Travis and Cindy, the tall officer turned away from the table. The badge fixed to his belt and the gun in his shoulder strap identified him as a detective, but the noticeable resemblance to Joe—although taller and a bit leaner—confirmed him as Joe's brother.

As she committed their names to memory, she walked to the back of the room and studied the bulletin board filled with information about seven missing children.

Joe came up behind her. "This display breaks my heart."

"I was just thinking the same thing." She touched one of the photos. "I wonder why there are only four pictures posted when seven children are missing."

He lowered his voice. "The rest are like Emily's case. There's no picture available."

Dominique's throat tightened.

"People are desperate. The number of pregnancies has dropped so low that some people will do anything for a child. It's gotten so bad a pregnant woman can't even walk the streets, and a mom with young kids can't go to the park alone."

A policewoman stepped in front of Dominique. "Excuse me." She pinned to the board a snapshot of a young boy with a huge smile. He clutched a toy car in a chubby hand. The name beneath the photo read Max Montgomery.

"Dear God, please help us." Joe rubbed the back of his neck.

His heartfelt prayer fueled both her investigative reporter side and her compassionate side. What would it be like to know your baby was out there somewhere, but you had no idea what your son or daughter even looked like? Were they being loved and cared for? Were they even alive? She stopped the unsettling questions … they cut too close.

She had to help. She would love nothing more than to help his family find Max. And hopefully, she could help Emily's family find their baby too. "They'll find him, Joe."

Her phone vibrated in her pocket. She checked the caller ID. "I have to take this." She squeezed Joe's arm and walked out of the room. Finding a break room with no occupants, she sat down and answered Stew's call. "You got my text. Thanks for getting back to me so quickly. Tell me our affiliates have some lead or information to share on the kidnapping."

"Yeah, they do, but it's a long shot," Stew huffed.

"Let's hear it." She rummaged through her purse for pen and paper. "I'll take anything you've got." She wrote down the information her boss relayed to her.

Crackhead

abandoned warehouse (10th and Sycamore)

South side

Illegal activity and exchanges

cargo van – white (parked in back alley)

"You're right; it's not much. But it's all we have to go on." Now, how could she pass this information to the police without blowing her cover? Her best bet would be to call the anonymous tip line.

She pulled up the voice-changing app she had downloaded in preparation for the assignment … just in case.

When the dispatcher answered on the first ring, Dominique let out a relaxed breath. Knowing her voice would be disguised as a man's gave her some measure of security. "I have information on the kid taken from the mall."

"May I have your name, please?"

"There's a warehouse on Tenth and Sycamore." Dominique peeked out from behind the blinds in the break room.

The dispatcher was motioning to Houston to pick up the extension.

Dominique chewed on her bottom lip. What if Houston somehow recognized her voice? Too late now. She continued, "Look for a white cargo van parked in the back alley between the two buildings. I think you'll find what you're looking for." She ended the call before the dispatcher could ask any other questions.

Several minutes later, she returned to the interrogation room. She handed Joe a cup of coffee and took a seat next to him. "Any news yet?"

"Houston's keeping close tabs on all the calls coming in. He thinks the last one we received may have some merit. The other officers aren't taking it too seriously because the caller wouldn't identify himself. It's hard to weed out the real leads from the quacks."

Her heart slammed in her chest. What if they didn't follow the tip? "I think they should take every single lead seriously." She paced in front of the bulletin board with the children's pictures. "What if they miss something important?"

Joe smiled. "Houston agrees. He took off while you were on the phone." He gave her hand a gentle squeeze. "Thanks again for driving me here. That was really kind of you, considering we've just met."

He was so sincere, while she hid behind a tall stack of lies. One wrong word and they would all tumble down. She shook the thought off. There were more important things to worry about—like finding Joe's nephew. "What prompted Houston to follow up on the tip the rest of the department wrote off?"

"Vinnie Fernandez."

"Who's he?"

"He's a guy that owns half of this town. Some of it legally, most of it not. The police have been after him for years. Whenever there's enough evidence to press charges, something happens and Vinnie goes free. Last year, Houston testified in a big case against Fernandez. The evidence was rock solid, but the jury didn't convict. Houston's convinced Vinnie got to more than one member on the jury."

Dominique processed Joe's response. "What do you mean something happens?"

"You know, evidence disappears, witnesses change their stories or end up dead. It's more than a coincidence, so Houston keeps after him."

Vinnie Fernandez. Dominique cataloged his name for future use. Maybe Houston was onto something and Vinnie was connected to the kidnappings. The story would make a great companion piece for the declining birthrate angle. Stew would love it. The big challenge would be proving Vinnie's involvement without becoming another statistic.

Chapter Three

Domestic violence and abandoned warehouses were two calls that put any police officer on high alert. With no time to lose, Houston sped to the address the anonymous caller had given.

The warehouse was located at the end of a long street. The farther he drove, the more graffiti defaced the decrepit, abandoned buildings. The few houses that remained had been boarded up long ago.

Houston parked in front of the warehouse and scanned the abandoned buildings of the warehouse district—a popular hangout for drug dealers, prostitutes, and the occasional homeless person. Gun secure, radio checked, he moved past a sagging chain-link fence and walked toward the warehouse. The back end of a white cargo van peeked out from an alley that separated two buildings.

The hair on his arms stood on end. He eased his gun from the holster and inched forward. His boss would have his hide for coming here with no backup, but if the tip was real and he didn't act immediately, Max would be lost forever.

Using the building's shadows as cover, he approached the back end of the van. The license plate hung at an odd angle. Probably stolen. Nevertheless, he memorized the number. He wiped the grime off the back window and peered inside.

Empty.

He opened the door and searched for anything that would confirm Max had been there. He slipped his hand under the driver's seat and pulled out one empty Mountain Dew can and a plastic bag with a pacifier in it. His shoulders slumped. Someone's child had been in the van, but not Max. He had never used a pacifier.

Houston stuffed it in his pocket. He took a few minutes to call in his discovery and request backup. Maybe forensics would be able to find some evidence that would be helpful in one of the open cases.

Where are you, Max? Houston swiped a hand over his face, and his jaw clamped tight. If he was going to find Max, he had to focus. Where should he start searching?

If his wife Becky were here, she'd tell him to pray. The thought poked his conscience.

A child's scream pierced the air. He jerked to the right and scanned the first building.

There! Movement through a window on the second floor.

He darted across the alley to the building on his right. His mike bounced with each step as he called again for back-up.

At the doorless entry, he flattened against the building. He flicked a glance inside.

Empty.

With light steps, he slipped in. He treaded softly as he crept up a dusty wooden staircase. The scent of motor oil and years of filth tickled Houston's nose, and he held back a sneeze. If Max was in here, he'd need a good scrubbing to strip away the stench.

A muffled crying came from above. He followed the sound to the top of the staircase, where he cracked the door open and peered down the long hallway, dotted with four doors on each side. All were closed except the first one on the right, across the hallway from the stairwell.

Another high pitched cry pierced the air. It came from the room with the opened door.

Houston darted across the hall, then flattened himself against the wall.

When the crying stopped, the silence felt more disturbing than the wailing.

He peered through the crack in the door. A disheveled man stood in the center next to a gray metal desk. Houston committed the man's description to memory: approximately six feet tall, dirty blond hair, dressed in faded blue jeans and a gray T-shirt. The most distinguishing feature was a prominent, deep purple birthmark on his neck.

A bundle wriggled atop the desk.

Houston's breath caught in his throat. *Max.* He laid a hand on the metal door, gun ready to shoot off the shaggy man's face if he made a move.

The stairs creaked behind him.

He snapped his gun around, aiming at the door and whoever might walk out.

The door cracked open, then Lt. Kenny Davidson stepped into the hallway, his own pistol drawn.

What was his boss doing here? He shouldn't have been able to get here from the station so quickly.

Houston lowered his weapon and placed a finger to his lips to warn Kenny not to speak. He pointed to the stairwell, then followed Kenny as he retreated back the way he came.

"Has something changed?" Houston asked. "Is there more news?"

His boss gave him a puzzled look. "No. Why?"

"Earlier, you said you thought the tip was bogus."

"I was nearby when you requested backup. Decided to respond, even though you shouldn't be here." Kenny glared at him for a moment.

"They have him across the hall, Kenny. They have Max."

Kenny's left cheek twitched. "How many are there?"

"I've only seen one. Did you bring anyone with you?"

"They're on the way." Kenny pushed past Houston, crossed the hallway, and glanced in. "I think we can take him. You get Max. I'll get the perp."

Houston hesitated only a split second. Something didn't feel right, but he'd worked with Kenny for seven years, and they had a job to do. "How much time till more backup arrives?"

Kenny ignored the question and barged into the room. "Freeze!"

The suspect dropped the medicine bottle he held and ran through a door that adjoined the next room.

Houston charged in just as Max started crying again.

"I'm going after him!" Kenny yelled as he sprinted after the kidnapper.

Houston returned his weapon to its holster, picked Max up, and pulled him close to his chest. "You're okay, you're okay." He kissed Max's forehead.

Max's sobbing quieted. "Huey." He rubbed his eyes and buried his head in Houston's neck.

Houston's eyes burned with unshed tears. Never had the nickname sounded more precious. "Let's get you home."

Clutching Max to his chest, he darted across the hall and made his way down the stairs. He nudged the door open and peered out. The front of the warehouse was deserted. It looked like there weren't any other perps, but they weren't out of danger yet—not with the suspect still loose.

He pulled Max closer and rushed to his car, but frowned at Kenny's car. He wouldn't be able to leave with it blocking him from behind. He pulled the standard-issue car seat from the trunk, maneuvered it into the back seat, and settled Max in, then moved to the front seat and picked up the radio. "This is Detective Armstrong. What's the twenty on our backup?"

"Be advised, Detective, there are two units with an ETA of six minutes."

Kenny walked toward Houston's car. No suspect in sight.

Houston rolled down the window. "What happened? Where's the suspect?"

Kenny held both arms in the air. "He got away."

Houston's eyes narrowed. "Is the van still here?"

"What van?"

Houston ran his fingers through his hair. "There was a white cargo van parked in the alley between the buildings. Just like the anonymous caller reported. The engine was still warm when I got here." How could Kenny not remember that tip?

"I'll go back and check."

Houston bit back a sarcastic reply. Instead, he checked Max for injuries. If that goon hurt one hair on Max's head …

Several minutes later, Kenny hustled back to the car. "It's gone."

Houston swore under his breath and reached for his radio. "I'll call in the plates. They're probably stolen, but it's worth a shot."

"I didn't get a good look at him, Houston. Did you?" Kenny asked.

Goosebumps spiked on Houston's arms. Instincts urged him to lie. He settled for a half-truth. "I saw what he was wearing."

"You sure?"

Houston nodded. That man's face was etched in his memory.

"At least you got the boy back." Kenny opened his car door. "I'm heading to the station. I'll look for your full report on my desk ASAP."

Houston kept his eyes on Kenny's car as it turned the corner and rubbed the tightness from his chest before reporting to dispatch.

In spite of an increasing sensation that something about Kenny's actions was off, Houston slid into the car and buckled up. This matter would have to be solved another day. Priority number one was to get Max back to his parents. He pulled out his cell phone and called his brother-in-law. Dispatch would relay the message to them, but he wanted to be the one to give them the good news.

Travis answered on the first ring. "You found him?"

Houston looked in the rearview mirror at Max's droopy eyes. "Yes, I have him." He choked out the words through a throat tight with emotion.

"Is he okay?"

Houston laughed. "He seems okay. He's still in the dress. But I think they may have given him some Benadryl. He seems a little groggy. Meet me at Valley Memorial."

He drove the short distance to the hospital, thankful Max slept peacefully in the backseat. Travis and Cindy were lucky. Max had almost been lost to them forever.

As he carried the toddler into the ER, Houston ignored the flashes from the reporters' cameras and the shower of questions they shouted out.

"Who kidnapped your nephew, Detective?"

"Is the suspect in custody?"

"Do you have leads on any of the other missing children?"

Houston lowered his head and maneuvered past several news cameramen in the waiting room.

A nurse pointed him towards the double doors into the ER itself. On the other side of the doors, she gave him the room number and waved in the general direction of the end of the hallway.

He walked past the nurses and doctors and the two officers outside the doorway of the last semi-private room.

Cindy, Travis, and Justin huddled around an empty bed. The moment they spotted him, they rushed forward.

Cindy pulled Max from Houston's arms. "Thank God, he's okay. Oh, thank you, Lord." She planted kisses all over Max's face and head. "Thank you, Houston! I don't know what to say."

Travis could only parrot Cindy as Max whimpered into her chest.

Houston wiped away the tears from his eyes. "I'm glad I could help. We got a good lead, and I'm thankful it panned out."

Travis ran his hand through Max's hair. "Did you get the man who did this?"

"No, but we're pursuing all leads."

Joe rushed into the room. "Mind if I give him a once-over? I want to make sure he's okay."

Everyone except Cindy stepped out into the hallway as she placed Max on the examination table.

Houston pulled Travis aside. "I need to speak with you."

"Sure."

Rubbing the back of his neck, Houston released some of the tension. "I know you've had an incredibly stressful day, but I need to ask you a few questions."

"Sure, but I thought we went over everything already."

He waited until they'd walked far enough away from the others not to be overheard. "How many people have you discussed the investigation with?"

Travis shrugged. "Including you? Two, maybe three. I can't be sure. I'm sorry."

Houston looked over his shoulder and turned back to Travis. "I just want to warn you to make sure you're very careful, because right now, I'm not sure who can be trusted."

Chapter Four

Two weeks later, Stew's threats still thundered in Dominique's mind as she rode the elevator to the hospital's maternity ward. *Bring me a story, Dominique, or I'll send a reporter there who will. You want that promotion? You have to earn it!* So far, despite interviewing pregnant patients in the waiting rooms, documenting pregnancy trends, and various other research tasks, nothing pointed to what might be causing the pregnancy crisis. This hospital boasted the highest birthrate in Ohio, yet nothing stood out to her.

The maternity records room. The one place she hadn't visited. The hospital computers contained some information on the pregnant moms, but in their last staff meeting, Penelope mentioned restricted files that were stored in the maternity ward. No chance for a computer expert to hack into the system, under lock and key twenty-four hours a day.

Trying to see if she could pass the security measures in place hadn't been worth the risk. Until now. She flashed her identification at the guard stationed to the right of the elevator. Her heartbeat thumped in her ears. Would he question her? She offered a small smile. The guard glanced over her badge and buzzed her in. Kind of scary that a mere badge allowed her access to vulnerable newborn babies, who were at the highest risk for being kidnapped. Because they had no traceable fingerprints, once kidnapped they were impossible to find. Dominique shivered at the thought.

She strolled down the hall and stopped outside the nursery window. Only two bassinets were occupied. Twenty empty ones lined the back of the nursery wall, a physical reminder of the birthrate problem. She inhaled deeply and let out a long, slow breath. She would piece this puzzle together. It was her job.

One of the nurses looked up and rushed toward the door. "Can we help you?" she asked through the window.

Yes ... can you tell me your theory on the empty nursery? She controlled the reporter side of herself. "I'm looking for the records room." She held up her hospital badge, which identified her as a social worker. Would it allow her access to the high security area? Moms, babies, and records were supposed to be guarded twenty-four hours a day.

The woman eyed Dominique's hospital badge and offered a slight smile. "Down the hall. Last door on the left."

Dominique thanked her and progressed down the hall. No guard was posted outside. She switched on the light and fought back a wave of discouragement. Filing cabinets lined the walls. Where should she begin?

One of the cabinets was labeled *Live Births.* That would be the best place to start. She opened the large drawer. She pulled out a large stack and sat at the table in the center of the room.

After reading one file, she lined up the rest and closely examined each one. What did they have in common? Nothing jumped out at her, and she didn't have time to thoroughly review the findings. She took out her camera and snapped shots of each of the records.

A draft of cold air hit her legs, and a chill of panic seized her. She slipped her camera into a front pocket and forced a smile before turning around.

Penelope Nordstrom stood in the doorway, arms crossed, a scowl on her face. "The security guard notified me you were here. This room is off limits to unauthorized personnel."

"I'm a licensed social worker, Ms. Nordstrom. My job requires me to have access to this information. If I'm not authorized, why was I permitted access?"

"I've been looking for you for over an hour, and you haven't returned any of my messages. I trust you have an excuse for missing the mandatory employee meeting?"

Dominique took a deep breath. "I'm sorry. It completely slipped my mind."

"In the future, Ms. Sherwood, if you intend to remain employed at the hospital, you'll pay more attention to your calendar. And furthermore, in matters concerning hospital finances and policies, you are to side with your immediate supervisor's position; even if it means losing a date with the hospital's most eligible bachelor."

Dominique took two steps toward Penelope. "I think we'll get along much better if we get one thing straight."

Penelope's eyes narrowed. "And what would that be?"

"I was hired to serve as a social worker at the hospital. I'm going to fulfill my duties to the best of my ability. If I permit you to make decisions for me, you'll have the determining influence in all of the cases we work on together. Which, I might point out, is a huge conflict of interest. I'm sure you wouldn't want me to report this to the ethics board."

Penelope let out a snort that made Dominique think of a fire-breathing dragon. Clearly her comment had gotten under Penelope's skin.

"Okay. You've had your say. Now I'm going to have mine." Penelope emphasized each word with her chubby finger pointed towards Dominique. "I don't like you, and I think you're hiding something. If it's not some romantic involvement with Dr. Armstrong, then it's something else. I won't be treated in this manner by some neophyte, barely-out-of-college girl. I will find out what you're up to, and when I do, you can be sure you won't have a job here for long."

Just as she was formulating her next response, Joe appeared in the doorway.

"Hi, ladies. Hope I'm not interrupting anything."

Talk about a knight in shining armor. "Not at all, Joe. I mean … Dr. Armstrong. Is there something I can help you with?"

Penelope's eyebrows shot up. "I see we're on a first name basis. How intimate."

Dominique chose to ignore the cutting remark. So did Joe.

He took several steps into the room. "Your secretary told me I could reach you here, Penelope, but I'm glad I caught both of you at the same time. I just wanted to let you know that I took Emily off life support."

Penelope smiled. "Well, it was the only sensible thing to do. After all, what quality of life could she possibly have … and at such a huge expense?"

"You've misunderstood me. I've taken her off the ventilator because she no longer needed it. She's breathing on her own. It's only a matter of time before she regains consciousness."

Penelope's cheeks flushed crimson. For once, she had nothing to say. She stomped out of the room like a pouting toddler who hadn't gotten her way.

"That's wonderful news about Emily. Her family must be so relieved."

A smile created dimples on both of Joe's cheeks. "Have you had dinner yet? I happen to be starving."

Mercy, this man was handsome. As if on cue, her stomach growled. Understandable, since she hadn't eaten a bite since breakfast. The sensible side of her told her to say no. Mixing business and pleasure was only going to lead to disaster. Somehow her heart didn't agree with her head. "Actually, I'm quite hungry. What's good around here?"

"There's a little restaurant across the street from the hospital. Do you like Chinese food?"

Dominique smiled. "It's my favorite."

"Let's go."

Joe held the door open for her. As she breezed past him, she couldn't help but notice the clean, masculine smell. He had such a gentle way about him, but he was definitely all man. Undercover stories, insane birthrates, nasty supervisors, and attractive doctors … the next few months would definitely be interesting. If she survived.

* * *

Travis counted four television news vans parked outside the gate that blocked the entrance to his subdivision. One advantage of living in a gated community was that the gate kept the nosy reporters and news trucks out. It had been weeks since Max's abduction, and still they hounded him.

"Mr. Montgomery." They rushed at his vehicle and tapped on the windows as he slowed to maneuver around several vans.

Travis pulled up to the keypad that controlled the gate and lowered his window.

Someone shoved a microphone into his face. "How is Max doing?"

Travis pushed the microphone away, punched in the security code, waited for the black iron gates to part, and drove into his neighborhood. He let out a long sigh when the gates shut behind him. Thankfully, the boys were so occupied with the new trucks Grandpa had given them a few days ago that they didn't notice anything.

Usually, a sense of pride filled him when his six-thousand-square-foot house came into view. Today, as he topped the hill, the sight of the massive house seemed tiny compared to his debt. Several payments behind on the mortgage, he was about sixty days away from receiving a foreclosure notice. Something had to give. Certainly one of the building proposals he had up in the air would come through, and he could dig himself out of this pit.

Travis pulled in.

Cindy paced the length of the driveway, cell phone in hand. Something must be wrong. Her blonde hair looked like she'd spent the morning running her fingers through it. Before the truck came to a complete stop, she ran to the passenger side door.

She unhooked Max from the car seat. Hugging him tight to her chest, Cindy kissed his head. She made no attempt to brush away the tears flowing from her eyes. "Where were you, Travis? I called you three times."

"Everything was okay, Cindy. I didn't take my eyes off the boys."

"Why didn't you pick up?"

He leaned into the back seat and took Justin out. Placing him on the ground, Travis fumbled for some type of explanation. "I didn't hear my phone. Sooner or later you're going to have to trust me with the kids."

"You could check your messages."

Travis met her eyes. Every response running through his mind sounded lame. So he chose to remain silent.

Cindy put Max down, grabbed both boys' hands, and walked toward the house.

He understood why she was still upset, but at some point she'd have to forgive him. He followed her through the garage and into the kitchen. "I'm sorry I didn't call you. I don't know what I was thinking."

"I'll tell you what you were thinking, you were thinking about yourself. I swear, I don't know what's wrong with you lately. It's like you're a completely different person." Cindy placed each of the boys in their highchairs and served them their afternoon snack.

"I said I was sorry." Travis set the twins' backpack on the table. "I have work to do. I'll be in my office."

Cindy blew the bangs out of her eyes. "You don't remember, do you?"

Travis stopped in his tracks. He didn't have the nerve to ask her what he'd forgotten this time.

"The meeting with my family … my father … is any of this ringing a bell?" She plucked a dishrag from the sink and ran it under a stream of water. "You promised me you would go. If I wasn't running this low-grade fever, I'd go. I don't want to risk exposing my dad."

Travis swore under his breath. Why had he promised to attend for her? He had a business meeting at five o'clock. Considering the subject matter, this family meeting could take a long time. He turned and met Cindy's angry glare. "What time do I have to be there?"

Cindy wiped down the already spotless counters. "Four-thirty. You could show a little more concern. We're trying to decide what to do with my dad. Houston wants each family's input."

Her eyes avoided his, and Travis's temper flared. "I have a business dinner meeting." He took a quick look at his watch. "I'll make an appearance, but I'll have to cut out early."

"I would like to have some say as to where my dad ends up." Cindy grabbed a fresh cloth and washed the boys' faces. "I'm going to lay down with the twins. Can you pick up the girls from school?"

"I can't. I need to prepare for my meeting." He hated the guilt that poured over him and stabbed at trying to salvage the conversation. "Maybe we can all do something this weekend."

Cindy walked out of the room.

Travis flinched. She didn't understand the pressure he was under, or how much he was trying to protect her. Two sets of twins under the age of six. He had been busting his back for months trying to keep them financially afloat. He was doing everything he possibly could to hold the family together. He took a deep breath and relaxed his shoulders. How much longer could he hide the truth from her?

He stalked into his office, shut the door, and sat down on the black leather chair. Once settled, he closed his eyes and focused his thoughts. How had things gotten so out of control?

One bad decision at a time.

The truth stung. He tapped his accountant's number on his cell phone. "Scott, it's me. Any news?"

The silence on the other end made his heart rate take a dive.

"I was just getting ready to call you."

Travis kept his tone light. "Don't keep me in suspense. Did Gladstone sign the contract?"

"He went with a different contractor, Travis."

He slammed his hand down on the desk. "What? We had a verbal agreement."

"He ran a credit check on the company. We haven't been in the black for a long time. It's time we start exploring other options."

"I'm not filing for bankruptcy. I've worked too hard to just give up."

Scott cleared his throat. "You may not have much choice. Payroll is scheduled to process next week. Right now we don't have money to cover it."

Travis rubbed the back of his neck. "You'll have it. One way or another, we'll make payroll."

He hit the off button and tossed his cell phone across the desk. A quick look at the clock on the wall told him he had two hours until he had to be at the hospital. But it wasn't that meeting causing his heart to race, it was the second meeting that he couldn't miss. Every instinct inside Travis screamed at him to cancel. He reached for the glass of water on the edge of his desk and swallowed its contents in one gulp. Vinnie had a reputation, but he was quickly becoming Travis's only hope.

He submerged himself in his work. When he finished the proposal, he arranged the stack of papers in a neat pile and placed a paperclip on the top left corner. The loan he sought might be short-term and at a rate significantly higher than a traditional loan, but in exchange, Travis would pay off the entire loan in twelve months. A year would give him enough time to acquire some new business and turn things around. It had to.

One look at his watch, and he shot out of the chair. Four-fifteen! Where had the time gone? Why hadn't Cindy poked her head in when she came home with the girls? He grabbed his briefcase and sprinted out the door. In the garage, Travis had his answer … Cindy wasn't home yet. He pulled out his cell phone and called his brother-in-law. "Houston, it's Travis. I got caught up taking care of some urgent business." He bit the inside of his cheek. "I'm still at the house."

"That's okay. We haven't started yet. We can wait for you."

"No. Just go ahead." Travis flung his briefcase in the truck. "I have another meeting scheduled for five. Cindy and I are fine with whatever the family decides."

Houston sighed. "I wish we could reschedule, but they want to discharge Dad from the hospital in a few days. We need to make some decisions today."

Travis pulled out of the neighborhood, thankful that the media had given up for the day. "Like I said, we're both comfortable with whatever the family decides." Not quite the truth, but he didn't have time to explain himself.

* * *

As he drove to the south side of town, Travis grabbed the bottle of Tums out of the center console. The antacid might help with the burning in his stomach, but he had nothing to calm his racing heart.

He was worth more dead than alive. If he died, his wife and kids would be provided for. They would have the life insurance money.

The truth struck a painful chord.

He vowed years ago that if he ever had a family, he would never do to them what his father had done to him ... take his own life. His present situation opened his eyes into what his own father might have been feeling prior to his death.

He pulled his truck into the parking lot and looked up at the sign displaying *Castalgia's Fine Italian Restaurant*. Although it had a reputation for good food, that of its owner was questionable at best. Tasteful landscaping surrounded a stone sidewalk, and an oak door fitted with beveled glass welcomed patrons into the restaurant. The extra touches spoke of undeniable wealth.

He took a deep breath. *It's just a business meeting. You've negotiated hundreds of deals.* He opened the door, and the aroma of fresh baked bread intermixed with garlic greeted him.

An attractive brunette in a low-cut black dress stood at the hostess stand. His eyes met hers, and he smiled. "Perhaps you can help me. I have an appointment with Mr. Fernandez."

"Welcome, Mr. Montgomery. We've been expecting you. Please follow me."

Travis fought to control his expression. She knew his name? Impressive. He followed her and took in the elegant ambiance of the restaurant. The tables and booths were spaced in a manner that provided a measure of privacy. The candles flickering on each of them added to the warm atmosphere.

His eyes then focused on the hostess leading him toward the back of the restaurant. Travis had seen his share of beautiful women, but this woman was exquisite. As she walked, her perfume left an enticing trail. He admired her silhouette from behind. *When was the last time Cindy wore a dress like that?*

"Here you are, Mr. Montgomery."

The hostess's voice jarred him from his thoughts.

She placed a menu on the table. "My name is Angelica. Please let me know if you need *anything*. Mr. Fernandez will join you shortly."

As Angelica sauntered away, Travis couldn't keep his gaze from following her swaying hips. A few minutes passed before he was greeted by a waiter, who set a basket of bread and a carafe of Burgundy wine on the table.

The waiter left, and a distinguished-looking man approached. Images of *The Godfather* came to mind. A touch of silver brushed the man's full head of dark hair at the temples. His tanned complexion made him look like he spent all day lounging in the sun, and a large, hooked nose overpowered his masculine face.

Travis extended his right hand. "Good evening, Mr. Fernandez. I'm Travis Montgomery."

Vinnie ignored Travis's hand. "No need for formalities, son. You can call me Vinnie."

"Thank you." Travis relaxed his shoulders and wiped his sweaty palms on his khaki pants.

"Let me pour you a glass of our house wine. My cousin runs a winery in Sandusky. I think you'll find it to your liking."

Travis rarely drank, but to refuse would be seen as an insult. "I would love a glass."

Vinnie hummed some tune under his breath while he filled both glasses.

Travis struggled to steady his hand as he lifted his glass. He was completely out of his league, yet what choice did he have if he wanted to save his business?

Only time would tell if this was the best decision he had ever made, or the worst mistake of his life.

Chapter Five

Houston paced past his wife, down the length of the hospital waiting room, and back to the door. He looked out into the hallway. Joe was still talking with the social worker on duty. Travis had been true to his word and had been a no-show. Despite meeting for an hour, things were still unresolved.

"I'm sure we'll be able to come to some sort of compromise with the hospital," Becky said. "What do you think, Houston?"

"Not if he doesn't give up this ridiculous notion. Can't say that I blame them."

"We'll work it out," Becky responded.

Houston bit back a sarcastic reply. *He'll never change.* He loved Becky more today than when he married her twelve years ago, but on this one issue, could she ever see his side? Almost every time they argued, it was over the same thing: his father, Samuel Armstrong.

Becky loved him. Houston tolerated him for his wife's sake. He looked around the sterile surroundings in the hospital waiting room. Although they attempted to make the atmosphere more comfortable, the tiled floors and metal furniture were a constant reminder that this place was not home.

Houston ran his hand along Becky's face. "I'm sorry, honey. I just don't see any other way."

Becky blew her nose into an already worn tissue. "There's always an alternative, Houston. I can't imagine putting your dad in that place."

"It's what the doctor recommended. You heard him; Samuel's mind is slipping."

"There's nothing wrong with Dad's mind. He's as sharp as a tack." Becky rose from the sofa and let out a sigh. "Are you ready to head home? I'm exhausted."

Houston came up behind her and wrapped her in his arms. Leaning down, he placed a kiss on her neck. "How about I make dinner tonight?"

"Now that's an offer I can't refuse." She returned his kiss. "Let's go."

Once in the parking lot, Houston said, "Please tell me you don't believe my father's overactive imagination. I can't believe he thinks God is allowing only Christians to get pregnant. I'm sorry, but in my book this proves the doctor is right."

Becky rubbed the goose bumps covering her arms. "I really don't know what to think."

He slowed. "I do. Dad's completely lost it. All those years of drinking finally caught up with him."

"Your dad hasn't had a drink in over fifteen years."

He opened the car door for her. Why was Becky being so stubborn? "I'm sorry I brought it up, but you have to admit that Dad's theory on the pregnancy crisis is a little far-fetched." He rubbed the back of his neck. Was something else on her mind? Once Becky was comfortable, he kissed her cheek.

Her knuckles, curled around the handles of her purse, were white.

Surely their conversation hadn't made her that tense. "You hiding a wad of cash in there?" He tried to lighten the mood with a joke.

Becky let out a tense laugh. "The contents of a lady's purse are private."

Silence possessed the next few minutes as Houston maneuvered them along local streets to the divided highway. He eased his way back to the topic at hand. "I don't think we'll ever reach a consensus. I am in complete agreement with the doctor. Joe thinks Dad will be fine without medication, and Cindy's in the middle—at least according to Travis."

"Do we have to decide this tonight?" Becky took off her glasses and rubbed her nose.

"We're going to have to make a decision sooner or later."

Becky turned the radio on. Classical music filled the car. "Let's sleep on it. Maybe tomorrow you can speak directly with Cindy and see what she thinks."

Houston nodded and dropped the subject. They traveled the next several miles absorbed in their individual thoughts. As they passed Castalgia's restaurant, his grip on the wheel tightened. Vinnie Fernandez. The mere thought of the man raised his blood pressure.

He slowed the car, unconsciously scanning the parking lot. A familiar truck caused his heart to skip a beat. *Travis's truck has that same bumper sticker on the rear fender.* "That's strange."

"What?"

He rubbed the back of his neck. "I think I just spotted Travis's truck parked outside Castalgia's."

"I thought you said he had a meeting with a client. Could that be where they're meeting?"

"That's not a typical meeting place. At least not for the type of meeting Travis would be having."

"I'm not sure I'm following you."

"Vinnie Fernandez owns that restaurant. We've been investigating him for years, but every time I accumulate enough evidence to go before a judge, something mysterious happens and the case dissolves." Houston waved a hand in the air.

Becky pointed her fingers at Houston as though they were pistols. "Are they the Mafia?" she joked.

Houston didn't respond, and the silence grew.

"Okay, now you have me worried. You don't think Travis is involved in something illegal, do you?"

"No. Of course not. I'm just tired. It probably wasn't even his truck. If it would make you feel better we can turn around and I'll double-check."

"I think we're both a little overtired. Let's just go home, have dinner, and go to bed."

"I like the sound of that. Especially the bed part." He winked.

She laughed. "I thought you were tired."

"You know me, honey, I'm never too tired." Houston let out a sigh. Although the conversation hadn't erupted into an argument, Becky's behavior troubled him. He couldn't shake the feeling she was keeping something from him.

* * *

Travis leaned back in the booth and pushed his empty plate to the side. One carafe of wine, a thoroughly delicious meal, and polite conversation. He couldn't remember the last time he'd experienced such a relaxing dinner. Perhaps Vinnie's reputation was built on nothing more than vicious rhetoric.

After the waiter cleared their plates and left, Travis grabbed the portfolio from the seat next to him. He placed the folder on the table and slid it across to Vinnie.

"I see you're ready to talk business."

"Yes, sir. I've prepared a proposal for your review."

Vinnie's gaze flicked to the file before returning to Travis. "I don't need a written proposal. Tell me how much you need, and I'll arrange it."

Warning bells went off in Travis's head. Although his friend John had referred him to Vinnie, Travis's own research had turned up mixed reviews. Houston swore the man was the devil, but he'd never been convicted of a crime. When he checked back with John, he waved it off and said people always spoke poorly of rich, powerful men, because they were jealous. Travis had never paid much attention to the gossip, but now he wished he had.

"I'm looking for a short-term loan to help me pay off debt and meet payroll for the next few months. A supplier went belly-up and left me with a lot of unpaid bills and projects I still need to finish."

Vinnie took a sip of his wine. "That doesn't sound like good business to me. I would never allow someone to leave their obligations unfulfilled. What are you doing to rectify the situation?"

"I'm not sure there's anything I *can* do. He went out of business. He was a close friend, but now he won't even return my phone calls." Travis drummed his fingers on the table. "My attorney said it would be tied up in court for years. I can't afford that."

"Travis, I like you. Because I like you, I'm going to give you a little business advice. Pay attention, because this is something you can't learn at a fancy university like Harvard or Oxford. Over the years, I've found that when I extend a little courtesy to someone, they take advantage of me. In order to prevent this, I've had to develop some stalwart business policies."

Travis swallowed the tumbleweed of doubt rising in his throat. "I had penalty terms in place, but they're no good if the other party refuses to acknowledge them."

Vinnie sneered. "When I make a business deal, the other party fulfills their obligation or faces the consequences. Sometimes these consequences aren't so pleasant, but I've found they're very effective."

Travis's heart pounded. Houston was right. He was the devil. There was no way he could ask Vinnie for a loan. "I'm sorry, Mr. Fernandez. I'm afraid I may have wasted your time. Thank you for meeting with me, but I think I'll look over some different options for a business loan."

Vinnie's right cheek twitched. He pushed the file back to Travis. "I think I understand you, Travis, my boy. But before you leave, let's get a few things straight. Number one, I don't like having my time wasted. Number two, if I find out you've disclosed any part of this meeting to anyone, I'll be extremely disappointed. I don't tolerate betrayals of *any* type. Are we clear?"

"I would never even think of betraying your confidence." Travis fumbled over his words. He grabbed the proposal and stumbled out of the booth, and his first several steps were unsteady from the wine. He needed to sober up before he left. Instead of heading toward the door, he walked to the bathrooms at the back of the restaurant.

Vinnie followed close on Travis's heels. "If you change your mind, Travis, you know where to find me."

Vinnie's laughter followed Travis down the hallway. Travis entered the men's room and splashed cold water on his face. *What am I doing? I have to get out of here.* When he left the restroom, he turned toward the red exit sign at the end of the hall.

As he burst through the door, the cool night air rushed over him. He took in a deep breath and slowly let it out. The relief was fleeting. He still had four kids to support, a mountain of debt, and a failing business. He sprinted down the dim alley, around the only vehicle, a white cargo van parked at the end, and rounded the corner to the parking lot at the front of the restaurant.

The space where he'd parked his truck was empty. He pulled out his key fob and hit the unlock button. Nothing. Where was his truck?

He pulled out his cell phone. Six missed calls—all from Cindy. But he couldn't call her back. Not until he figured out what had happened to his truck.

He pressed the alarm button on the fob, maybe it was parked nearby. Silence. His cell phone chimed to indicate he had received an email.

To: Travis Montgomery

Re: Notice of Redemption and an Affidavit of Defense.

He swiped a finger across the screen to pull up the full message. It described the year, make, and model of his truck and what he needed to do to get it back. Travis swore under his breath. What now? Cindy's Land Rover was sure to be next on their list.

He looked over his shoulder at the restaurant. Maybe he should go back and strike a deal after all. He'd probably have his truck back first thing in the morning. He'd be able to make payroll and start turning his personal finances around. *No! I will not make a deal with the devil.*

He walked the length of the parking lot, ignoring the heavy feeling in his chest. His choices were to fess up to Cindy or turn around and make the deal. Both left him with a pit in his stomach that wasn't from the effect of the wine.

He needed to make his decision with a clear head. He called for a taxi and waited in the far corner of the parking lot for it to arrive. On the ride home, he mulled over his options. Cindy would be so disappointed; he couldn't let her down. But did he really want to be under Vinnie's thumb?

When the cabbie parked in the driveway, Travis paid the fare and shuffled to the front door. It opened before he had a chance to put his key in.

"Where have you been?"

"Can we take this inside? I'd rather the neighbors not hear us arguing."

Cindy turned around and stomped through the living room and into Travis's office. "I tried calling you several times. You had me worried. Where were you?"

"I told you I had a business meeting." Travis shut the door, walked around the large cherry desk, and dropped into the black leather chair. He gestured for Cindy to sit across from him.

"I'm too upset to sit." She paced the width of the office. "Why did you take a cab home? Have you been drinking?"

"I had some wine with dinner."

"So you left your truck at the restaurant?"

Travis met Cindy's glare. Trepidation filled her eyes, and her expression radiated a mixture of anger and concern. He longed to hold her and reassure her that everything would be okay. Maybe he could talk with a few more banks and see if something would work out. "I don't want to argue. Not tonight. Let's call a truce."

Cindy crossed her arms over her chest. "We're far from a truce, Travis. I know you're tired, but that doesn't let you off the hook. The least you could have done was call and let me know you were running late. We have things we need to talk about."

He stiffened. "What's so important that it can't wait until tomorrow?"

Cindy's expression softened. She was almost beaming as she rubbed the slight expansion of her belly. "I'm pregnant. We're going to have a baby."

The joy on her face only fueled his anger. "You've got to be kidding!"

Cindy frowned. "Not exactly the reaction I expected."

He spun the Montblanc pen on his desk. "How could something like this happen?"

Cindy smiled. "I would think you'd have figured that out by now."

"You know what I mean. I had surgery so this would never happen again." He waved his hand in the air. "How can you be pregnant?"

"Just what are you insinuating, Travis?" Her eyes darkened. "Are you accusing me of having an affair? Just when would I have time for that?" Her volume grew with each question she threw back at him.

"I don't know what I'm saying. I just know I paid the doctor a lot of money to prevent this from happening." He leaned back as far as the chair would go. "When *did* this happen? Are you absolutely sure? You're telling me in the middle of a nationwide pregnancy crisis you're pregnant … *after* I've had a vasectomy?"

Cindy ran her hand over her belly. "I've been in denial for some time. I just took the test yesterday morning. If my calculations are correct, I'm way past my first trimester."

Travis rubbed the stubble across his jawline. "Have you been to the doctor yet? Those home tests can be wrong."

She pulled her shirt tight and showed him her profile. "That doesn't explain my growing belly. And don't go placing all the blame on me, Travis. After your vasectomy, the doctor left you several messages asking you to come back in for a final check. If I remember correctly, you never went."

His temples throbbed. How in the world could he support another child? He took a deep breath. "I can't talk about this tonight. I'm going to bed."

"We're going to have to talk about it sometime. We have a lot of things we need to decide."

"We'll talk later." Taking the stairs two at a time, he reached the top floor and walked down the hall. He didn't even stop to check in on the kids. He went straight to the master bathroom. Maybe a hot shower would clear his mind. He needed to come up with a plan. If he didn't, he'd lose everything.

Chapter Six

Dominique ran her hand along the side of the smooth, mahogany table, enjoying the quiet atmosphere of the restaurant after a long, hard day.

"Are you a Christian, Dominique?" Joe asked.

Her hand stopped with a glass mid-way to her mouth. Where had that question come from? But, deep inside, she had known the question would come up. He'd not made a secret of his faith. Now the dreaded question hung in the air.

She didn't want to discuss religion, or Jesus, or anything spiritual with anyone. She knew what God had against her. It was unforgivable. She knew the popular Christian lingo. Her mother had hounded her long enough that she had all of the correct responses memorized. She could get away with lying. But the guilt of pretending to be a licensed social worker hounded her enough. Lying about her faith, or lack thereof, was a different story.

No, she couldn't lie to him, not about this. "Let's just put it this way: I have a mother who's a religious fanatic, so I'm not sure what that makes me."

Joe burst out laughing. "I take it you've been asked this question before."

"Yes, and to be honest, I never quite know how to answer it. I believe Jesus existed. Does that make me a Christian? I don't know, Joe. I guess I'm not a very religious person."

Joe pushed his plate to the center of the table. "I'm sorry, Dominique, I don't want to make you uncomfortable. My relationship with Christ is a large part of my life, but I don't consider myself a religious person either."

"Now you have me confused." *Weren't all Christians religious?*

"Religion is a strict set of rules and regulations. Being a Christian is about your relationship with Christ. In the book of John, he tells you the truth, and I believe him."

"You make it sound so simple. My mom usually gives me a laundry list of what I'm doing wrong and how I should change."

"That's religion at its best— " The ring of his cell phone cut off the rest of his words.

"You'd better get that. It could be the hospital." Guilt stabbed at her. He didn't deserve to be toyed with. She should end this relationship before it began. She should never have accepted his invitation in the first place.

The candlelight hit Joe just right as he rose while pulling out his cell phone. It bounced shadows across his handsome face before he walked to the lobby.

But how could she resist someone so handsome and kind?

The waitress stopped next to Dominique and set a leather case containing the bill in the middle of the table. Joe came back just as the woman returned. "I'm sorry about that. Interruptions are part of the job."

Dominique handed the waitress the folder with her credit card protruding from one end before Joe could object. She touched his arm. "I understand. I hope everything is okay."

"Actually, I need to get back to the hospital. Emily is awake and very alert. Her family wants me to be there when they tell her about the baby, in case the bad news affects her condition. If that isn't bad enough, we had to do a complete hysterectomy, so if she ever has children, it will have to be through adoption."

"Such a tragedy. I wish I could do something."

He sighed. "It would help if the police found their baby."

The waitress returned, and Dominique accepted the black leather billfold with a smile. She quickly added a generous tip and retrieved her credit card.

"That doesn't seem fair, Dominique. I ask you out to dinner, and you pay the bill. Please let me make it up to you."

"You don't have to do that, Joe. I really enjoyed talking with you. Please don't worry about it."

"Have lunch with me on Sunday. This time I'll pay." He gave her an irresistible smile.

She fiddled with the zipper on her purse. She could never be the woman Joe was looking for. He needed a woman who shared his faith, someone who was pure and acceptable. The exact opposite of her. But she couldn't resist his charm. Instead, she threw reason aside. "Where would you like to meet?"

"How about I pick you up?" he suggested as they stood.

How could she explain living in a long-term motel? "That's okay. Just give me a place and a time, and I'll be there." She held her breath. Would he agree or push the issue?

"There's a great Mexican restaurant on Fifth Street." He gave her directions as they walked outside. "See you at one on Sunday."

She waved as he headed to his car. She breathed in the scent of his pleasant masculine cologne that trailed behind him. What was she doing? She was in way over her head. He was a Christian, and her mother always told her that unless she changed her ways, she wasn't *fit* or *equally yoked,* or however she termed it.

As she walked to her car, she considered the huge barrier her lie created between them. She flopped down in the front seat of her rental and took a deep breath. Then there was the other matter. The spiritual element. If she revealed her past to Joe, he would drop her. Only one other person knew her shameful secret, two if you included God, and she preferred not to include Him. There had to be a limit to what He would forgive.

Her cell phone vibrated. Channing. *Oh, brother. What does he want?* There was a time in her life when seeing his name on her phone brought a jolt of happiness—but now it gave her an ache in the pit of her stomach. But after two more rings, curiosity got the best of her. "Hello, *Channing.*"

"Hi, beautiful. You miss me?" His smooth baritone taunted her. She rolled her eyes and resisted spewing forth the sarcastic reply on the tip of her tongue. "What do you want?"

"Do I have to want something in order to talk with my favorite correspondent?"

She pictured him sitting on a warm California beach, his blond hair tossed by the gentle breeze, his rugged physique covered in sunscreen. Work and relaxation flowed together so easily for him. Somehow he always succeeded, relying on the labor of other people. How could she have been so blinded?

"With you, there's always a reason. Are you calling to brag?"

"Spoken like a reporter who doesn't have a story. Things a little slow in southern Ohio?"

She played with the dials on the car radio. He might have gotten the coveted assignment—to expose a giant, money-hungry corporation—but she wouldn't let him get the best of her. She'd find a newsworthy story, even if she had to embellish one of her current leads. "As a matter of fact, things are coming together quite nicely. I have a lead on the population story, and I'm working on another angle. One I think Stew will want to feature."

"You're lying, Dominique. There's nothing going on in Ohio. No story there."

The bulletin board of missing children flashed in her mind. "If you call a black market baby ring nothing, then you don't know a good news story when it hits you square in the face." She cringed.

"You have a lead on the baby black market? I don't believe it." The challenge in his voice carried through the phone.

The words flowed out of her mouth before she could stop them. "I have a solid lead that's sure to be the head story for weeks on end. Pollution is boring compared to murder and missing children. Think about it." She hung up without saying good-bye.

She slumped back in the bucket seat. Channing had a big mouth. Better to end the conversation before she got in any deeper.

At the rate Dominique was going with her investigation into the higher pregnancy rate here in Ohio, maybe she'd have better luck if she shifted the focus of her story to the kidnappings. But where should she start?

What about Emily and her missing child? Maybe she could offer to help Emily's family deal with the loss of a child. Their conversations would inevitably involve the horrifying event. She had to remember something that would help. If it led to finding one child, maybe others would be found too.

Joe's brother was a police officer. As she pulled up to a red light, she considered how she could question him without raising suspicions. Her credentials as a social worker would help. The fact that she had to use a lie nagged at her. But maybe it would be worth it if she could help find Emily's baby.

Channing's smug face popped into her mind. She couldn't completely neglect her original assignment, but she needed a direction for the investigation to follow. Then she could prove to Stew and Channing and everyone else that she wasn't just another pretty face to put in front of the camera with no more ability than to read what scrolled along the teleprompter. She would prove she was a qualified news reporter who could uncover the truth no matter the consequences.

If only she could ignore the red flags and warning bells cautioning trouble ahead. It was the same admonition she had before she made the worst mistake in her life. The one sin God would never forgive.

* * *

Houston reached across the bed to draw Becky closer to him, but his hand hit a cold, empty sheet. Sleep fled from him as he sat up.

Light shone from underneath the bathroom door, along with muffled crying. He knocked twice, then gently pushed the door open. "Everything okay, honey?"

Becky sat next to the tub, crying into her hands.

The sight broke his heart. He knelt beside her on the hard tile floor and pulled her into his arms. "What's wrong?"

She grabbed a tissue from the box on the floor next to her and blew her nose. She pulled the pregnancy test strip from the counter and waved it in front of him. "Negative. I was so certain this time would be different."

Houston took the strip from her hand. A single pink line glared from the small window. "It'll happen. I know it will. No one would make a better mother than you."

She shook her head. "I'm three weeks late. I don't understand. Unless … "

He let out a long, slow breath. She was surely thinking about their conversation with Samuel. "Let's go talk in bed. We'll be more comfortable there."

He helped her up from the floor, grabbed the box of tissues, and they settled next to each other in bed. "Please don't let what my dad said earlier cloud circumstances. Maybe this test is wrong. The only other time you were this late, you were pregnant."

"That's why I was so certain this was it. I wanted to get to the doctor early and hopefully prevent another miscarriage."

He drew her closer and placed a kiss on her head. "Make an appointment. That test could be wrong."

"It's not wrong."

"How do you know?"

"I just do." She leaned on him. "It's so hard not to give up … especially after what your dad said. I know you don't believe him, but I don't think he's lost his mind."

Houston kissed her again. "We had this problem long before he started spouting religious banter."

Becky sat straight up. "Don't do that."

"What?"

"Completely dismiss what's been going on. What if he's right ... have you even considered that?"

Houston's cell phone buzzed from the top of his nightstand. This late, it was probably work-related. "This is Armstrong."

"There's been another murder," the on-call dispatcher relayed. "Lt. Davidson wants you on the case."

Houston rolled off the bed and reached for the notepad on the nightstand. "What's the address?"

"Two-hundred Damascus Street."

His heart slammed in his chest. *The address of the church Becky, Joe, and Cindy belong to.* "I'll be there in fifteen." He ended the call. "I'm so sorry, honey. I have to go." He kissed her forehead. "I hate leaving, especially when you're upset, but this can't wait."

Becky pulled the comforter up to her chin. "Bad news?"

"There's been another murder."

"Please tell me it's not another mother and child. I don't think I could handle that, not after the night we've had." He grabbed his badge, cell phone, and Glock. "I won't know till I get there." But the thought haunted him. He leaned and kissed her good-bye. Becky deepened the kiss, making it difficult for him to break their embrace. "I'll call you when I can. Try to get some sleep."

At the church, Houston approached the group gathered around the body, waiting for the coroner to arrive.

The body lay face down underneath a large oak tree at the back of the church property.

Houston pulled on Latex gloves and moved closer. Faded jeans, gray T-shirt—he held his breath as he turned the victim over.

The officer behind him flashed a light on the dead man's face. The deep purple birthmark glowed, even in the poor lighting.

Houston swore.

"You know the guy, Armstrong?"

"Yeah. He's the man who kidnapped my nephew."

Chapter Seven

Light streamed in through the church's stained glass windows, casting a rainbow shadow on the tweed-colored carpet in front of Travis. If only he could be out in the sunlight. Anywhere but on this hard, wooden pew.

His gaze drifted to the other side of the aisle. A guy from his weekly Bible study group waved, but Travis looked down. He hadn't been to the men's group in several months. He'd get back to it, as soon as he could get his life back on track.

Next to him, Cindy looked beautiful in her pink silk blouse and blue trousers. Her hair was fastened in a neat braid, and everything was in place, in spite of crying most of the night. At least, on the outside. But when his leg had brushed hers, she pulled away.

He owed her an apology, but he wasn't ready to talk yet. No, it would be better to tell her about his struggles when he was more certain of a solution. She would blame him for their predicament, but he wasn't the one who had insisted on private school or a closet full of designer clothes.

He clenched his jaw and stared straight ahead as the choir filed onto the stage. Truth be told, he was still angry. He felt like an animal with its foot in a trap.

Another baby.

How could Cindy be pregnant when he'd had a vasectomy? *This isn't happening. Did she cheat on me?* When they were dating in college, rumors circulated about Cindy and some football player. He chose not to believe the gossip, had never even asked her about it. He'd been afraid of the answer and what her reaction might be. Now, years later, he suspected her of committing adultery again. She didn't deserve that. A breath caught in his throat.

He twisted the gold band on his left ring finger as the choir sang. If he truly loved her more today than the day he'd married her, how come he felt so trapped?

He should be thrilled about the baby, but his true feelings cut to the heart. He didn't want another child. Babies cost a lot of money, and the timing couldn't be worse. In fact, he couldn't foresee a good time—he was drowning in debt.

He thought about the pile of unpaid bills hidden in his desk drawer. Seemed like the harder he worked, the deeper he sank. When was the last time he spent an entire day with the family? Business dealings had sapped more of his time than he thought possible. Cindy and the kids deserved better than him. On more than one occasion, Cindy had pleaded with him about spending more time with her and the kids. Adding another child into the mix would only stretch him thinner. He didn't have enough time for the four kids he already had.

"Did you bring the tithe check?" she whispered as the choir finished their song.

The question only intensified his troubled thoughts. "No, I'll mail it this week." The lies were becoming a habit. He'd had to tell a lie about the missing car. Told her he parked in a no-parking zone, and it got towed. He was trying to protect her from the ugly truth. The kids kept her busy enough. Why burden her with their money problems?

Travis opened the bulletin and read the day's topic: "Integrity – How to Live an Authentic Christian Life." *Maybe I should leave. I could tell her I'm not feeling well.* Perspiration formed on his brow, he fanned himself with the bulletin. He pulled at the knot on his tie and undid his top button.

As he leaned over to let Cindy know they needed to leave, Joe slid in at the end of their pew. "Well, if it isn't my favorite sister and her husband." Joe hugged Cindy, then shook Travis's hand.

"I'll take that compliment, even though I'm your only sister."

No hope of leaving now. He'd just have to suffer through the service. He had too much on his mind to concentrate on a sermon, especially one on integrity. *Lying, poor business decisions, a failing marriage … you're a great example of integrity!*

If only he were on the end so he could make a quick exit at the end of the service. He didn't feel like making small talk with anyone.

"We have news," Cindy whispered to Joe.

Travis leaned in close to her, "Let's not get into that right now, Cindy. We need to discuss it further."

She glared at him. "What's to discuss?" She turned back to Joe. "Ignore him. Travis is just a little shocked right now and not himself."

Joe's eyebrows shot up. "This must be good. Let's hear it."

Before Cindy could spill the dreadful news, the worship leader asked the congregation to stand. Travis had never been more relieved. Somehow sharing the news with family would make the pregnancy more real. Maybe Cindy had made a mistake; she hadn't even seen a doctor. Perhaps the home pregnancy test gave her a false positive. It was a slim possibility, but it did give him some measure of hope.

The service flew by. If given a test on the sermon, Travis would certainly fail. He placed his hand on Cindy's arm. "Let's get the kids and get out of here. I have work to do."

"Joe's meeting a friend from work for lunch, and he wants to know if I can join him. I'll only be a few hours. Do you mind watching the kids?" Cindy looked at Travis with such hope in her eyes.

With a pile of work waiting for him at home, he'd planned on Cindy feeding the kids lunch. He could get a lot of work done while they napped. "Can you make it another day?"

The disappointment in her eyes made his stomach tighten, but he pushed the guilt aside. Once they were out of this mess it would all be just a bad memory. "I'll tell you what. I'll get the kids and load them into the Land Rover. You can visit for a few minutes."

His offer did little to appease her, although he did notice a slight smile on her face. He excused himself and headed back to the nursery and Sunday school area. After collecting the kids, he dashed for the door. If he could make it to the parking lot, he could avoid having uncomfortable conversations with anyone else.

Carrying one twin boy in each arm, he urged the five-year-old twin girls to hurry.

Audrey pointed, "What's that man doing with our car?"

Travis looked up. The Land Rover was hooked up to a red tow truck. When the man at the wheel stuck his arm out the window and waved, the truck pulled out of the church parking lot.

How was he going to explain this to Cindy?

Chapter Eight

Fifteen minutes late for her date with Joe, Dominique hurried to the small wooden table at the back of the restaurant. Her stomach growled at the mingled aroma of cumin and oregano. Joe stood when she arrived at the table, and the napkin from his lap fell to the ground.

She picked it up and handed it to him. "If you're half as messy as I am eating Mexican food, you're going to need this."

"Thanks. Did you have trouble finding the place? I would have been happy to pick you up."

Dominique sat down. "I'm sorry I'm late. I thought Gladys would keep me from getting lost, but I guess I was wrong."

"Gladys?"

"Yeah, that's my GPS system. I gave her a name so I wouldn't resent her telling me where to go all the time."

Joe laughed. "I'm more of a map lover."

The waiter set a basket of warm tortilla chips and salsa on the table.

Dominique grabbed a chip. "How was church this morning?"

Joe leaned forward. "It was a really nice service. I enjoyed the message, and I got to see most of my family."

"Do you all go to the same church?" Dominique unwrapped her straw, then knotted the wrapper.

"Everyone except my dad."

"Doesn't he attend?"

Joe sipped his iced tea. "No. He's in the veteran's hospital. He's disabled, and now they're trying to convince us he has dementia or is mentally unstable."

"Is he misplacing things or wandering off?"

"No, nothing like that." He dipped a chip in the salsa. "They're concerned that dementia is exacerbating his supposed delusions."

Her eyebrows shot up. "I'm sensing from your tone that you aren't in agreement with this diagnosis."

"You're right about that one." He popped the chip in his mouth.

The waiter arrived and took their order, and Joe handed the menus back.

"I can't say I blame the doctors for their diagnosis. My dad is making some pretty unusual claims, but weird claims aren't always the same thing as delusion. There aren't any other symptoms consistent with mental trouble."

"What kind of claims is he making?" Dominique grabbed another tortilla chip and dipped it into the sauce.

Joe leaned forward. "He's telling everyone he knows the cause of the pregnancy crisis."

How could some old man have it figured out when the government, doctors, and respected scientists were stumped? *That would be a story.* "Does he have proof?"

"Not exactly. My dad grew up in this area, so he knows everyone. One day after a story ran on the news about the lack of newborns, he started tracking local births. His research showed that those babies were born only to couples who were committed Christians. He thinks the Lord is raising up a new generation."

The waitress returned to drop off some bread, which allowed Dominique time to let the words sink in. Not exactly what she expected. "You don't believe him, do you?"

Joe leaned back. "Actually, I do."

"Really?" Dominique did nothing to conceal her surprise. Yet her curiosity gnawed at her. At this point she was desperate for any direction in her investigation. "Why would God do something like that?"

"Because He can."

Goosebumps ran up her arms. *Is this God's judgment?* Her own conscience battled with her investigative instincts. "Isn't God supposed to love everyone, not just Christians?"

"The question isn't whether or not God loves us. He does. It's whether we accept His plan, even when it doesn't match what we think it should be."

Dominique shook her head. "I just don't believe God would single out a group of people like that. Why Christians? Why not a different group of people?" She fought to control her tone.

"I don't have the answer. There are places in Scripture where the Lord did open and close women's wombs." Joe paused for a moment. "Maybe He wants us to have a greater appreciation for life."

"That's a pretty big stretch, claiming He would single out Christians. Maybe it's a coincidence. Isn't it just as important for us to care for the life that's here already?"

Joe seemed to search for just the right words to say. "Have you ever been present when someone died?"

She rested her hand on the belly that once carried a child and swallowed her pain. *Does my own child count?* She cleared her throat. "No."

"I've witnessed a lot of deaths, and the thing that amazes me is the uniqueness of that single human life. It can never be duplicated. In the weeks following the death of a loved one, we contemplate what we wouldn't give for just one more moment with that person. Life is so very precious. Our society places such a lack of value on human life." Joe's eyes held hers, as though he was trying to gauge her reaction. "Since abortion has been legal in this country, over fifty-six million babies have lost their lives. The numbers are devastating."

My child was one of those statistics. Her throat swelled, and she wasn't sure she could say anything even if she knew how to respond.

The waiter headed toward their table with a tray holding their order. She let out a long breath.

After the waiter placed their plates in front of them, Joe said, "Do you mind if I say a blessing?"

She nodded and hoped his prayer would be short.

He said a quick grace, then resumed their discussion. "So, do you think I'm crazy, too?"

She felt drawn to at least investigate Joe's dad's claims, no matter how farfetched they seemed. As a woman who had undergone an abortion, she was heartsick. How could she ever confide in him now, knowing how he felt about abortion? "I think you're a man who loves his dad. There's nothing crazy about that."

"That's a nice way of avoiding the question. Do you think his theory holds any merit?"

"Let's just say I'm extremely skeptical."

"Then come see. Come to with me to our evening worship service tonight. You'll see something you haven't seen in a long time."

"What's that?"

"Pregnant women."

Chapter Nine

Travis stood at the end of his driveway and waved good-bye to the church member who had been kind enough to give his family a ride home. The short journey had taken forever. Although they only meant to be helpful, their endless suggestions grated his nerves. *No, I don't need the name of your mechanic, or an honest car salesman. Can you help me out of this financial pit I'm in?*

What would have happened if he'd blurted out the revolting truth? Would they have walked away and withdrawn their offers to help? What would Cindy have done? With a sigh, he followed Cindy into the house. They drifted further and further apart with each passing day. At this rate it would take forever to find their way back to one another.

Travis settled himself in his office and fired up his laptop. The girls went upstairs to play dress-up, and the boys giggled and chased each other in the living room.

Cindy leaned against the door frame. "Are you going to help with the pancakes? It *is* Sunday."

He longed for simple family tradition, but— "I can't today, honey. I know I don't usually work on Sundays, but I'm swamped."

"That's two weeks in a row. I hope this isn't going to become the norm." She took two steps into his office. "Is something troubling you?"

Tell her. Help with the pancakes, then have an honest conversation and open up.

After an awkward silence, she started to leave, then stopped and turned to face him. "Oh, I forgot to tell you, the school called and said we're two months behind on the girls' tuition. You said you paid that."

Travis opened the desk drawer and pulled out the checkbook. He casually flipped through the ledger, pretending to look for the entry. "I'll call them tomorrow. I'm sure it's just a mistake." He shoved the checkbook back into the drawer. "Sorry about lunch. I'll make it up to everyone next week." He stared at the computer screen, hoping she would drop the subject. He still caught the glare Cindy shot him when she left the office. Guilt stabbed at him, but he focused on the spreadsheet on the screen. The best thing he could do for his family was come up with a plan to save his business, not waste time making pancakes.

Unable to concentrate, he pulled out his phone. Three missed calls from his accountant. *This can't be good.* He couldn't return Scott's calls until he completed a business outlook plan for the next six months. Then Scott could let the bill collectors see the projected revenue increase. They would be paid the money owed them plus interest. The plan was sound. After putting it in motion, Travis would turn his attention to growing the business.

Two hours later, Cindy walked into his office and planted her hands on her hips. "What really happened to the Land Rover? First the truck, now the Land Rover."

"I told you, Cindy, I couldn't get the Land Rover started. And the truck was towed because I parked in a no parking zone. I'll handle it."

"Great!" She stormed out of the room.

Travis swore under his breath. What little he'd heard from the morning's sermon popped into his mind. *Integrity is what you do when no one is looking. We must be authentic before the Lord and others.* He didn't want to think about that. The pastor had probably never faced the kind of problems he was facing. What could he know about a failing business or crumbling marriage?

His cell phone rang again. He knew without looking that it was Scott. *Just get it over with.*

"I'm glad I finally got a hold of you. Payroll is scheduled to cycle on Tuesday." Scott let out a sigh. "You still don't have the money to cover it."

Travis clutched the phone tighter. "Move it from another account."

"There is no other account, Travis. You've depleted all of your resources. Do you have anything in one of your personal accounts you could transfer?"

His personal finances were in worse condition. He didn't know where next month's mortgage was coming from, never mind finding the money to cover an entire payroll. Where was he going to come up with that kind of money in just two days? He swallowed past the pain in his throat.

Vinnie Fernandez's face flashed across his mind.

Even though he'd already turned down the man's offer, it was looking like it might be his only choice. He looked at the figures he had been scribbling out for the last hour. Nothing but red. He wadded the paper into a ball and hurled it across the room. "Give me twenty-four hours. I'll see what I can do." He ended the call and tossed his cell phone on the desk.

His business had always operated on the up-and-up. Where had that gotten him? Bankruptcy, both personal and professional. Although Vinnie's reputation was less than stellar, he'd talk with him one more time. Now that he'd met the man, he would be better prepared. It would be such a relief to catch up on some bills. Travis smiled for the first time all day.

Bad company corrupts good character.

Travis tapped his fingers on his desk, ignoring the warning from this morning's sermon. The arrangement would be temporary. He would make sure of it.

The ticking of the clock on the mantel seemed loud. The kids must be napping. He climbed the stairs two at a time. When he reached the top, he heard it.

Sobbing.

Pain stabbed at his heart. Cindy was crying and he was to blame. For one brief moment, he thought about turning around and ignoring it, but he couldn't bring himself to do it. He headed down the hallway, his wingtip shoes silent on the plush carpet.

He tried turning the knob to the master bedroom, but it didn't move. He knocked softly, careful to not wake the kids.

The minutes seemed long before the door opened slightly. Cindy backed into their bedroom and sat down on their king-sized bed.

He sat next to her on the bed. "Cindy, I'm sorry. I know I've been distant lately, but I've been under a lot of pressure."

Silence.

"Please talk to me. I need to know you forgive me."

She grabbed a tissue from the box on the nightstand. "I don't know what to say, Travis."

"Well for starters, you can say you forgive me. You're right, I haven't been myself lately. I've been short with you."

"You just don't get it, do you?"

"Get what?"

"Are you even a little happy about the baby, Travis?"

The baby. Why did she have to bring that up? He wasn't ready to accept the fact that their family was going to grow by one. Or two. The knot in his stomach twisted tighter. Another set of twins would be incomprehensible. "Have you been to the doctor yet? Sometimes those home pregnancy tests are wrong."

"Guess that answers my question, doesn't it?"

He sighed. "I'm sorry. You've had a little more time to process this than I have." He brushed a stray strand of hair away from her face, and tucked it behind her ear. "Can we talk about this later? I have to go to a meeting."

"What kind of meeting? It's Sunday."

"Something came up that requires my immediate attention. I don't want to go, but I have to. I'll bring home a pizza for dinner. After the kids go to bed, we can talk."

Her face relaxed but her eyes still held questions.

"Try to take a nap before the kids wake up. I'll do my best to keep this meeting brief." Travis kissed her on the cheek.

He didn't wait for a response—her slumped shoulders and dull eyes told him she accepted the fact that he was going out. It wasn't as if he had a choice. He rubbed the knot out of his neck. If he didn't come to some sort of agreement with Vinnie, he would lose everything.

Careful to keep quiet, he went outside to the detached one-car garage where he kept the old truck. With its rusted-out body and leaky engine, it wasn't fit to be kept in their oversized three-car garage, but it was debt free. No one could repossess it. Hopefully, Vinnie would be at his restaurant and agree to meet with him.

While driving, he reviewed his final business proposal. He'd guessed what Vinnie might want in return for the loan: money laundering. Vinnie had been accused of it many times, even though he always evaded conviction. He would ask for a one-year business venture. His contracting company would provide a legitimate avenue for Vinnie to funnel his capital. But it was illegal and dangerous. Travis gripped the steering wheel as though his life depended on it. Maybe it did. The plan he'd drawn up assumed this was what was going on, and it was fair for both parties. In exchange for the currency he channeled for Vinnie, he would receive a cash advance and a small percentage off the total amount of money he moved each month. The advance would provide enough to get his vehicles back, pay the kids' tuition, and process the next two months' payrolls.

With a boost in revenue, he would devote some time to increasing new business and hopefully collect some of the money his vendors owed him. After one year, the contract would expire, and he would never have to do business with Vinnie Fernandez again. *Make the deal, fulfill your part of the contract, then get out!*

A different hostess greeted him, one much older, who had a warm, motherly look about her. Her voice was so soft, Travis almost didn't hear her. "Table for one?"

"Ah, no. Well yes, there's just one in my party. Actually, I was hoping to see Mr. Fernandez."

"Do you have an appointment?"

"No. I'm sorry, I don't. I met with him the other day, and I was hoping to discuss things a bit further."

"One moment please." The hostess headed toward the back.

His heart pounded so loud, it seemed like everyone in the restaurant could hear it. Never in his life would he have imagined even entertaining the idea of doing business with a criminal like Vinnie Fernandez. What would he do if Vinnie wouldn't let him out of the arrangement? Maybe he could hide the fact that his brother-in-law was a police officer, then use that as an excuse to dissolve their contract. Surely Vinnie wouldn't want the police looking too closely into his business affairs.

Before he had a chance to question his decision any further, the hostess reappeared.

"Mr. Fernandez will see you, Mr. Montgomery. Follow me."

His relief that Vinnie would see him was short lived. The hostess knew his name, but he hadn't given it to her. He followed her to the back of the restaurant and focused on the red-square linoleum floor to avoid making eye contact with the customers they passed.

She took him down a long hallway lined with four solid oak doors, tapped twice on the last door to the right, and opened it. "Mr. Fernandez will be right in."

As a building contractor, Travis appreciated the luxury and craftsmanship of the office. With its large cherry desk in the center of the room and a stately chair behind it, the office clearly belonged to a wealthy and powerful man. If Travis wasn't mistaken, it was positioned slightly higher than the chairs on the opposite side. Probably to make the person meeting with him feel insignificant. He was familiar with that feeling.

The expensive art, plush carpeting, and Italian designer furniture clearly spoke of power. Before he had an opportunity to inventory the entire room, the door opened.

"Hello, Travis. I've been expecting you."

Why had Vinnie been expecting him when he hadn't known he was coming here until a few hours ago?

Something wasn't right. Every instinct screamed at him to leave. Nothing good could come from this meeting. He would just end up being another one of Vinnie's pawns. *Think about Cindy and the kids ... what are you going to tell her?*

Travis took a deep breath, but instead of walking away, found himself saying, "Thank you for seeing me on such short notice, Mr. Fernandez."

"Let's forego the formalities. You can call me Vinnie. Have a seat."

Travis ran his hands over his legs to stop their trembling. He had been right. Vinnie's chair *was* elevated, leaving Travis feeling like a troubled, defiant student sitting in the ever-powerful principal's office.

He wouldn't give in to his feelings of insecurity. *Time to lay all the cards on the table. Either I make the deal, or I lose it all.*

"What can I help you with, Travis?"

"I may have spoken in haste at our previous meeting. I would like to talk about a business deal with you. I hope you'll be agreeable to my terms."

"I only work under my own terms." Vinnie tapped his thick index finger on the desk. "I thought I made that clear at our last meeting."

Sweat trickled down his sides and dampened his eyebrows. This wasn't going as planned. He needed to start fresh. How could he turn the tables? He'd present his offer, but leave out the one-year arrangement—he'd bring that up later when he sprang the whole brother-in-law-is-a-cop bomb.

"Of course. I'm familiar with your terms, Vinnie." Using the man's first name felt awkward. Travis hoped it didn't show in his voice. "I've just had some things come up, and I was hoping we could come to a satisfactory arrangement for both parties."

"How much do you need?"

Travis's heart thudded in his ears. Vinnie seemed to know his next move before he even had a chance to express it. How many other people had sat here, desperate for financial assistance, and had no choice but to allow this man to bully them into accepting his terms?

Vinnie leaned back in his chair. "You seem surprised I knew you need an advance. Let me tell you, son. I've been in business long enough to know there's only two things that drive a man. Money and women. Am I right?"

"Yes, sir." Again, Travis felt like a small child in a principal's office. It was difficult to breathe. He loosened his collar.

"Will one hundred grand cover your needs?"

Just like that. Vinnie could offer him one hundred thousand dollars without even batting an eye. It would definitely help him ... temporarily. He could get his cars back and make payroll. His other debts would still need attention, but at least he would have more breathing room.

"Yes, that should be sufficient." Travis put on his best poker face. He couldn't afford to let Vinnie know how desperate he'd become, or he'd lose what little negotiating power he had.

"Here's my terms, Travis." Vinnie leaned forward. "You filter some surplus funds I have through your corporation. You take a ten percent cash payback from the top. Your first obligation will be to pay me back the original loan, plus interest. After that, I don't care what you do with the money. I treat my business associates very well, but if you betray me, you'll regret it."

"Understood."

"Do you have any questions?"

"You mentioned interest. What is the rate you'll be charging?"

"A lot higher than those banks that keep turning you down. Don't worry, I'll let you know when the loan is settled. Any other questions?"

"Yes. How am I going to get this past my accountant? He's a pretty sharp guy and meticulous with the books."

"That's easy: You're going to fire him. I'll provide you with an accountant, and you can pay her the same salary you paid your previous one."

Fire Scott? He'd worked for Travis for as long as he'd been in business. They attended the same church. Scott had a wife, and three kids. What would he tell him?

Travis swallowed the lump in his throat. "That's fine. I'll handle that matter immediately." He gripped the arms of the chair.

"You're going to enjoy working for me, Travis." Vinnie slid a thick manila envelope across the desk.

Travis took it with trembling hands and stuck it in his briefcase. If only this money didn't come with so many strings. "Thank you, sir. What do I do if I have further questions?"

"Ask your accountant. Let's keep our communication to emergencies only."

Travis stood and offered his hand across the desk. "Thank you again for your help. I won't let you down." His arms tingled.

Vinnie shook his hand, then pulled out another envelope and handed it to him. "Consider this a little bonus. A welcome-to-the-company gift."

Travis opened the envelope. Inside were two keys. "I'm not sure what these are for, sir."

"Leave through the back entrance. You'll understand."

"Okay … thanks." Travis stuffed the envelope with the keys into the side pocket of his briefcase. Just outside the back door, he stopped short.

Parked in the alley were his truck and Cindy's Land Rover. Both sparkled from a recent washing and a fresh coat of wax.

How had Vinnie gotten them from the repossession company? He walked back into the restaurant and knocked on Vinnie's door.

"Come in."

The questions he had been so eager to fire at Vinnie now stuck in his mouth. "I don't understand. How did you get my cars?"

Vinnie closed the distance between them and stepped into Travis's personal space. "Never underestimate me. I have connections everywhere."

Travis backed out of the room, his thoughts bouncing around in his head. He had been played. Vinnie knew, even at their first meeting, that he'd be back. His feet dragged. Now he had to go home, call Scott, and fire him.

He looked down the alley at his two vehicles. How was he going to get Cindy's Land Rover and his two trucks home?

Two young men came out the back door, both taller, slimmer versions of Vinnie. The older one said, "Uncle Vinnie says you may need some help getting your trucks home."

"Do you both have your driver's license?"

When they laughed, Travis tossed the keys to his trucks to them. He would drive Cindy's Land Rover. "Follow me."

"We already know where you live."

A chill ran up Travis's back. *What have I gotten myself into?*

Chapter Ten

Dominique grasped the steering wheel and stretched her arms. A little over ten minutes late. Not because she had any problems finding the building, but because she'd sat outside in her car for over twenty minutes deciding whether it would be worth it to go inside. The only reason she showed up at Joe's church was to see if there was a slight possibility that his father's crazy theory held any truth.

Finally, her curiosity won out, and she headed inside. The first thing she saw was two women standing together talking. Her heart jumped when she noticed their expanded bellies.

"Are you getting any sleep?" the woman on the left asked.

"No. Too much back pain. How about you?"

Dominique pulled out her phone, turned off the sound, and pretended to check the time while she snapped a quick picture of the women.

Her footsteps were silent on the navy blue carpet as she walked into the sanctuary. She tucked a stray strand of hair behind her ear and glanced at the rear of the church.

Joe stood behind the last row of wooden pews. He raised his hand and offered her a winning smile. Things were looking up.

An elderly man with round glasses handed her a bulletin as she passed.

"I'm glad you made it," Joe whispered as she reached his side.

"Sorry I'm late." Looking around the room, she counted four more pregnant women, bringing the total to six.

"Do you mind if we sit with my sister? Cindy is by herself tonight."

"That's fine." She followed him down the aisle, thankful his sister wasn't sitting in the front row. Just being in a church was difficult enough to endure. It seemed like they'd just taken their seats when the worship leader asked for everyone to stand. The worship team played a version of "Amazing Grace" she had never heard.

Shivers ran throughout her body, giving her chills. She should have worn a sweater—air conditioning always made her cold. Maybe she'd snuggle up close to Joe and cause a stir. The thought brought a smile.

At the end of the song, a large, stately man bounded forward with a hearty, "Praise the Lord! What a worship time that was!"

Her shoulders slumped, and she took in a deep breath. Next would come the talk about how unholy she was. How God was perfect, white as snow, and she was nothing but a filthy rag. She'd heard it all before. From preachers and her mother. No one knew that fact better than she did.

She wasn't worthy. She'd *never* be worthy. There was nothing she could do to earn God's favor. Case closed. Why even try?

"God loves you. Period. There's not a thing you can do about it," the preacher began. "He loves you, and He wants you to give your life over to Him. Not so He can control your every move, but so He can bless you."

What? She leaned back. She'd never heard those words before. That contradicted everything she'd learned about religion. Why would God want her? She had a laundry list of reasons why He shouldn't love or accept her. She sat up straighter. What would the preacher say next?

Instead of continuing his message, he introduced a woman in her late forties, early fifties. What could this woman possibly have to say?

"Hi, my name is Amanda Clearwater. Most of you know me as Mandy. I'm here today to share with you a story of the Lord's grace and forgiveness, and to tell you about the miracles He's performing, even today."

Joe leaned over. "Sunday evenings are more of a time for personal testimonies and prayer requests. They're always encouraging."

Mandy's voice shook as she spoke. "Never in my life would I have imagined standing up in front of an entire congregation and sharing my past. I grew up in the average American home. My dad worked two jobs to keep food on the table, and my mom did her best to keep track of me and my four brothers and sisters." She ran her free hand through the length of her hair. "Once I hit my teen years, I went a little wild. My first pregnancy occurred at the age of fifteen. I knew I was too young to have a baby, and my boyfriend at the time wholeheartedly agreed. So he drove me to, and paid for, my first abortion."

Dominique sat up. She'd never heard this issue discussed in church.

Mandy relaxed her grip on the microphone. "I was devastated. Completely alone and devastated. The counselor at the clinic told me I might feel that way for a while and supplied me with a box of condoms. I immediately regretted my decision, but I didn't have anyone to talk to. I became depressed, and soon afterwards, my boyfriend, who had promised to stay by my side through thick and thin, dumped me.

"I soon found another boyfriend, and it was less than a year before I ended up in the same predicament. That time I made a different choice. I confided in my mother, but I failed to tell her about my first abortion. She didn't want to tell my father because she was afraid of his reaction. So she drove me to the clinic. I had a second abortion. The clinic didn't tell her about my first visit, because my records were my business, not my mother's.

"I was inconsolable." Tears streamed down the woman's cheeks.

Dominique was hypnotized. She knew this woman's pain. She shared in her anguish. Emotions welled up inside, and Dominique reached into her purse and grabbed a tissue.

"I swore off men and dating. At the ripe old age of sixteen I had already had two abortions. I couldn't get my babies off of my mind. Would I have had girls or boys? One of each? The brochures they hand out inform you that it's not a baby, it's nothing but a clump of tissue."

She licked her lips. "They lie."

Mandy moved the microphone to her other hand. "We know from the technology now available that by the time you find out you're pregnant, your baby has a beating heart. Six weeks after conception, brainwaves can be detected. He or she is a beautiful bundle of life just waiting for the opportunity to take his or her place in the world."

Mandy took a sip of water. "The remainder of my high school years went by somehow. I was determined to never put myself in that situation again. But my secret pain was never more than a heartbeat away. Anniversaries came and went, and I didn't have a single person with whom I could share my grief.

"I decided if I was going to make something out of myself, I needed to get away from my past. I was accepted at a small out-of-state college and couldn't wait to start my life over. I moved into a co-ed dormitory and immediately began enjoying college life.

"My two roommates introduced me to the college party scene. I'd never tasted alcohol, but I found that I loved it. Not only did getting drunk make me feel good, it numbed the pain. I'd do anything to escape the pain.

"But drinking to excess creates other problems. So, by my second semester as a college freshman, I found out for the third time that I was expecting a baby.

"I was at a crossroads. I didn't know what to do. Should I have the baby and do the best I could to be a good mother? What would be involved with the adoption process? A third abortion was absolutely out of the question.

"My boyfriend said he would support whatever decision I made. I called a local pregnancy crisis center and made an appointment. I was determined not to have another abortion and wanted to look into adoption. I informed the father of my decision, but he wasn't as supportive of my choice as I'd hoped he would be.

"He told me he was hoping I would do the sensible thing and end the pregnancy. We both had college to get through, and he wasn't ready to be a husband or a father. He was also against putting the baby up for adoption. Claimed he didn't want some child of his popping up twenty years down the road and possibly ruining the life he had worked so hard to build. What if he had a wife and children? What would they think? He told me he would pay for an abortion. I'd never confided to him that I'd already had two, so he couldn't understand why I was so resistant to the idea. From what he'd heard, it was a very safe and easy procedure. He didn't know the truth."

Dominique looked around the room. Every eye was focused on Mandy. Surely she wouldn't have a third abortion, not after all of the pain she had endured in the past.

"I insisted on keeping the appointment with the pregnancy crisis center. I told him I would let him know my final decision. To my surprise, he agreed to go with me. Things were looking up … or so I thought. The next week we went to the center. They sat us down in a conference room and talked with us about abortion. They told us the truth, information the abortion clinic conveniently avoided talking about. The simple truth that I was carrying a baby, not a clump of tissue, and that if we chose to have an abortion we would be ending a human life. And not just any human life, but our child's. Our very own flesh and blood.

"The next step was a basic physical. This confirmed that I was indeed pregnant, in fact, I was four weeks further along than I had originally thought. I was twelve weeks pregnant. I was stunned. Also shocking was the fact I was pregnant with twins."

Dominique's cell phone vibrated, and she chose to ignore it. She didn't want to miss a word of what Mandy had to say. She was right there … absorbed in the midst of Mandy's turmoil.

Mandy ran a trembling hand through her hair. "After hearing I was expecting twins, my boyfriend asked the counselor if we could have a moment alone. When the counselor left the room, he took an envelope from his jacket and placed it in front of me. He told me it contained $567 and to use it toward an abortion. He reasoned there was no way either one of us was ready for the responsibility of two babies. He wished me luck and told me not to call or contact him again. I pleaded with him to stay and speak with the counselor, but he refused and left. I had never felt more betrayed and alone in my life."

A collective gasp resounded in the room. Dominique cleared her throat and adjusted her necklace.

"When the counselor returned, she asked if we'd made a decision. I told her I wasn't sure and left. I decided to walk the five miles back to campus and use the time to think. By the time I arrived back at my dorm, I was no closer to reaching a decision than when I'd left.

"Two babies? I was overwhelmed with the prospect of trying to raise one baby. What about adoption? Could I even give up two babies? I didn't know what to do. I just wanted to wake up and have it all be a bad dream.

"The next day, my literature professor asked if he could speak to me after class. He informed me that he'd submitted some of my essays and poems for consideration to a prestigious magazine that had contacted him in hopes of finding an intern. He told me they were impressed with my work, and I'd earned the position. That meant my sophomore year would be spent as an intern at the magazine, and I would also be earning college credit.

"That turn of events threw me the lifeline I thought I was looking for. How could I have a baby and do an internship? My pregnancy would get in the way. I made the appointment and had the abortion. The procedure didn't go as planned. Because I was further along, the bleeding was severe. I developed a serious infection and suffered other complications.

"My sophomore year turned out to be a disaster. I continued to make the same poor choices, which left me broken and bitter. I became depressed, and three weeks into the internship, I was fired. In time, I managed to earn my bachelor's degree and obtain a good job, but personally I was suffering. I completely shut myself off from the opposite sex, turning down all offers for dates. If a friend offered to set me up on a blind date, I would refuse. I wanted to live the rest of my life as I felt I deserved ... alone.

"But that's not where God wanted me. The Lord had different plans. One evening when I was home alone, Billy Graham came on the television. He spoke of a man named Saul who had been completely transformed. That's what I needed—complete transformation. That night, I gave my life to Christ.

"Eventually, I met and married Tony. We were very happy, and we both longed to be parents. When I told Tony about my past history and my brokenness over all the children I would never hold, he hugged me, and told me he loved me and that we would meet those precious babies in heaven. He wiped my tears and bathed me in compassion and forgiveness.

"We were thrilled when we found out we were expecting our first child, only to be disappointed when I miscarried in my first trimester. That was followed by three years of not being able to conceive again. After consulting with a specialist, the news was almost more than I could bear ... I was infertile. I had a condition known as Asherton's Syndrome."

Dominique looked down. She was holding Joe's hand. When had that happened? His touch was warm and comforting. She turned her attention back to Mandy, but kept her fingers intertwined with Joe's.

Mandy continued, "Asherton's Syndrome is caused by scar tissue left in the uterus. I was devastated. Why did Tony have to pay for my past mistakes? He would have made a wonderful father. We accepted our situation and even thought about adopting a child. We had two adoptions fall through, and after much prayer, decided the Lord must have other plans for us.

"You may be wondering why I'm up here, publicly confessing my past sins. I'm doing it because the Lord asked me to. He wanted me to give the testimony of my heartbreaking past, so you could fully grasp the incredible miracle that is going to be my future.

"Tony and I just found out that we're going to be parents. Yes, after multiple abortions, years of infertility, and two miscarriages, I'm going to have a baby!"

When the room broke out in applause, Dominique clapped with them, but her heart wasn't in it. Instead, her mind slowed to a crawl as it tried to absorb this woman's words.

How was this possible? Could there be hope for her?

But Dominique's thoughts were drawn back to her conversation with Joe about his dad's theory. A chill ran up her back, and goose bumps appeared on her arms. The logical side of her wanted to throw the idea out as completely impossible. *But why would God limit pregnancies to only Christians, especially if God was as loving as Joe's preacher said?*

"Are you cold?"

Joe's question jolted her from her disturbing thoughts. "I'm fine." She glanced down when Joe took her hand again.

When the applause settled down, Mandy took a deep breath, then smiled. "I'm here tonight to tell you that nothing is impossible with God. He forgave me completely, and He longs to forgive you. All you have to do is ask."

Joe squeezed Dominique's hand, then released it.

Heat flooded her cheeks. She hadn't felt cared for in such a long time. What would he do if she confessed everything to him? Her cell phone vibrated again. She checked the caller ID and rolled her eyes … a text from Channing.

Channing: *Where r u?*

He would never believe her if she told him. She texted back: *Work*

Channing: *Any leads?*

Dominique: *Just got a big one!*

Channing: *Call me.*

Instead, she put her cell phone away and asked Joe. "I know this may sound strange, but do you think I could meet your dad?"

Chapter Eleven

Dominique balanced her laptop bag and the tray of food as she navigated through the hospital's cafeteria, thankful she hadn't spilled her chicken noodle soup when she bumped a rack of chips. She took her place in the long line of restless people waiting to pay for lunch.

She cocked her head and studied the man in front of her. Where had she seen him before? Ah, of course. "You're Houston Armstrong, aren't you? Joe's brother?"

"I guess I can admit to that." Houston let out a slight laugh. "You're his girlfriend, Dominique, right? We were going to meet for lunch, but he got paged and had to leave."

She blushed. Unsure of how to respond, she changed the topic. "Would you like to join me? Seats can be hard to come by in this cafeteria."

He smiled. "Thanks."

After they paid for their lunches, she led him toward an empty table along the back wall. "I need a place to plug my laptop in later. I have a lot of work to do, and my office can be so distracting." *Especially when Penelope is on the prowl.*

She placed her lunch tray on the table and tucked her laptop safely away under the seat. Now all she had to do was to figure out a way to steer the conversation to the recent baby kidnappings. "Are you coming off a shift or getting ready to start one?"

Houston sighed. "Finishing a long one. I got called in to work last night. I wouldn't work another case like this one if you paid me a million dollars."

"Rough night?"

"You could say that."

She stuck a spoon in her soup and stirred the contents. "Another kidnapping?"

Houston took a sip of his coffee. "No, but the case is related."

This was her chance. "Do you have any other leads or suspects?"

"Nothing so far."

"Any gut instincts?"

"You're not a tabloid reporter are you?" He examined her through narrowed eyes. Just as she thought he might have recognized her, his face relaxed and he grinned.

She laughed, maybe a little too hard. "No, no. It seems like the cops investigating the actual crime scenes usually have a different perspective, that's all."

"Well, if I were in charge of the whole investigation, I'd start with the person who's usually behind ninety-nine percent of the crime in this city."

"Who's that?"

"Vinnie Fernandez. If he's not responsible for the crimes himself, I'm willing to bet he knows who is."

That name again. Dominique made a mental note, as she tried to think of a good follow-up question.

"You and Joe been dating long?"

Houston's question took her by surprise. "Well, I don't know if I'd use the word dating."

"I'm sorry, I just assumed. You were with him at the station, and your name has come up a few times in conversations lately."

"No need to apologize. Several nurses have asked me the same thing today after one of them saw me with Joe at the church service last night. Apparently, the rumor mill at the hospital is going full force."

"I'm sure you devastated a slew of pining nurses when they heard the news." Houston's smile reminded her of Joe's.

"I'm sure they'll be relieved when they find out the truth. We've shared a few meals ... and I do enjoy his company." Heat traveled up her neck and face. She must be deep red. Without a clever comment to make up for her babbling, she let out a laugh. "I don't know what I'm saying. It's just that what people saw last night, isn't what they *think* they saw. Does that make sense?"

Dominique caught movement out of the corner of her right eye. Penelope was headed straight toward them, her face sporting a sour look.

She stopped in front of their table and poked a finger towards Dominique. "Are you aware you missed another staff meeting?"

"Yes. I sent you an e-mail to let you know that I couldn't attend. I have loads of work I need to catch up on."

Penelope scrutinized the table. "Is this your idea of working?"

This woman was a piece of work! Dominique's short temper flared, but she attempted to keep it at a low burn. "No, this is my idea of lunch. Is there anything else I can help you with?"

Penelope cleared her throat. "There are several items that need your immediate attention. One in particular. There are a few discrepancies with your social worker's license. I'm afraid the hospital can't wait on this matter."

Darn that Penelope. Leave it to her to bring this matter up in front of Joe's brother—a cop no less! Dominique stole a glance at Houston, who apparently wanted to hear her response as much as Penelope did.

"That's odd. What did Kevin in Human Resources say? He handled all of my paperwork." Always answer a question with another question, a standard reporter technique.

Penelope looked aside and let out a sigh. "I haven't spoken with him yet."

"Well then, I would start there. Anything else I can help you with?"

Penelope's left eyebrow raised. "You weren't much of a help at all. I'll be back in touch." She turned and stomped off like a child who'd just been told she couldn't have a second ice cream cone.

Houston laughed. "Nice lady."

"She's a real challenge to work for."

"Joe told me about some of your dealings with her. Better watch your back."

He has no idea!

"I'd better get going. I've been working all night, and I still have hours of paperwork to do before I can head home." Houston rose and grabbed his tray, still laden with his half-eaten lunch. "Are you done with your lunch? I can take your tray up."

She gathered her things together and handed them to him. "Thanks, Houston."

He took a step away, then turned back toward her. "Oh, if I see Joe, I'll let him know I think he'd be a fool to let you get away."

She cradled her head between her hands. How could she continue lying to these people? They were all so nice. She needed to speed up her investigation.

64

Today's project: review again the list of patients who had given birth within the last eighteen months. But first she would focus on the baby snatchings.

After her computer fired up, she went to Google search and typed in the name Vinnie Fernandez.

Chapter Twelve

Vinnie Fernandez was behind this latest murder—Houston was sure of it.

He drove down the country road he lived on. Several horses grazed in the field across the street from his house. When he pulled into the driveway, his shoulders relaxed for the first time today. Houston loved their home, a large two-story farmhouse with a wrap-around porch. It was peaceful living out in the country away from the noise and crime. Becky made everything pleasant. He was a lucky man, and he knew it.

He took the porch steps two at a time. When he looked up, she stood at the top with a worried expression on her face.

Houston enveloped her in a big hug, breathing in her familiar scent. Lord, he loved this woman. "I missed you." He spoke softly into her ear. He tried to kiss her, but she pulled back slightly. "We need to talk, Houston."

He brushed his lips on her forehead. "Sorry I didn't call earlier. How'd it go at the nursing home? Is he all checked in?"

She averted her eyes.

"Is everything okay?" The hair raised on his arms. "The admission was routine, right?"

"I'm not sure where to start."

Not good. Becky always was straight forward. He rubbed the back of his neck. "Can we talk inside? I'm a little tired." Houston reached for the door handle. "We'd be more comfortable inside." He kissed her lightly.

Instead, Becky took a seat on the old wooden porch swing. "I did something I truly believe was the right thing to do, but you may not see it that way."

What could be so bad that she insisted on beating around the bush so much? "It's okay, honey. You know I love you; we'll work it out. It can't be as bad as you think." He sat next to her and draped an arm around her shoulders. "You know you can tell me anything."

She hesitated. "I didn't put your dad in the nursing home the hospital recommended. It was awful. I couldn't leave him there." She bit her lip and looked away.

Houston stopped the swing. "Is he back in the hospital?"

"No."

"Where is he?"

Becky took his hand. "Right now, he's resting in the spare bedroom."

He jerked back. "What did you say?"

"He's in the spare bedroom." Pain filled her eyes and furrowed her brow. "Please don't look at me that way. The place smelled of urine. I saw a few cockroaches. And when I went in the residents' rooms, most of them had empty water pitchers and dirty linens on their beds. I couldn't leave him at the nursing home, Houston. In fact, I wish I could have brought every last one of those patients home. Nobody should have to live like that."

He let the full impact of the news sink in. His father, here, in his home. *Impossible.* He couldn't live under the same roof with him, not after what his dad had done. He could never forgive him. Would *never* forgive him.

Becky's eyes pleaded with him. How could she do this to him? She knew how he felt about his dad. "Why didn't you call me?" He kept his tone even. "He was discharged to a nursing home, Becky, not our home."

"I'm sorry. I should have called you." She rubbed both her arms. "I didn't know what to do. I spoke with the hospital. He's been officially released, against medical advice. I know this comes as a shock to you, but I couldn't think of any other place to take him."

"What about Cindy and Travis? They have plenty of room."

"They also have four kids, and I think they may be having marital problems."

"What? We just saw them yesterday, and everything seemed fine."

"Things aren't always as they appear. It's a strong feeling I have. Anyway, I felt bringing Samuel here was my only option."

Joe's place was out of the question. It was too small, and he was never home. "Couldn't you have taken him back to the hospital? Sheesh, Becky, now what are we going to do?"

She chewed on her lip. "I'm not sure. The hospital won't re-admit him unless he agrees to take the sedatives. He refuses. And I've got to tell you, I think he's right."

Houston paced on the front porch. This was his worst nightmare. He could barely tolerate being in the same room as his father, let alone living under the same roof. "How long will he be here?"

"So he can stay?"

"I don't really think I have a choice now." His words were cold, but he'd been forced into this position. Silence filled the air for several moments. He let out a slow breath. If he refused to let his dad stay, he'd look like a jerk. But if he allowed him to stay ... How could Becky have put him in such a situation?

"Houston, I'm sorry. You know I would never do anything to intentionally hurt you." Her hands trembled. "Please forgive me." Her eyes pooled with tears.

He leaned against the railing. Their arguments never lasted long—he could never stay angry with her. But this was different. Why couldn't she let things be?

He hung his head. He'd never shared it with her ... how could she know the full impact of this decision? He should've shared the truth with her a long time ago.

He glanced at Becky huddled on the swing, and his anger deflated. Her kind heart was one of the things he loved most about her. How could he ask her to be anything less than what she was?

He opened his arms, and she stepped in and hugged him tightly.

"I'm so sorry. Please know I would never hurt you intentionally. I truly didn't know what to do."

He pressed her closer. She always smelled so good, and she felt just right in his arms. He would not let his dad come between them. His father had ruined what little family life Houston had growing up. He wouldn't let him ruin his marriage.

Houston kissed Becky lightly. "Shhh, I love you, Becky. It'll be okay. I love your caring heart. It's what makes you such a wonderful wife and nurse. We'll figure something out."

Wrapped in each other's arms, Houston drank in the stillness. After a few minutes, he kissed her forehead. "Let's go inside."

When he took a step into the living room, he broke a vow he'd made to himself years ago—the promise that he would never again, under any circumstances, live under the same roof with Samuel Armstrong.

Chapter Thirteen

Tuesday morning, Travis pulled into the parking lot of the model home at the front of an upscale subdivision which doubled as his business office. The two-story brick home, with custom stained glass windows and professional landscaping, showcased his talents as a professional builder. Normally, he also considered it a private getaway, but today it felt like a prison. He could almost hear the metallic sound of a cell door slamming when he closed the door behind him.

The empty lot made his stomach churn. He never thought he'd miss seeing Scott's beat-up Ford Windstar, but now he'd be happy to see it every day for the rest of his life. He'd never forget the expression on Scott's face when he told him he was letting him go. Even worse, he hadn't been able to answer any of the questions Scott fired at him. All he'd been able to say was that his final paycheck would be sent in the mail. He shook his head at the dismal memory.

Travis checked his watch. The new accountant would be in at nine, which left him a little over a half an hour to get things ready. First, he needed to deposit cash into his bank account so payroll could process.

Inside, his footsteps rang out on the hardwood floors as he passed the empty reception desk. Thankfully, it wasn't one of the days the part-time receptionist came in. This would give him a chance to talk with his accountant without the risk of their conversation being overheard.

A car pulled into the parking lot, followed by the slam of a door. Probably the new accountant. He hurried to his office, the room which would have served as the master bedroom in a residential home, and grabbed a few files from the in-box on his desk. It would be better to look busy, as if he were carrying on business as usual.

The front door opened, and heels clicked on the hardwood floors. Someone gave a soft knock on his door.

"Come in!"

"Hello, Travis, it's good to see you again." Angelica, the hostess from Vinnie's restaurant, stood before him. Her long dark hair was pulled over to one side, and the cut of her red dress left little to the imagination. Words stuck in his mouth.

She raised her eyebrows. "Didn't Vinnie tell you to expect me?"

"No … I mean … It's just … " Heat spread throughout his body, and his hands felt numb. The effect she had on him now was just as strong as the first time he met her. This could be a problem.

They were completely alone, just the two of them. How was he going to fight this temptation? He looked at the picture of Cindy and the kids on his desk. He loved his family; he needed his family. He would have to keep things strictly professional.

"Where's my office?" She smiled. "Or are we sharing this one?"

How could her smile be friendly and seductive at the same time? He ignored her innuendo regarding sharing the same bedroom. "Upstairs, first door on the right. After you get settled, please come back down. There's a few things we need to go over." Travis tried to make his tone authoritative and professional. He must maintain the upper hand in this relationship.

"I'll be down shortly." She turned to leave, then came back. "I don't know how much Vinnie told you, but you work for me, Travis, not the other way around. We'll get along just fine if you remember that." She left the door open behind her. The smile she gave him this time didn't match the cutting tone of her words.

Fifteen minutes passed before she made her way back down the stairs. Reporting to Angelica wasn't part of the deal he'd made with Vinnie. Or was it? If he couldn't establish control, he'd never be able to sever the contract.

She entered the room. "You ready to get down to business?" She placed several file folders and a large ledger on his desk.

He eyed the folders. "Are those for me?"

"Very good. You catch on quick." She winked. "You need to keep these in a safe with a combination lock, which, of course, I will have access to. From now on, you'll have two sets of books. One for the IRS to see and another that will document new business. I'll handle both sets of books. You need to familiarize yourself with these eight companies, enough so that if you're questioned, you'll be able to talk intelligently about them."

"Are these actual companies?"

"To you they are. I can't really divulge a lot of details, Travis. You've just begun working for Vinnie. Trust must be earned."

He didn't miss her choice of words emphasizing he was working for Vinnie. He needed one victory, however small it may be. "I have a secretary who comes in three times a week. She'll put your employee information into our system."

"I need a list of all of her responsibilities."

"She answers the phone, handles some scheduling, and does a hundred other miscellaneous things I usually don't have time for."

"Vinnie doesn't like outsiders interfering with his businesses, but I'll speak with him and see if she can stay."

This wasn't going as he'd planned. "I won't let her go. She's been with my company since day one. She's an elderly woman, and she needs this income to supplement her social security." He hoped Angelica didn't detect the panic in his voice.

"Relax, Travis, I'm sure it will be fine. Trust me, you're going to like working for Vinnie."

The last thing he could do was trust Vinnie, or Angelica, or even himself for that matter. He desperately needed help.

Chapter Fourteen

Dominique tightened her grip on the steering wheel. For the next step in her investigation, she needed to dive deeper into Vinnie's world. The kidnapping investigation continued to consume more of her time. Avoiding Penelope had become somewhat of a new game—dodging down the hallway at just the right time, checking caller ID, and letting the pesky call roll to voice mail. Dominique was becoming quite the expert. She left a rather hurried message on the busybody's voicemail, advising her that she would be taking a few days off.

It was time do to some heavy-duty investigating.

First, she would become familiar with Vinnie's surroundings. She pulled her rented blue Taurus into the parking lot of Castalgia's, the melting pot of his businesses, both legal and illegal. She had driven by the restaurant on multiple occasions, and each time, Vinnie's car had been in the lot. With a little luck, she would get her first glimpse of him.

She pulled her notebook from her purse and read her notes. The district attorney had charged Vinnie with racketeering, money laundering, and a series of misdemeanors, but he could never get a conviction. That was going to change.

An elderly hostess greeted Dominique and escorted her to a booth by the window. Dominique's stomach growled in response to the heavenly smells of garlic, tomato, and fresh bread coming from the kitchen. She'd expense the meal to Stew as a working lunch. Only six other tables were occupied. It was a little past the lunch hour. Maybe that's why they were slow. Toward the back of the restaurant, a few private booths were set off to themselves. That must be where all the real business took place.

Waiters, bartenders, and doormen always had the most intriguing and helpful leads, so when the waiter brought the tea she'd ordered and a small basket with two biscuits, she said, "That was quick. You work here long?"

"I've been here a little over a year."

Dominique leaned forward. "Do you like it?"

"It's a job. I don't like it when things are slow." He placed his empty tray underneath his arm.

"Which is worse? The customers or the management?" She gave her best smile in an attempt to pry a little information from him.

He laughed. "That's a loaded question."

"No seriously, I may be looking for a part-time job, and I was wondering if the management is good here." She took a small sip of her tea and averted her eyes. "I've waited tables in other restaurants, and bad management can make for a terrible working environment."

The waiter leaned in closer and lowered his voice. "I'd apply elsewhere."

She met his gaze. "Any particular reason why?"

"You ask too many questions." He frowned. "That's not a good habit to get into around here. Have you decided what you'd like?"

After he left, she scolded herself. *Could you be a little more obvious?*

The meal arrived in a timely manner. It looked and smelled delicious. As she plucked a piece of bread from the basket, a very pregnant woman entered the restaurant. The hostess sat her at the table directly across from Dominique's booth.

The woman smiled at Dominique. "I love the food here. I can't seem to get enough of their Caesar salad."

Dominique put her fork down. "Try the ravioli, it's amazing."

Movement in the back hallway caught her eye. Two young men were deep in conversation. They pointed at the woman across from Dominique. They focused in on her like lions hunting prey.

What little was left of Dominique's appetite diminished. What if the woman was in danger? How could she help her? *Maybe it's nothing.* Her stomach clenched. Other than her gut instincts, she had no proof. But each time she had ignored that internal nudging, she'd lived to regret it. *Not this time. There's too much at stake.*

"Can I get you any dessert today?" the waiter asked when he stopped at Dominique's table.

She declined and asked for the check. He returned with the bill and placed it on the table. Dominique slipped her credit card into the black leather case and waited for him to return. *What should I do? I can't leave her here all by herself.*

Images of the kidnapped women and children shown in the news flashed in her mind. Their pictures had haunted her for several days. She had to help this woman, even if she didn't realize she was in danger.

The men had disappeared from the hallway, but it couldn't have been her imagination. They had stared at that pregnant woman with dollars in their eyes. When the waiter returned with her card and receipt, Dominique left a generous tip, then stopped at the expectant woman's table. "Enjoy your salad."

"I decided to try the ravioli too." She patted her belly. "I'm eating for two, you know."

"Well, I hope you enjoy your meal."

"Thanks."

At the front door, Dominique grabbed her cell phone to take a picture of the pregnant woman. She adjusted her position to make it appear she was texting. Just as she was about to snap the photo, the woman bowed her head in prayer. A chill ran up her spine. *Another pregnant Christian.* Joe's dad's theory was becoming more realistic with each passing day. She busied herself by looking at the various paintings on the wall. When the woman was done praying, she quickly took the picture.

Outside, she hurried to her rental car. Four other cars besides her own were parked in the front.

Two spots over from her car, one of the men who had been staring at the pregnant woman stood next to the back of a white Toyota Camry.

Just as she unlocked her door, she noticed the other man who'd been in the hallway crouched behind him.

Dominique slid into her car, but instead of leaving pretended to look for something in her purse.

A few moments later, the second man stood, and both sauntered back into the restaurant. She wasn't a betting woman, but she'd lay odds that car belonged to the pregnant woman … and that she was in danger. Should she call Joe and ask him to contact Houston? But how could she explain why she was here? No, if she was going to maintain her cover, she'd have to handle the matter herself.

She pulled around to the side of the restaurant to keep an eye on the Camry.

Her heart pounded at the sight of a white conversion van parked in the alley.

She pulled out her phone and took a picture of the van. She couldn't be certain that it was the same one involved in the kidnapping of Joe's nephew, but some of the articles she read about other kidnappings mentioned that a similar van had been spotted near the location of a few of the abductions. Her experience as a reporter told her when coincidences started adding up, she was onto a tremendous lead in a case.

Dominique kept her eyes trained on the door. A little over twenty minutes passed before the woman emerged from the restaurant.

Dominique checked her mirrors. The alley was still deserted.

The pregnant woman made her way toward the white Toyota.

Dominique tightened her grip on the steering wheel. *Should I warn her?* No. It would be too obvious if someone was watching. She would follow her, and when she was sure no one had trailed either of them, she would decide what action to take—if any.

She remained a few car lengths behind the white Toyota. With the light traffic it was easy to keep the car in sight, even though it had been over a year since she had tailed a car during an investigation.

The stoplight ahead of her turned yellow just after the Camry passed. Dominique slowed to a stop and reprimanded herself for drifting too far back. She pounded the steering wheel when a delivery truck turned onto the road in front of her, blocking her view ahead.

The moment the light turned green, she floored the accelerator until she caught up to the truck. Before she could decide whether she should try to pass it, the Camry made a right turn. She stomped on the brakes and squealed into a turning lane to follow.

She checked the rearview mirror. A white cargo van pulled into the lane behind her. Was she being followed? Her heart slammed in her chest. When the van turned left at the next light, Dominique let out a slow breath.

After about fifteen minutes, she followed the Toyota into a Kroger parking lot, and she finally released her tight grip on the wheel. She parked her sedan two rows over and waited until the pregnant woman was inside the store before approaching the Camry. What had the man crouched behind the car been doing?

She took a quick glance around. Good, no one seemed to be watching. She knelt behind the car and felt underneath the bumper. She wasn't exactly sure what she was searching for, but that man must have put something underneath. She ran her hands underneath the bumper until they hit something. A little tugging pulled it off with the sound of a rip. A small black box lay in her hand, with Velcro covering one side—a GPS tracking device. The news station used them sometimes when they investigated someone.

"What do you think you're doing?" The woman's voice.

Dominique stood slowly. "My name is Dominique Sherwood. Believe it or not, I'm trying to help you." She held out a hand so the woman could see the device. "I'm an investigative reporter with a news station in Florida. I'm working undercover on a story related to the baby kidnappings. When I left the restaurant and saw some men hanging out by your car, I was afraid you might be in danger. But I couldn't risk speaking with you there." She held the device up. "This is a tracking device."

"Why would anyone want to follow me?"

"The people who placed this on your car want your baby."

The woman paled so much, Dominique feared she might pass out.

"Are you okay?" Dominique took a step forward and placed her hand on the woman's arm. "Is there someone I can call for you? I'm sorry, I don't even know your name."

"Sharon."

"Sharon, who can I call?"

The woman placed a shaky hand over her expanded belly. "My husband's out of town, and my parents don't live in this area. I haven't lived here long, so I don't know many people Why would you go to all of this trouble to help a stranger? What should I do?"

Dominique retrieved one of her business cards from a pocket. "I'm here on business, and got tangled up in this mess. I wish I could explain further, but I can't." She handed her card to Sharon. "Please believe me. You are in danger!"

She deactivated the tracking device and handed it to Sharon. "Take this to the police station and ask to speak with Detective Houston Armstrong. He's a good cop, and he'll know how to help you. Tell him exactly what happened. He'll know best how to proceed." She leaned forward. "Please don't give the police my name or show them my card. It's imperative my identity remain a secret, at least for a little while longer."

Sharon's eyebrows rose. "Will you come with me?"

Dominique chewed on her bottom lip. She still needed her cover as a social worker for at least another week. "I can't. Please try to understand."

She squeezed Sharon's arm. "I'll follow you to the police station to make sure you get there safely."

Sharon wiped a tear from her eye. "I would like that."

"Is there someone you can stay with until your husband gets home? I don't think you should be alone."

"My parents live about two hours away. They didn't like me being at home by myself for a week anyway. I'm sure they'll be glad to have me stay with them a few days. I don't know how to thank you, Dominique." Sharon gave her a tight hug.

Dominique's throat tightened. "You don't have to thank me, but please don't give the police my name."

"I understand." Sharon wiped her nose with a tissue. An awkward silence hung in the air.

Dominique hesitated a moment, then asked. "May I ask you a personal question?"

"Okay."

"Are you a Christian?"

Sharon's eyes lit up. "Yes, I am. Are you?"

That question again. The great chasm. Dominique looked away. "I believe in God, but I'm quickly realizing that's not enough. Guess I still have a lot to work through."

Sharon squeezed Dominique's arm. "Thanks for sharing with me."

She let out a big breath, relieved Sharon didn't say she'd pray for her. Dominique's mother had been praying for years, but for some reason it just didn't seem to take. "I'll be right behind you. You be careful, you hear?"

Sharon gave her a quick hug and got into her car.

As Dominique walked toward her car, her cell phone vibrated. Caller ID showed it was Joe. He heart skipped a beat as she accepted the call. "Well hello, doctor," she answered as she got in her car.

"Hello yourself. I stopped by your office to see if you wanted to have a late lunch, and you weren't there."

"I took a couple days off. I have some personal matters that need my attention."

"Well, I missed seeing you. I also wanted to ask you if you're free this Saturday."

"I think I am." She pulled out behind Sharon's Toyota.

"Good. My sister-in-law Becky is having a birthday party for my dad. You said you wanted to meet him, so I was wondering if you'd like to come to the party with me."

A family get-together was a big step. Everyone, including Joe, would assume they were getting involved. But maybe once she talked with Joe's dad she could get the answers she needed and finish her research. Then she could be completely honest with Joe. Dominique paid close attention to Sharon, changing lanes at the opportune time.

"Not exactly the response I'd hoped for."

Joe's comment brought her back into focus. "What? Oh, I'm sorry, Joe, I'm driving, and I lost my train of thought. Of course I'll go with you. Can I bring anything?"

"No, I'll take care of that with a bowl of my famous potato salad."

She navigated her car onto the divided highway, keeping pace with Sharon. "I happen to love potato salad. Can you e-mail me the address, so I can program it into my GPS system?"

"I'll pick you up."

She hesitated. Would Joe question why she didn't have a more permanent residence? But it would be worth the risk to talk to his father. She gave him the address and ended the call just as Sharon pulled into the police station.

Houston would know what to do with the tracking device. It would be the lead he'd been searching for. Saturday's party could provide her with the remaining missing pieces she needed to complete the investigation.

She smiled and let out a soft sigh. Then maybe she could start fresh with Joe.

Chapter Fifteen

Houston slammed the refrigerator door and muttered, "He'll probably be here for his next birthday too."

"What exactly are you trying to say, Houston?" Becky jammed the remaining birthday candles into the cake.

"I was just asking how much longer he's going to be here, that's all." He plunked the plate of hamburger patties on the counter. His dad had been there for a little over two weeks, and he wasn't sure how much longer he could stand being under the same roof.

"He's your father." She rinsed off the few pieces of silverware left in the sink. "I know he's made mistakes, but this grudge you're holding against him is affecting more than just your relationship with him."

Why does it always turn to religion? "What's that supposed to mean?"

"You know what I'm talking about."

"Why don't you spell it out." He punched down the trash in the can, pulled the bag out, and tied the top in a knot.

"Okay, I will." Becky let out a deep breath. "The bitterness you feel towards Samuel is a stumbling block for you." She lowered her voice. "How can you have a relationship with your heavenly Father if you're not even on speaking terms with your earthly one?" She closed the gap between them. "I know you think he's crazy, but look at all of the evidence that's accumulated over the past six months or so. There are several pregnant woman at church, and Shannon from work said it's the same at her church. How many pregnant women do you encounter on a daily basis?"

His mouth drew into a tight line but he said nothing.

"The only ones I've seen are at church. You can't continue to ignore the facts."

"So it's my fault we can't have a baby?" Houston ran his fingers through his hair. "Come on, Becky, we had problems conceiving long before this crisis began."

She placed her hand on his arm. "At least consider my position. Every day you go in to work and see the evidence that God is building up his church. He's raising up a generation. I want to be a part of it. It's your pride that's holding you back."

"My pride … *my* pride. Nice to see who's side you're on."

"Why do there have to be sides?" She placed a stack of paper cups by the punch bowl. "It's killing me to see you consumed with this bitterness against your father. You're only hurting yourself. Forgive your dad for whatever it is you've held against him for so long. You'll never have any peace until you do."

He pulled away. Heat traveled up his neck. "He's responsible for my mom's death. That's unforgivable."

"She died of breast cancer. How can you hold Samuel responsible for that?"

Houston took in the confusion on his wife's face. It was long past time for him to share the details with her. He let out a long breath and nodded. "Early detection of breast cancer is vital for a patient's survival. She was always a huge advocate for mammograms, and it angered her when insurance companies changed their policies so they paid for the first screening at age fifty instead of age forty."

"Right. I can understand that."

"Mom had been saving money to pay for a routine mammogram. Breast cancer runs in her family, and she wanted to take good care of herself. She almost had enough to pay for one when she discovered that the jar she'd been saving the money in was empty. Dad had found the money and blew it all on several benders."

Becky sank into a chair at the kitchen table, but didn't interrupt.

"Then Dad found God. Eventually Mom had the test, but by then it was too late. She already had stage-four breast cancer. From there she went downhill fast and died a painful death. All because Dad chose alcohol over his family." He couldn't manage to say the last sentence without a heavy dose of bitterness.

The sound of tires on the stone driveway alerted them to guests arriving. Becky wrapped her arms around Houston. "Can we finish this discussion later?"

He nodded. "I don't like it when we fight, honey, especially about my dad."

"I know, but this has to be resolved once and for all." She stepped back. "Did you remember Cindy wanted you to talk with Travis?"

"I'm planning on it. Sounds like my brother-in-law needs a little friendly advice." He placed a quick kiss on her cheek.

"Maybe he just needs another man to talk to. Cindy said he hasn't been himself for several weeks." She caressed his arm. "I'm sorry to dump so much on you right before everyone gets here."

She had no idea just how much that was. She didn't know what it was like to grow up with an alcoholic for a father. He couldn't even count how many times he'd made excuses for his father's drunken behavior.

His mother had begged him on her death bed to forgive his dad and accept Christ as his Savior, but he couldn't do either. He did vow that if he ever married, he would cherish his wife and kids. He let out a short sigh and kissed Becky again. "Let's just let it go for now. Okay?"

"Agreed."

He opened the front door. His nieces, Megan and Audrey, rushed ahead of their parents while Cindy and Travis unbuckled the boys from their car seats. Becky greeted the kids and directed them to the porch to play with the litter of kittens they found in their barn earlier in the week.

* * *

As Travis unbuckled Max from his car seat, children's laughter filled his ears. If only his life could be as carefree as a child's. Instead of being laden with financial burdens, his primary concern would be whether he'd get seconds of dessert.

He allowed his thoughts to mentally log the list of problems he wouldn't have to deal with if he were a child. Topping the list was that no new business had come his way. It was as if there were a sign posted outside his office that read "closed to new business." He'd made no progress on repaying his loans from Vinnie.

"Did you remember to grab Dad's gift?"

Cindy's voice pulled him back. She hadn't said a word on the entire trip over here.

"It's in the boys' bag." He straightened as he pulled a backpack loaded with all of the kids' supplies for the day out of the back. "Are we on speaking terms now?" He didn't disguise the sarcasm in his voice.

"That depends." She reached for the casserole.

He resisted the urge to roll his eyes. Always some condition with her. "On what?"

"Are you going to leave me here and go in to work?" She placed the casserole she'd brought on the roof of the Land Rover and grabbed the cooler filled with water bottles. "Angie might need you." It was her turn for sarcasm.

He slung the backpack over his shoulder and slammed the door. "It's Angelica, and I've told you a hundred times that hiring her had nothing to do with her looks." He stared at the ground. "She's an excellent accountant, and she's a lot cheaper than Scott."

She didn't resist rolling her eyes. "You can say that again."

"Can we talk about this later?" *Or never.* He had a hard enough time setting aside his attraction to Angelica at work—especially when she made no secret that she would welcome his attention.

Cindy turned her back on him and stormed into the house, arms loaded with the casserole and cooler. She wouldn't accept his help even if he offered; she needed time to cool off. Would things between them ever return to normal?

"Hey, Travis. Got a minute?" Houston leaned against the door frame.

"Sure, let me put this inside."

Houston followed him as he made his way into the house, let Cindy know where he'd be, and agreed to keep an eye on the kids while he talked with Houston. At least she was talking to him in front of the family.

Travis waved toward the back door, and Houston followed him outside where the kids gathered around some kittens. "Looks like the kids are having fun. What'd you want to talk about?"

"Are you in some kind of trouble, Travis?"

His heart skipped a beat. Did he know about Vinnie? How could he? Did the police have a man on Vinnie's payroll who told his brother-in-law about their business deal? "What do you mean?"

"Exactly what it sounds like. What's eating at you?"

He shrugged. "Just some stress at work. I think I'm through the worst of it, though."

"Anything I can help you with?" He took a step toward Travis. "Cindy told Becky she's worried about you. If you need some help, I hope you know you can come to me."

He looked past Houston to the kids. "Cindy has blown things out of proportion. Everything's under control. Thanks for the offer, though." He folded his arms across his chest. If only he could confide in Houston. But involving the police would be a disaster. He'd just have to avoid him until he could get out of the business deal with Vinnie. "C'mon, kids. Let's go play in the barn while they get all the food ready."

Houston snagged him by the arm. "You're not by any chance involved with Vinnie Fernandez, are you?"

Chapter Sixteen

Dominique stared out the window of Joe's Ford Mustang and repeatedly clicked her handbag opened and closed. Even though she looked forward to spending the day with Joe, asking to meet his father might prove to be a big mistake. He was bound to be a male version of her own mother. Was she ready for piercing, judgmental eyes to stare straight into her soul? It would be reminiscent of the Scripture her mother had pounded into her head: *You have been judged and weighed and found wanting.* No matter what she did, it was never good enough. She would never be able to gain her mother's approval, or the Lord's.

"Are you nervous?"

Joe's question jolted her out of her fretting. "A little."

"Well, you've already met everybody but the kids and Dad." He raised his eyebrows.

"You're not scared of my nieces and nephews, are you?"

She let out a laugh. "If you must know, I'm a little scared to meet your dad."

"I thought you *wanted* to meet him. Actually, I was hoping maybe you could give our family a little professional input."

This could be trouble. She licked her lips. "What kind of input?"

He took a deep breath. "The hospital thinks my dad is in the beginning stages of dementia, and they want to medicate him and put him in a nursing facility. Unless we agree to their treatment plan, he can't be re-admitted. We're just looking for fresh ideas or information on a nice facility. Anything you can suggest would be appreciated."

Things had gone too far, she had to tell him. She couldn't let him go on thinking she was a social worker. Confession is good for the soul, her mother always said. "Joe, we need to talk."

He pulled the Mustang into a long driveway and parked behind several other vehicles. "Here we are. Looks like we're the last to arrive. Please don't be nervous about meeting Dad; he's going to love you."

"There's something I really need to talk with you about first. Can we drive around a little before we go in?" She hoped he would pick up on her insistent tone.

"We're already here. Why don't we go for a walk after dinner? Will it wait until then?"

Her instincts screamed at her to get everything out in the open immediately. But what if he told her to leave before she had a chance to speak with his dad? She nodded slowly. Maybe it was for the best. "Sure. We can do that." But a pit opened in her stomach and wouldn't go away. She was losing her edge. In the past assignments, she'd been forced to lie and con her way through in order to get a story. Not once had it ever bothered her. Until now.

Joe gave her hand a light squeeze. "Just be yourself, Dominique. You're an amazing woman."

Shivers ran up her arms when she met his gaze. Desire filled his eyes. He brushed a stray hair from her face. He was going to kiss her, she just knew it.

Pounding on the driver's side window shattered the romantic moment. Houston peered in through the closed window, a huge grin on his face. "Come on, Joe, you'll have plenty of time for that later. I need your help on the grill."

Heat crept up Dominique's face. The last time she'd felt like this, she'd been an awkward teenager caught making out behind the bleachers at the football game.

"Do you have any brothers, Dominique?"

His question brought a smile to her face. "As a matter of fact, I don't. I'm an only child."

"You're lucky." Joe lowered the window and called out to Houston's retreating form, "I'll be right in, give me a minute." His eyes met hers once again. "After dinner, we can pick up where we left off."

"I'd like that." She willed her heart to slow down. Did he mean the conversation or the kiss? She would just have to wait and find out.

"You ready to meet my dad?"

His question brought her back into the present. "Yes. Of course. Do you need help with anything?"

"No, I think I have it covered. I'll take you into the house and introduce you to Dad, then help Houston on the grill. I'll be out on the deck if you need me."

On the way into the house, Joe took her hand again, and she couldn't contain her smile. "I'm sure I'll get along just fine with your dad. I don't know why I was so nervous."

But she knew exactly why she was nervous. She experienced nausea and jitters each time she was on the brink of breaking a story wide open. Meeting the man who held such an intriguing theory was an incredible opportunity. What if it were true? Yet, she regretted living a lie. What if this insightful man exposed all of her deep, dark secrets? Once Joe knew the truth, he'd want nothing to do with her. She would be alone ... again.

She followed Joe into the house and greeted his family. As they walked into the living room, she was completely taken aback by the man who sat in the brown leather recliner. Instead of the overbearing, staunch gentleman she'd anticipated, Samuel Armstrong was a kind-looking, frail older man. The left side of his mouth tilted down, and the whole left side of his body seemed to droop, evidence of the stroke Joe said he'd experienced a couple of weeks ago. But his light-blue eyes held a gentleness that instantly put her at ease, and she offered him a genuine smile.

His left arm hung awkwardly, but Samuel pointed a finger at her with his good hand. "I know you! I've seen you on TV." His words slurred a bit as he spoke.

Her eyebrows shot up. He'd recognized her!

Joe rested his hand on the small of her back. "I think you may have Dominique confused with someone else, Dad." He turned to her. "He watches a lot of television since being in the hospital. Dad, Dominique works with me in the hospital as a social worker."

Samuel scratched his head. "Well, I'll be. You look just' like this news reporter. She's from Georgia, or Florida, or somewhere down south. Wherever she's from, she's your identical twin. Now what was her name?"

The slight slur tempted her to write off his words as those of a drunkard, but her heart still leaped into her throat. He knew. She needed to talk with Joe immediately. She tugged on his sleeve and whispered, "I need to speak with you in private."

Before he could respond, his cell phone rang. He retrieved it and checked to see who it was. "I'm sorry, Dominique, I have to answer this call. I'll be right back."

She sat in the overstuffed chair next to Samuel. How could she start a conversation on the pregnancy crisis and his prayer without seeming awkward? How could she lie to this gentle, God-fearing man?

You shall know the truth, and the truth will set you free. The verse she had memorized as a child challenged her to confide the truth to him.

Samuel's eyes met hers. "I'm right aren't I, Miss Sherwood?" he whispered. "You're not a social worker, you're a reporter."

Chapter Seventeen

Houston flipped the burger on the grill while keeping an eye on Joe, who was introducing Dominique to the kids. Had he noticed tension between Cindy and Travis? Travis had been spending a lot of time at work. Maybe that was the source of the problem. Family should always come first.

Joe joined him at the grill and gave him a slight punch in the arm. "Didn't need my help after all?"

He laughed. "Sorry to interrupt you and Dominique. I did need—"

"There you are, Joe." Becky handed Houston an extra pair of tongs. "Do you have a minute?"

Joe looked back and forth between Houston and Becky. "Are you two up to something? It feels like you're conspiring against me."

"This is a little awkward." She glanced at her husband. "Houston tells me he intruded on a private moment between you and Dominique."

Houston held both hands in the air, spatula and all. "Leave me out of this."

She tucked a stray hair behind her ear. "Fair enough." She turned her attention back to Joe. "I noticed you were holding Dominique's hand on the way in."

"Guilty as charged." Joe smiled.

"She is a beautiful woman and seems very sweet." Becky lowered her voice. "But do you know if she shares your faith?"

Houston tightened his grip on the spatula, and the muscle in his right cheek twitched. "Maybe he doesn't feel as strongly about the subject as you do."

"He does. Or at least I hope he does." She raised an eyebrow.

Joe ran his hand along the back of his neck. "Becky's right, Houston. I'm not certain where Dominique stands."

Houston focused on the grill, but couldn't hold back his opinion. "She seems nice enough to me. I don't see what the problem is."

Becky squeezed Joe's arm and pointed to a couple of chairs by the grill. "I know Houston thinks it's none of my business, but I didn't know if you had talked with anyone."

Joe sat on a lounge chair. "I know what the Bible says on the subject. What's confusing is the relationship you and Houston have. It's not like it can't be done."

"I became a Christian after we married. He's a wonderful husband, but I think if you asked him, he'd tell you our religious differences have caused difficulties."

Houston put the burgers on the platter and turned his attention to the hotdogs. He seemed to be looking anywhere but in their direction.

Joe stood. "Think I'll see how Dominique and Dad are getting along."

"Is that a subtle way of telling me to mind my own business?" Becky laughed.

"I know what you're saying, Becky. It's just one of those things that's easier said than done."

Megan rushed up to the patio. The hair had come loose from her French braid, and her face had smudges of dirt on it. She gasped to catch her breath. "Audrey fell from the hayloft and won't wake up. Daddy said to come and get you, Uncle Joe."

Houston reached for his cell phone. "I'll call 911."

"I'll grab my bag and meet you down there!"

After being assured an ambulance was on its way, Houston ran over the hill toward the barn. Becky trailed behind him, carrying an icepack and some towels from the kitchen. He picked up his pace when he passed over the ridge and could see the barn ahead.

He raced through the door and stopped short at the sight in front of him. His beautiful niece, Audrey, lay on the ground, completely lifeless, her face and lips ashen. Travis was bent over her, desperately trying to breathe life back into his daughter.

Houston rushed forward and placed a hand on Travis's shoulder. "Becky and I will take over. I called for an ambulance; they'll be here shortly."

Travis stared off into the distance. All color had drained from his face. Houston had seen that look countless times before—when he told parents their child was gone, a life cut short by some senseless accident.

He checked for a pulse.

Nothing.

Despite his earlier claim that he possessed no faith, he silently cried out, *Help us, God!*

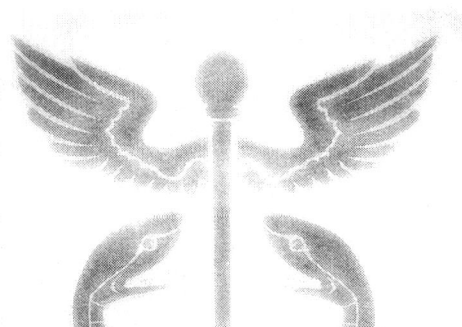

Chapter Eighteen

Dominique pulled a bag of chips from the top of the refrigerator and put a generous amount on each of the two plates that already held sandwiches, then rejoined Samuel in the living room. "The boys finished their lunch and I put them down for a nap. Do you think you could eat a little something?" She tried to keep her tone light.

"Any news yet?" Concern filled Samuel's eyes.

"Joe said they got a faint heartbeat on the way to the hospital. I'm sure he'll call as soon as there's another update." She placed the plates next to the coffee on the side table and sat down beside him.

"Will you join me?" He bent his head in silent prayer.

She waited until he finished before speaking. "Do you want me to tell you why I'm posing as a social worker?"

"I am a little curious."

"Well, to begin with, I want you to know I would never intentionally hurt Joe. I've grown quite fond of him." She took a bite of her sandwich.

"I can tell you care for him." He wiped his mouth with the paper napkin. "Why not tell him the truth?"

She abandoned her sandwich. "It's complicated. Although I did try earlier today." She picked up her mug and took a sip of coffee. "As you know, I work for a television station in Florida. After the birthrate dropped, I was assigned to cover the story. It didn't take me long to notice that in certain areas of the country, the birthrate hadn't dropped nearly as much as for the rest of the country. Most of the cities are in the Bible belt, but this area is in the top five. My manager sent me here and another reporter to California." Dominique shifted in her seat. "My responsibility is to collect demographics of the women having babies and then connect the dots to see what they have in common."

"And you found out they were all Christians?"

"Not right away. To be completely honest, I wasn't looking for anything spiritual. I was looking more for an environmental connection." She sipped her coffee.

"Then you met Joe."

"Yes. We worked together on a different case and became friends. He shared your story, and it intrigued me. I've interviewed several families—some of them I met at church. All of them were Christians. As hard as it is to believe, I can no longer deny the spiritual connection."

Samuel raised his good arm. "Praise the Lord!" He touched her arm. "What did your boss say when you told him? I'm sure you'll be the lead story."

"Well ... that's where it gets complicated. I told him what direction I was heading, and he highly encouraged me to find another one. He doesn't want to run with this story; he says it's offensive. So now I'm focusing on the baby snatchings."

"But it's the truth." He slammed his hand on the table. "Isn't he interested in the truth?"

"Apparently not."

The disappointment on Samuel's face mirrored her own emotions.

She placed her hand on his. "Samuel, I'm not listening to him. I'm still wrestling with this spiritual connection and why God would do such a thing. I'll continue to dig and find some way to get the truth out."

Samuel's blue eyes held hers for an uncomfortably long moment. He seemed ready to say something, then the moment passed and he picked up his sandwich awkwardly with one hand.

A companionable silence passed as they finished their lunch. Dominique gathered the empty plates and placed them in the sink.

"What's holding you back, Dominique?"

Her eyebrows shot up. "From reporting the truth?"

He shook his head. " I mean, what's holding you back from the Lord?"

What *was* keeping her from the Lord? She rubbed her temples. The answer seared her conscience. *The abortion*. Did she dare share the truth with him? She had never told a soul. She looked into Samuel's gentle eyes and knew he wouldn't judge her the way her mother did. Somehow, she knew she could trust him. She returned to her seat next to him. "I've made a lot of mistakes. I'm not so sure God would want me."

"I happen to know for a fact He would. Besides, if He would have the likes of me, I know He would welcome you into the fold."

"I can't imagine what you could have done, Samuel, but believe me, I have a lot of regrets in my life." She warmed her hands on the mug.

"We all do."

She stared at the floor until her longing for forgiveness overrode her reservations. "I've had an abortion," she blurted. "I heard Mandy's testimony and I know she believes God forgave her for the abortions she had, but I don't know if I can believe that for myself. I killed my own flesh and blood. How can God possibly forgive me?" Tears streaming down her face, she mustered up the courage to look at him, but his eyes held no condemnation.

"Can I share something with you?" He grabbed a well-worn Bible from the end table next to his chair. "I'm not going to pretend I know the anguish you're living with, but I do understand the emptiness."

Without responding, Dominique focused on Samuel. He seemed deep in thought for a moment, then looked her straight in the eye. "Did you know I'm an alcoholic?"

Her heart skipped a beat. How could this gentle, understanding man be an alcoholic? Her brain couldn't reconcile the two images. Joe's family had seemed so perfect. "I didn't know that."

"I haven't had a drink in over twenty years," he continued, "but that didn't stop me from causing a lot of damage. In fact, my relationship with Houston suffered the most. It's still damaged to this day."

"I'm sorry, Samuel. I had no idea."

"Well, I don't want you to feel sorry for me, I just wanted you to know I'm not some perfect person. What I am is an old man who still has to rely daily on God's grace to make it through life. God isn't looking for people who are perfect, He's looking for people who are broken."

She smiled. "Now there's something I can relate to."

"We're all broken, Dominique. There's nothing worse than a broken person who thinks he's perfect. The truth is, God loves you, and there's nothing you've done that He isn't willing to forgive. All you have to do is ask."

"You make it sound so simple. Why has it always seemed so hard?"

"Because of our pride. We want to do something to earn it." He shook his head. "I remember thinking I would straighten up my life first, make myself a little more presentable for the Lord. That doesn't work either. If it did, I'd still be working at it."

Memories of her mother's words pointing out her every flaw flooded her mind. *You're a sinner, Dominique. You want to spend eternity in hell? You better change your ways!* The words haunted her. "Can we change the topic, just for a moment?" She ran her hands over her khaki skirt. "I need to ask you a few questions."

He spread his good arm in front of him. "Ask away."

"What purpose can this whole pregnancy crisis serve? If God is behind this, why would He do it? What point could He be trying to make?"

"Life!"

"What?" Her eyebrows shot up. "I don't understand."

"Life is so precious. We are *all* so very valuable to God. He makes each one of us unique. Scripture say we are knitted together in our mother's womb—fearfully and wonderfully made. And yet, in our pride and selfishness, when we are inconvenienced with what we term as an unwanted pregnancy, we put our own desire and needs above that of an innocent, helpless baby."

She let out a slow breath. "And now we've become desperate."

"Exactly." He nodded. "People finally see the value of children. The same people who campaigned for choice now pay large sums of money trying to conceive, or worse, seek illegal ways to obtain a baby and raise it as their own."

Tears flowed unchecked down Samuel's face. "Have you seen the pictures or studied the statistics? We've destroyed human life and acted as if it were our right. It breaks my heart, Dominique. I can't imagine how much it grieves the Lord."

She shook the images from her mind. After her abortion, she continually read over the pamphlet the clinic sent home with her. Its contents assured her she had not destroyed a human life, she had just removed the *product of conception*. Really? How could she have been so easily deceived? What else could the *product of conception* be other than a human life? Exactly when did they think that happened?

Her heart knew the truth; it ached with the truth. She would never witness her child's first steps or words or birthdays or graduation. Nothing. Only empty arms. Her throat filled, making it difficult to speak. "How could He forgive me, then? I let them destroy my baby. Deep down, I knew the whole time it was wrong. How could I do that to my own child?"

She curled up in a ball on the chair, and sobs wracked her until her sides ached. She snatched several tissues from the box on the side table. Her eyes were sore, and her nose was completely stuffed up.

She wasn't sure how much time had passed when she heard Samuel softly praying. His well-worn hand gently stroked her back. Slowly, she raised her head. "I'm sorry. I've never told anyone about my abortion. I never wanted to face the truth."

"I didn't mean to upset you. I believe the Lord brought us together for a reason. Don't you see, honey?" Samuel paused, seeming to choose his next words carefully. "You're valuable, just like your baby. The doctors and nurses who work in the clinics, they're important too." He squeezed her hand. "Life is a precious gift from the Lord. It should be embraced and cherished. God values and loves you so much that He sent His son Jesus to die in your place, to pay for your sins. He longs to be with you. He went to a lot of trouble … jus' for you! Make no mistake, sin is serious business, but the Lord has a solution for that problem."

Silence filled the room.

Dominique's shoulders relaxed. This wasn't the first time she'd heard the gospel, but somehow the way he explained it offered hope that God would actually desire a relationship with her. She was a sinner—that fact had been drilled into her since her early teens. What held her back? The abortion. She could never wipe that clean.

Samuel shifted in his chair. "I wish I could say the right words or recite the perfect verse to show how much the Lord loves you, and how much He longs for you to ask for forgiveness. I can promise you I will pray for you, Dominique. I will pray that you accept His forgiveness."

Joe's friendship, Mandy's testimony, and time spent with Christians during her investigation all served to soften her heart to God's truth. Samuel's kind and wise words further melted her resolve. Slowly, she took his hand. "Would you pray with me, please?"

He squeezed her hand. "It would be my privilege."

She cleared her throat and bowed her head, shutting out everything around her. Verses from her youth, Joe's steady faith, and Samuel's words of encouragement spurred her on. "Lord, forgive me …" They were the only word's she could vocalize through the tears. She raised her head and took in the joyful smile on Samuel's face. His eyes brimmed with unshed tears.

The telephone ringing interrupted the quiet moment.

Dominique quickly grabbed the handset from the table before it could wake the napping toddlers. "Hello?"

"Hi, Dominique, it's Becky. I have news about Audrey."

Chapter Nineteen

Travis paced along the row of windows in the hospital waiting room. Why did they always make them so cramped? The doctor's words jumbled in his mind. *We're trying to determine the extent of the brain damage. We don't know when, or if, she'll regain consciousness. The CT scan was inconclusive. These next hours are crucial.* He hadn't been able to offer them any words of hope.

Cindy rubbed the back of her neck, then massaged her expanding belly. She looked so uncomfortable sitting on the faux leather couch. In the past he would have offered to massage her neck, anything to help relax her. But earlier today she had pulled her hand away when he tried to hold it, and whenever he looked at her, she turned away. They'd barely said two words to each other since they'd arrived at the hospital. Clearly, she didn't want to be in the same room as him, let alone have him touch her.

Becky sat beside her and draped a sweater over her shoulders. "Can I get you anything? How about a cup of coffee?"

"No, nothing. Audrey is scared of heights. What was she doing in the loft? I just don't understand how this could have happened." Cindy glared across the waiting room at him, her unspoken words louder than the ones she'd voiced.

Megan plopped down next to Cindy.

"How about you, Megan? Can Aunt Becky get you something?"

"I want a milkshake," she responded with a smile that didn't quite reach her eyes.

"Travis?"

"No, I'm okay. Thanks anyway." He reached for the *Sports Illustrated* on the side table and sat in the chair across from the couch.

"One milkshake coming up." Becky headed out the door.

Cindy reached for the small pile of coloring books, crayons, and markers provided by the caring staff at the hospital. She presented them to Megan, then sat in the chair beside Travis. "We need to talk."

He leaned back in his chair. "It's not my fault, Cindy. Accidents happen every day." He tossed the magazine back on the table. "I know what you're thinking. First Max, and now Audrey."

She crossed her arms. "I'm not saying it's your fault. I just want to know what happened."

"She fell from the loft. I didn't see it happen, I only saw her lying on the ground."

"How high up was she?"

His mouth was dry, and a pressure headache throbbed behind his left eye. He lowered his voice. "I told you. I didn't see anything."

She took in a deep breath. "Did you know she was up there? Did you see her climb the ladder?"

"Daddy was on the phone," Megan said as she continued to color. "I told him she was climbing, but he said the call was important."

Travis leaned forward with his elbows on his knees and buried his face in his hands. He hadn't paid attention to what Megan said. All he heard was "climbing," and then he tuned her out. Since Audrey was afraid of heights, he thought she wouldn't go up more than a few steps … "

Cindy glared at him.

Megan looked up from her coloring. "I told her to get down, but she wouldn't listen. Then she fell." Megan's face crumpled. "I'm sorry, Mommy."

Travis's heart broke. How could Megan blame herself?

Cindy scooped Megan into her arms and planted kisses all along her forehead and hair. "It's okay, sweetie. It's not your fault. You did the right thing telling Daddy." She set Megan on her lap and gently rocked her back and forth.

Once Megan's crying had slowed, Cindy sat her down at a small table in the corner and took out a book. After several minutes, she made a beeline for the seat next to Travis. Voice low and seething, she let her accusation fly. "You were on the phone? You told me you would watch the kids. Tell me, Travis, who were you talking to? What could be so important you would neglect your own child?"

Audrey hung onto life by a thread—all because he had to make a phone call.

"What's happening to us, Travis?" The question was so quiet, Travis almost didn't hear it.

He had no answer, only regrets.

She walked over to the window. "Does the baby make you that unhappy?"

"I can't talk about this now." He stood. "I'm going to get a cup of coffee. I'll be right back." He pulled the door open, and a middle-aged woman wearing the customary navy blue blazer of a hospital employee stepped into the room. She held a clipboard and wore a determined expression, "Excuse me, is Travis Montgomery in here?"

His heart picked up its pace. "I'm Travis Montgomery. Is there a problem?"

The woman's eyes scanned the room, as if taking an inventory of the people. "I have a private matter I need to discuss with you. Is this a good time?"

Travis followed Martha down the long hallway and into a consultation room. The plate hanging on the door at a slight angle read *Private, please do not disturb*.

Martha sat in the wooden chair behind the desk and gestured for him to sit in one of the overstuffed chairs across from her. She cleared her throat. "I know this is a difficult time for you, Mr. Montgomery, but we've had a problem with your insurance provider."

"What kind of problem?" He asked the question because it was expected, but he had a feeling he knew where this conversation was going. They'd only received a few late payment notices, not a notice of cancelation.

"Your insurance provider said your policy has been cancelled. Perhaps you gave us an expired insurance card? It does happen quite frequently."

He leaned forward. "Which card did I give you?"

"PrimeHealth America." She slid a photocopy of the card across the desk. "Their representative said you aren't covered under their COBRA plan either. Do you have a new provider?"

He rubbed his temples against the persistent tension headache he'd been fighting since he arrived at the hospital. Apparently, the headache was going to win. Why hadn't Scott had taken care of the matter, or at least let him know?

"I don't know what to tell you, Martha. I'll have to look into this. Do you have a business card, or a way I can get in touch with you?"

She handed him her business card. "Please let me know as soon as you have any information. We need to get this cleared up. I apologize for the timing, but if you don't have coverage, we'll have to see if you're eligible for the National Healthcare Plan."

National Healthcare? The words hit him like a physical blow. How much time would they give Audrey? "As soon as I know something I'll contact you. I apologize for the mix-up. If you don't mind, I'd like to get back to my daughter."

He left the room, but instead of heading back to the trauma waiting area, he walked toward the cafeteria. A cup of coffee would help clear his mind. What could he do? How could he pay the bills with no coverage? There was no way he was going to tell Cindy. She was already upset enough without adding financial worries.

In the cafeteria, he mechanically filled the Styrofoam cup with coffee, paid, then added two packets of sugar. With his brain barely functioning, he felt like a zombie as he lumbered to a table in the corner of the room. What was he going to do? The hospital bills would be astronomical with no insurance. His shoulders slumped and his head fell forward. He could only think of one person who would be able to help him. What other option did he have?

He dialed the number on his cell phone and hoped he could get hold of her. She answered on the third ring. "Angelica, this is Travis. I need help."

Chapter Twenty

Houston slammed on the brakes as three deer darted in front of his car. It was bad enough he had to leave the rest of his family at the hospital while they waited for news on Audrey. The last thing any of them needed was another accident. At least Audrey was holding her own, even though she wasn't responding yet.

He tightened his grip on the wheel and accelerated. Another pregnant mom murdered. This time the baby hadn't survived either. The heartless thugs had discarded both bodies in an abandoned farmhouse on the west end of town.

Houston took a sip of coffee Becky had poured for him from the thermos she'd taken to the hospital, anticipating a long night. The good-bye kiss she had given him made it even more difficult to leave. *Come on now, I've got to focus if I'm going to be of any use.*

Thoughts of the scene that would greet him made him reflect back to the message the pastor had preached last Sunday. *Most people think the majority of people are good.* Ha! One ride with him would change their opinion. He'd seen the depravity of man firsthand.

He hadn't bothered to listen to the rest of the sermon. He assumed the pastor was going to go off on a tangent about how all men are sinners. Houston agreed with that; no one was perfect. His own sins were always before him. His struggle lay in the area of forgiveness.

Some things were unforgivable.

He slowed to check the street sign. This was it.

How could a truly just God forgive? What about the despicable criminals who killed pregnant women and stole their babies without remorse, all for a little bit of money? Did God expect the victims' families to forgive them? That hardly seemed fair.

Lights flashed up the road on the right. Four police vehicles, an ambulance, and the coroner's car crowded the driveway. Houston parked his car on the side of the road and took one last sip of coffee. Twenty or so people converged on the scene, yet silence filled the air.

At the end of the driveway, Kenny waved him forward. "Thanks for coming in, man. I know tonight was your night off, but I thought you might be particularly interested in this one."

"How so?"

"Come on inside. You'll see."

The steps leading up to the sagging porch reminded Houston of a rickety house of cards. He doubted they could support his weight.

"Watch your step. This place isn't exactly up to code." Kenny tossed a cigarette butt on the ground next to a discarded screen door on the side of the porch.

Houston took one big step up onto the porch. The moment he passed the splintered wooden door that barely hung on its hinges, the smell of death and decay inside made him retch.

Several emergency lights, strategically placed, lit the living room. An old, forgotten piano sat against the far wall with a sheet of music centered on top, as if some past resident would step onto the scene and start playing.

Houston took out his Latex gloves and joined the cluster of policemen processing the bodies, but immediately turned away.

The bloody body of a perfectly formed baby with the umbilical cord wrapped several times around his neck. He would never be able to erase the image from his mind. Who could do something like this?

He took a deep breath and examined the scene further. It looked like the baby had been born dead, and, not knowing what to do, the criminals had just left the corpse. At least the baby was with his mother and not in the hands of some heartless criminals.

The mother lay in a disheveled heap, but she looked familiar. "I know this woman. Her name is Sharon. She's the woman who came to the station the other day looking for me. She gave me a GPS tracking device that had been attached to her car." Anger welled up inside him.

"Did you get any information off it?" Kenny asked.

"No. When I asked the judge if I could investigate it further, he said no. Because there was no warrant issued, any evidence obtained from the GPS would be thrown out of court."

Kenny's cell phone rang. He shook his head and walked away from the scene.

Did he know more about the victim than what he was letting on? Suspicions about his boss were piling up. Until he knew for a fact that Kenny wasn't involved with Vinnie, he'd be careful about how much information he shared with him.

He surveyed the rest of the room, and his gaze was drawn to a darker spot in the shadows under the piano, about the size of a wallet or a small purse. He knelt beside the piano and ran a hand underneath the pedals until he felt something. With only his thumb and forefinger, so he wouldn't contaminate the evidence any more than necessary, he pulled it out and into the light.

A thick, black leather wallet.

Houston scanned the room—no one had seemed to notice what he'd discovered. He opened the wallet and quickly found the driver's license, which contained a smiling picture of the victim standing next to a tall man. He was just about to announce his discovery when a business card fell out of the wallet.

His stomach sank. The card had two words and a phone number printed on it.

Dominique Sherwood.

Why would the victim have a business card with Joe's girlfriend's name on it?

Chapter Twenty-One

Travis shifted his position on the uncomfortable green faux leather loveseat in the hospital waiting room, carefully trying to re-adjust his position. Cindy's head rested against his shoulder. He closed his eyes and breathed in her familiar scent. He'd missed that incredible scent of jasmine and patchouli. At least she'd finally sat next to him, and even relaxed enough to fall asleep. Maybe there was hope for making their way back to normal.

His gaze traveled down to her expanding belly. The due date had been moved forward, and he still wasn't prepared for another mouth to feed. How had things gotten so out of control?

One bad decision at a time.

The convicting thought nagged at him. He should have called Houston or tried to handle the benefits fiasco himself instead of calling Angelica. One more bad decision to add to the growing list.

A quick glance at the clock told him he had a little over an hour before they would be allowed to visit with Audrey. *Lord, please don't let her die.* But why should God help him? He couldn't remember the last time he had prayed. His relationship with the Lord grew more distant with each passing day. That needed to change—his situation had to change. But first he had to free himself from Vinnie Fernandez.

Cindy let out a sigh and moved closer. Their marriage was in a shambles, and he was to blame for the majority of it. If Audrey died, his marriage wouldn't survive. Another failure. But this time his children would pay the price.

Thankfully, the last report had been a little more hopeful. All of her numbers were stabilizing. When the swelling in her brain went down, they could run more tests to check for any permanent damage.

A slight brush of cool air drew his eyes to the left, where Angelica stood in the doorway. His heart skipped a beat. In skinny jeans and a flimsy tank-top, Angelica could command the attention of any man. But he dared not allow Cindy to wake and see her. He'd never survive the ensuing war.

He placed a finger to his lips. Carefully, he pulled his arm from beneath Cindy's neck and moved her gently to the side. He eased up from the sofa, walked out into the hallway, and closed the door behind him. "Thanks for coming. I hope you have good news."

"You look terrible. Let's get out of here." She touched his arm, and it sent a trail of fire burning through his veins. "I'll take you out and buy you a cup of coffee. You can't get anything decent in a hospital."

"It'll have to be the cafeteria. I can't leave my family."

She rolled her eyes. "Your loss. Let's go. It looks like you could use a break."

She attracted him like a moth to fire. The soft scent of spices in her perfume only heightened his desire for her, but he must maintain control for his family's sake. *Keep it short. Tell her your problem then get back to your family.* Because he needed Vinnie's help, he'd have to trust her—but he also had to resist her.

Travis followed her into the elevator.

The way to the cafeteria had become too familiar. Although the accident had happened only a day ago, it felt more like a week. At least at this early hour, they didn't have to worry about finding a seat. He poured an extra-large cup of coffee and added a little cream and sugar.

Angelica waited for him at a small table in the corner of the room. One leg crossed over the other, and a bejeweled sandal dangled from her foot.

He took the seat across from her. "Were you able to clear up this insurance thing?"

She winked at him. "You get right down to business. I like that."

"I'm sorry, Angelica. It's been a long night, and finding out that the policy lapsed only made it longer." Annoyed at the tab on the plastic lid over his coffee, Travis opted to remove the lid and drink his coffee straight from the Styrofoam cup. "If we don't have coverage, I have no idea how I'm going to pay for this." With the current rate at which they were laundering money, it would take him over ten years to pay back his loan plus interest. Who was he kidding? Unless the deals he'd been working up on the side panned out, he would never get out of Vinnie's clutch, much less pay off the loan early.

Angelica scooted her chair forward, and her leg brushed up against his. "You've had a few things on your mind." She took a sip of her coffee and licked her lips. "I can understand how this could've slipped through the cracks."

He should move his leg away from hers, but he enjoyed sitting across from her, having her hang on his every word. It was so nice to have someone understand him. To not be accused or blamed for something. "Thanks. You have no idea how much I needed to hear those words."

A knowing smile highlighted her delicate cheekbones. She looked absolutely beautiful. "Well, I have good news for you." She took a sip of her coffee. "Not only was I able to get your health coverage restored, but when Vinnie heard about your little girl, he insisted on paying your deductible."

The unexpected news halted Travis's wayward thoughts. He looked past Angelica and stared at the television mounted on the wall behind her. A few minutes passed in silence as he tried to process her words. "What's the catch?"

Her eyebrows rose. "Don't be so cynical, Travis. Vinnie just wants to help."

Travis let out a small huff. "I simply find it hard to believe he would pay the past due premiums and the deductible without wanting something in return. I already feel like I'm in way over my head." He hadn't meant to reveal so much, but he didn't have anyone else to confide in.

She took his hands in hers. "I know you may find this hard to believe right now, but once Vinnie trusts you and takes you into his inner business circle, he's extremely loyal." She squeezed his hands. "His business associates are his family. He's not the heartless criminal some would have you believe."

He thought back to his conversation earlier with his brother-in-law. Houston already suspected something. He had come right out and asked him if he was working with Vinnie. What if he got wind of this insurance problem? His stomach churned. He'd have to tell more lies, but Houston wasn't easily fooled.

Not knowing how to respond, he remained silent. Angelica's hands still touched his own—what would she do if he pulled her closer? *Focus!* He shook the wayward thought from his mind.

She pulled her hands away and tapped a shiny red fingernail on the paper in the middle of the table. "All I need is your signature, Travis, and this all will be taken care of."

He stared at the paper. How could he even contemplate getting in any deeper with Vinnie? *Just one more time.* Then he'd get those building contracts. He could keep those additional funds hidden from Angelica ... and Vinnie.

He steadied his hand and signed the paper. His plan would work. It had to.

"You made the right decision." She smiled. "I just have one more question, Travis."

He couldn't quite decipher the look in her eyes. And the tone of her voice had an edge to it.

She leaned forward, with a gleam in her eyes. "Why didn't you tell me your wife is pregnant?"

Chapter Twenty-Two

Dominique raced down the hospital corridor toward her office. The staff meeting had taken way too long. She plopped down in the chair behind the desk and checked the caller ID. Two missed calls. Maybe one was from Joe.

No such luck. Both were from her boss Stew. Whatever he wanted would have to wait. Before she went any further with the story, she needed to speak with Joe. She had two very important things she wanted to share with him: her decision to become a Christian and the truth about why she was in town. *Lord, please help him understand why I lied. Give me the courage I need to be completely honest with him.*

Her cell phone beeped, indicating an incoming text. Stew again! He was never this persistent. Something must be wrong. Her hands shook as she read the text.

Cover blown. GET OUT!

How had *that* happened? It had to be Penelope and her snooping around. No doubt the spiteful woman was to blame. But there was no time to investigate the cause. She needed to pack up her stuff and get out of the hospital before Penelope threw her out. She wouldn't give her that satisfaction.

Dominique opened her e-mail account and attached the files containing her research. While the computer copied the files, she popped a flash drive into a USB slot and moved the files.

Come on … hurry up, computer. The bar made slow progress as she copied the necessary files. Her station's policy was to have documentation backed up in two different locations, and it had saved her on more than one occasion. But now, she didn't even have one full copy, much less a copy emailed to her personal account.

Footsteps echoed down the hallway. From the heavy, clunky rhythm, she guessed they belonged to a woman. More specifically, an angry woman, which could only mean one thing. She was just seconds away from being busted.

She dashed to the door, locked it, and turned off the lights. That would buy her a few extra moments to hide. The bar across the computer screen indicated that her download was almost complete.

The footsteps stopped in front of her door. The doorknob jiggled.

Out of time, she minimized the window, scooted underneath her desk, and pulled the chair in as far as it would go. An obvious place to hide, but hopefully Penelope would open the door, see she wasn't in the office, and leave.

Keys jangled in the door. The knob clicked, and the lights flashed on. Dominique let out a long, slow breath.

"Come in, gentlemen." Footsteps softened by carpeting traveled around the desk and stood right in front of Dominique's hiding spot.

If she'd wanted to, Dominique could have reached out and grabbed Penelope's thick ankle. Instead, she held her breath and willed herself to remain silent in spite of cramping in her legs from remaining in a folded position.

Penelope mumbled under her breath. All Dominique could catch was the word "evidence."

"What would you like us to do, Ms. Nordstrom? Do you want us to contact the police?"

"No. That won't be necessary. We don't want to draw any unwanted attention to the hospital. I don't think Ms. Sherwood is aware we're looking for her. Let's keep searching. She'll turn up somewhere."

She finally walked away from the desk, and Dominique let out a long breath.

"Replace the locks as soon as possible," Penelope ordered the guards, "and contact the IT department to have her account deactivated." Penelope stomped toward the door. "Hospital information should remain with hospital employees."

They mumbled their agreement to follow through with the orders. The last few words were muffled as they left the room.

Dominique remained under the desk for several more minutes as an extra precaution. *It's now or never.*

With painstaking care not to rush, she pushed out the chair and peered as far around the desk as she could. She was alone. She didn't know whether she should laugh or cry. How was she ever going to get out of here? She stood, straightened the wrinkles from her pants, and wiped off any dirt and dust she might have collected from the floor.

One last thing before she left. She reached for the flash drive, but nothing was there. Suddenly, it seemed like someone sucked all the air out of the room and she couldn't breathe.

Penelope must have it.

Dominique clicked a key, and the screen saver on the computer disappeared. A window showing that the download had completed sat in the middle of the screen, her e-mail program the background behind it.

Dominique's heart pounded, and her mouth went dry. Her story had been compromised. If Penelope realized what was on the flash drive, Dominique's career would be over.

She jumped when the desk phone rang, but her heart leaped at Joe's name on the caller ID. "Hello?" She kept her voice just above a whisper.

"Dominique? Are you there? I can barely hear you."

"Sorry, is this better?" She increased her volume slightly.

"Much better. Are you free for coffee?"

"Not exactly. But I do need to speak with you. I have so much to tell you." Her words all jumbled together, but she had to get out of the hospital immediately.

"Is everything okay?"

"I can't really explain it over the phone, but I would love to see you—I need to see you."

"Well, I was going to stop and check on Audrey. Can you meet me up there?"

Would Penelope check the ICU? Probably not. She might not even know Joe's niece had been admitted. "Okay, I'll meet you up there in five minutes."

"See you then. Oh, and Dominique? I spoke with my dad, and he told me everything."

The phone went dead. Samuel told Joe, and he still wanted to meet with her? *He forgives me!* Everything was going to work out. All that remained was to make it to the ICU without Penelope and her goons spotting her.

As quietly as she could, she opened the door a crack, listened for anyone in the hallway, and was met by comforting silence. She opened the door a little further, looking both ways down the hallway.

Looks like the coast is clear. She headed down the hallway toward the stairs. The fewer people who saw her, the better. With her head held high, she resisted the urge to look over her shoulder or dash down the hall. She just needed to pretend like she had every right to be there. But her heart beat double time until she pulled open the stairwell door. She stopped for a moment to catch her breath, then took the stairs two at a time, up three flights without stopping.

She opened the door at the ninth floor carefully. Except for a few nurses attending to patients' charts, the hallway was completely empty. She headed toward the waiting room at the end.

As she passed a cross hallway, the click-clack of Penelope's thick pumps echoed down the narrow corridor. Too late, she spotted Penelope marching away from her, toward the nurses' station. No doubt she'd ask if they'd seen her. The faithful security guards followed several steps behind her, struggling to keep up. This was probably the most exercise they'd had in a long time.

With no time to think, Dominique ducked inside the first room that didn't have a patient's name posted next to it, entered the patient's bathroom, and closed the door. Her eyes adjusted quickly to the darkness. *Lord, please keep me hidden and help me to get out of here safely.* She leaned back against the wall and worked to slow her pounding heart.

A whoosh of cold air hit her face as the door opened, and she stood face-to-face with Joe Armstrong.

"What are you doing in here?" he asked. "I was waiting for you by the elevators, but it took so long, I thought maybe you'd come up the stairs to get some exercise—"

"Quick, close the door. I don't want her to find me."

He pulled the door shut. "You don't want who to find you?"

The tight space in the bathroom shrank after Joe entered.

Dominique stumbled forward in the darkness, but Joe caught her by the arms and steadied her. "Dominique ... "

The fresh scent of his cologne and close proximity proved to be too much for her to resist. She wrapped her arms around his neck, drew him closer, and brushed her lips over his.

Joe pulled her tightly to his chest as he deepened the kiss.

She'd waited a long time for their first kiss. His gentle, passionate response was better than anything she had imagined in her wayward thoughts and dreams. It took everything in her to pull away. "Joe, we have to talk."

"Am I moving too fast? I've wanted to kiss you for such a long time, but I've had to hold back ... "

"Because of my faith ... or lack thereof?"

He kissed the nape of her neck. "Yes." He ran his hands along the length of her arms. "Samuel told me your news." He lulled her with another kiss.

Suddenly it hit her—he hadn't say anything about her being a reporter, or the investigation. She pulled away. "I have to ask you a question."

The bright light flooded the bathroom and blinded Dominique for a moment.

"There you are," Penelope said. "You two are creating quite a stir at the nurse's station. Lucky for me, one of the nurses saw you both sneak into this room. I should have known I would find you in some sort of compromising position."

Dominique scooted past Penelope and the guards. Joe followed right behind her. "Let's talk in your office, Penelope. This is private."

Penelope shook her head. "There's nothing to talk about. You're fired!" She turned to the guards. "Escort her off the property."

Joe held up a hand. "Hold on. That's a bit extreme, Penelope." He placed his arm around Dominique's shoulder. "Surely we can't be the first employees to sneak a kiss during working hours. You're blowing things way out of proportion."

He doesn't know. The thought made Dominique nauseous.

Penelope's lips turned up in a smirk. She would make a terrible poker-player. Her expression gave away the fact that she held a straight flush. She stepped toward Joe. "I'm sorry you've been deceived just like the rest of us, Dr. Armstrong. Dominique doesn't really work here; she's been lying to us all. She's a reporter, working on some tabloid story." She dangled the flash drive from a lanyard like a pendulum. "I found this in her computer. My guess is that she got word that she'd been discovered and she was copying confidential hospital records before being booted out."

Swiping her hand like a bear after a salmon, Dominique grabbed the flash drive, darted out of the room, and took off down the hall.

She opened the stairwell door and ran for all she was worth. Judging from the shape the security guards were in, she could outrun them with no problem.

Footsteps echoed behind her, but she didn't look back.

She darted out of the stairwell on the ground level and raced for the front door. A couple walking out of the gift shop shot her odd looks.

Dominique reached the front doors and stepped around a man pushing a boy in a wheelchair. A small measure of relief washed over her as she ran out from under the drive-through entrance. She'd made it. As she neared the employee parking lot, she slowed her pace.

"Dominique, wait!" Joe called after her. He must have taken the elevator. How else could he have caught up with her?

She turned to face him but wished she hadn't.

The eyes that had just held such love and desire were now filled with trepidation. No doubt Penelope had ruthlessly poured out all the sordid details. His expression propelled her forward again. She'd seen that look all throughout her childhood … disappointment.

She swallowed the lump in her throat. She couldn't deal with him. Not yet. With tears burning her cheeks, she yanked her car's door open, started the engine, and pulled away. The tires squealed as she tore out of the parking lot.

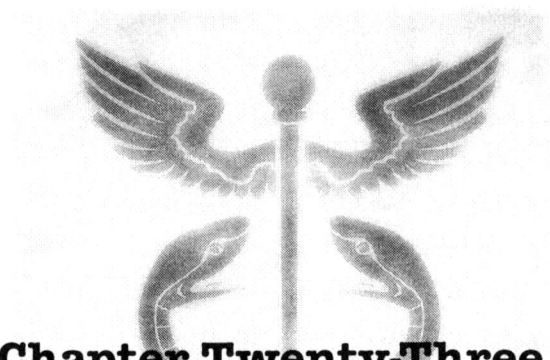

Chapter Twenty-Three

The hospital loudspeaker paged several doctors and issued a few medical alerts. Travis ignored the announcement and pulled the heavy oak chair closer to the round table. Three days since the accident and nothing but bad news about Audrey. *Please let this meeting have good news. Please don't let my child die.*

He grabbed a few tissues from the Kleenex box on the middle of the table and handed them to Cindy.

She accepted them and offered him a sad smile. He took it as a positive sign, so he took her cold hand and gave it a squeeze, but she didn't respond. Her eyes looked lifeless and glassy. He'd known her since college and had never seen her so beaten down.

You're responsible for most of it. The condemning truth haunted him.

Finally, he couldn't stand the silence between them. "Do you want some coffee or something?"

"Not right now. Thanks for asking."

Another conversation that resembled those of polite strangers more than between man and wife. That had to change. But how? He needed to confess to her and beg for her forgiveness. She deserved to know the truth about their finances, his business, and his entanglement with Vinnie. But if she knew everything, she would surely distance herself from him even more. He would tell her all in good time. He'd clear things up, then fix his marriage. Travis had told himself this so many times he was almost starting to believe it.

Audrey's pediatric neurologist entered the room. His white hair was combed over in an attempt to hide his balding head, and the long white coat concealed his over-sized belly.

The doctor placed a file folder on the table and sat. "I'll get right to the point. After reviewing all of the test results from yesterday, I see no reason why Audrey shouldn't make a full recovery."

Travis let out a huge sigh.

Tears streamed down Cindy's face.

A small but reassuring smile broke on the doctor's face. "The edema has subsided significantly. I'm expecting her to regain consciousness any time now."

"Thank you, Doctor." Cindy choked out between sobs.

Travis squeezed his wife's hand. "Do you think she's completely out of the woods?"

"I would say so. We'll know more once she wakes up." The doctor tapped the file twice with an index finger. "These past few days have been very difficult, but I'm extremely optimistic about the outcome. I'll check in on Audrey later this afternoon. If you have any questions, have one of the nurses page me." He stood, grabbed the file folder, and left the room.

Words refused to come to Travis. He couldn't even imagine where to begin.

His cell phone broke the silence. The caller ID said it was Angelica. With the way their last meeting ended, he couldn't risk avoiding her phone call—she could make him look bad in front of Vinnie. "I have to take this, Cindy."

Her silence, dull eyes, and slumped shoulders expressed exactly what she was thinking even without words.

He walked out into the hallway to answer. "What can I help you with?" His tone held an edginess he'd never used with her before.

"Well hello to you, too, Travis. It's not me who needs help, it's you. Vinnie wants to meet. Today."

"I can't. Not today. You know why."

"You don't have a choice. He wants to see you at one o'clock. If I were you, I wouldn't miss it."

He swore underneath his breath. His chest felt like it was pressed in a vice grip. The tension rippled across his shoulders and spiked down his back. "Do you know what it's about?"

"I have no idea. I'm just the messenger."

A muscle in his cheek twitched. "All right, I'll be there."

"Good decision." The line went dead.

Back in the consultation room, Cindy sat on the end of the sofa, head cradled in her hands. "You have to go, don't you?" Her words were so quiet he almost missed them.

"There's something I have to take care of. I can't handle it over the phone. I'll be back as soon as I can."

"Okay." Her tone sounded so dejected and downcast, he wished more than anything he could stay. "Want me to stop at home and bring you a fresh change of clothes?"

"That sounds heavenly." Cindy stood and embraced him. Her arms tightly bound around his neck as if she were hanging onto a life preserver.

Warmth spread through his body as they stood wrapped in a hug—the firm roundness of her protruding belly against him. This was what forgiveness would feel like. He wanted to hold onto her and never let go. Instead, he planted a quick kiss on her cheek and began to step away.

A slight nudge poked his abdomen. "Did you feel that?" he asked Cindy. "The baby just kicked!"

The wonder of life overwhelmed him, and he placed his hands on her stomach. When the baby kicked again, Travis laughed and bent over. "Hey little one, it's your daddy." Cindy placed her hand on top of his. Not only was it the first time he'd felt the baby kick, it was the first time he'd experienced any paternal feelings toward this new growing life.

He straightened. "I'm so sorry, but I have to go. I'll be back as soon as I can." He brushed another quick kiss across her cheek and marched out the door. Whatever it took, he had to begin the long process of getting his life back. And when he was firmly on that road, he would come clean with Cindy and tell her the truth.

The drive to Vinnie's restaurant took less than twenty minutes. Despite it being the lunch hour, only a few cars dotted the parking lot.

A quick look in the rearview mirror depleted Travis's new self-confidence. His face desperately needed a shave, and both hair and clothing were rumpled. The dark circles under his eyes told the tale of two nights with little sleep.

As he entered the restaurant, the same elderly hostess who had met him the second time he'd visited Vinnie greeted him. "Good afternoon, Mr. Montgomery, I'll let Mr. Fernandez know you're here."

Travis searched in his pocket for the roll of antacids he always carried with him. His stomach churned in protest to his uneasy nerves.

Several minutes later, the hostess returned. "Mr. Fernandez will see you now."

He lumbered down the long hallway. At Vinnie's office, he knocked twice.

"Come in." Vinnie's commanding voice called from the other side.

Travis opened the door and stepped into the room. Before he could say a word, a fist slammed into his jaw and set him staggering into a leather chair. The chair slid away under his weight, and he collapsed onto the hardwood floor. Pain radiated from his cheek and shock dulled his brain. The room reeled.

"Get up," a rough voice growled.

Travis placed his hands on the ground in front of him and struggled to sit up. He took another blow to the ribs. He doubled over and tried to suck back the air that had been knocked out of him.

Another blow, and another—and when he curled into himself to protect his stomach, a boot hammered into a kidney. He wailed in agony. "Stop!"

A popping sound came from somewhere beyond the thug. "Enough, Derek!" Vinnie sounded off. "Make sure he's not armed or wired."

Derek threw Travis against the door and ran his hands along Travis's side. He took no steps to avoid his sore ribs. Travis grunted through the pain. Derek spun him back around, and Travis averted his eyes. Was this how it was going to end? Would Vinnie's next order be to kill him?

"He's clean."

Vinnie pointed at the door. "You can leave us alone now. Don't go too far."

Travis waited in silence until Derek left the room. He held his side and stumbled into the chair. "What exactly did I do to deserve that?"

Vinnie placed both his hands on the desk and leaned forward. "Didn't I tell you there are consequences for betraying me, Travis?"

"I haven't done anything to betray you." He wiped the blood away from his mouth. "You owe me an apology."

"Let's just get one thing straight. I don't apologize to anybody. Do the names David Klems or Brian Warner mean anything to you?"

There go my two deals. Could they be under Vinnie's control too? Was that how he found out? "Yeah, I know them. What does that have to do with betraying you?"

"Your business is my business. You're trying to make deals on the side and cut me out. All of your business goes through Angelica. Are we clear?"

Sirens blared outside. Footsteps pounded in the hallway, and Derek burst through the door. "It's a raid. We've gotta go!"

"Get him out of here," Vinnie ordered.

Derek grabbed Travis by an arm and pulled him up out of his seat. He pushed him toward the door, then gave him a shove into the hallway. When they reached the back door, he scanned the alley looking for a way to escape.

Vinnie squeezed his way around Travis and Derek, then turned back suddenly and poked a thick finger in Travis's chest several times. "We're not through with our meeting. I'll be in touch."

Derek opened the passenger door of the black Mercedes Benz that pulled up next to them. Vinnie stepped into its dark insides, and it whisked him down the alley and onto the street, the cops none the wiser.

Travis stumbled up the alley to the front of the restaurant, relieved to find that police cars didn't block his escape. The cars' lights flashed, and a few nosy spectators had gathered across the street. He wiped his mouth and glanced down. Blood smeared the back of his hand.

There had to be a way to get to his truck on the far side of the lot without drawing too much attention to himself. Hopefully, the cops would be occupied with trying to locate Vinnie.

Two police officers conferred at the entrance. Their radios sounded off and informed them that the restaurant was clear. Two more officers exited, followed by the elderly hostess.

"I told you he wasn't here," the hostess said. "Make an appointment, and Mr. Fernandez will be happy to meet with you."

"Sure will," an officer replied sarcastically.

Nearby, Travis remained hidden in the alley.

After talking for a few more minutes, the officers got in their vehicles and left.

Travis took advantage of their absence and jogged to his truck. He breathed a sigh of relief as he turned the key in the ignition. That was too close. What would have happened if they'd found him there? He pushed the unwelcomed thought away as he drove home. Instead, he tried to focus on what he needed to do to get out of this mess.

A rectangle of bright orange decorated the middle of his front door when he pulled into his driveway, but he couldn't read the word at the top of the note until halfway to the porch.

Foreclosure.

The sign advised him they had thirty days to vacate the premises.

Clenching his fists, he resisted the urge to shout out several profanities. Instead, he tore the notice off the door and stuffed it in his pocket. Vinnie's tentacles had no limits. No area of Travis's life was free from his clutches.

Enough.

If I'm going down, I'm taking Vinnie with me.

Chapter Twenty-Four

The country scenery Houston drove past on his way home offered him no peace today. Not with the knowledge that he would have to present Joe with evidence that could hurt him. The business card with Dominique's name on it sent his imagination swirling in a million different directions. How had he misjudged her so much? But if she was lying to them all, it was better that Joe know now, before he got too involved with her.

As he turned on the road leading to his house, his thoughts shifted to Becky, and the images from the early morning crime scene returned to haunt him. More than once as they processed the scene, his mind played tricks on him, replacing Sharon's face with Becky's. He pulled into the driveway of his home in the country and was relieved to see Becky sitting on the porch. He approached the porch and took the steps two at a time.

Becky looked up from the Bible in her lap, and waved. "Hey there, handsome. I was just thinking about you."

Houston didn't bother to answer. He scooped her up in his arms and took in the fresh scent of her hair. *I must be the luckiest man alive.* He kissed her softly, then deepened the kiss. He put her down but kept his arms wrapped around her waist. So often they could communicate as much with their actions as with words.

Becky ran a hand along the side of his face. "Rough morning?"

"You could say that." He grabbed her hand and kissed it.

"You want to talk about it?"

He drew her closer. At that moment his boss was probably notifying Sharon's husband of her death. *What if it were Becky and my child?* He shook the horrible thought from his head, yet it was someone's reality.

He had to find out who was committing these heartless crimes. The only lead he had pointed him in a direction he didn't want to go. "Where's Dad?" he asked Becky.

She tucked a stray hair behind her ear. "Everyone's still sleeping. I think having the kids here has made him more tired than usual."

"You talk to Joe this morning?"

"No. He usually calls later in the afternoon with any updates on Audrey." Becky hugged him again. "What's bothering you, Houston?"

He looked deep into eyes that held such innocence. As a nurse, Becky saw a lot of gruesome things, but they lacked the malicious intent of a crime scene, where the violence sometimes hung in the air like a dense fog.

Houston debated how much to share with her, hoping to spare her some of life's ugliness. "I stumbled upon an unusual lead this morning, and I was hoping he could help."

The boys' crying traveled through the open windows and interrupted any response Becky may have had. He didn't miss the look she shot him as she entered the house. It was clear she wasn't finished with the subject.

He sat on the old, white wicker chair, pulled his cell phone out of its black leather case, and dialed Joe's number. "Hey, little brother, got a minute?"

"Yeah. Did you hear the news about Audrey?"

Houston listened while Joe shared the good news. "That's fantastic. Becky will be relieved."

"Dad too." Joe responded.

It only took two little words to snap his defenses in place. "Now's not the time to go into it, Joe." The last thing he needed now was Joe's encouragement to fix his relationship with their dad. He could still hear the words he said right before the hospital released him: *Time's running short. We don't know how much time Dad has.* But he didn't want to be coerced into some kind of false reconciliation.

Thankfully, Joe remained quiet.

"I need a favor, Joe."

"Anything for my favorite brother."

He laughed at the old joke. "I need to speak with Dominique. When you see her could you ask her to call me?"

"Sure." There was another moment of silence. "May I ask why you need to speak with her?"

The apprehension in Joe's tone made the hairs on Houston's arms stand on end. Maybe there was more to Dominique then met the eye. "I have a few questions for her."

"Personal or business?"

He shifted in the chair. Again with the uneasiness. Something was definitely up. "Is everything okay with you two?"

Several seconds ticked by with no response, then Joe cleared his throat. "To be completely honest, I'm not sure."

"You guys have a fight?"

"We didn't have a chance. I found out Dominique's not the person she claims to be. But before I had a chance to talk to her, she ran out of here. I've tried calling several times, but all I get is her voice mail. Is she in some kind of trouble?"

So the woman was hiding something. Was she somehow involved with Fernandez? He let out a slow breath. "I found Dominique's business card at a crime scene earlier today. I really need to speak with her."

"You've got to be kidding! Dominique didn't murder anyone, Houston. She's a reporter, not a killer."

Houston clutched the phone tighter. "Take it easy. I didn't say I think she's a murderer. I have to find out why the victim had her name. She may be able to help."

"I'm sorry. It's been a stressful couple of days. I'll give her your message when I see her."

Houston rubbed the back of his neck with his free hand. "Thanks. Say hi to Cindy and Travis for me. I'll stop in as soon as I grab a few hours of sleep."

"I'll tell Cindy, but Travis took off. Said he had some business to attend to."

He ended the phone call and bit back the urge to find Travis and shake some sense into him. What kind of business was more important than your daughter?

Chapter Twenty-Five

Dominique apologized to the gentleman in the seat to her left as she accepted a cup of water from the stewardess. As she swallowed two Advil, she gazed longingly at the window on the other side of the teenager wearing earbuds and nodding to his music. The seats in coach were confining, especially the middle seat. She had hoped to get a window or aisle seat, but took what she could get last minute. She'd still end the flight with a giant-size migraine.

The large dose of regret and anxiety only made things worse. Regret because of the way she'd left things with Joe, and anxiety over the upcoming meeting with her boss. Their last conversation still rang in her ears: "Just bring me the story I want, Dominique. Not some fairy tale."

"I'll bring you the truth," she said before she hung up on him. Why was he so resistant to her angle on the birthrate story when he was definitely interested in the baby-snatching story? But every time she'd dropped hints about the spiritual aspect of the birthrate crisis, he'd redirected her focus to researching the toxins in the environment. This time he'd have to listen to her. She wouldn't take no for an answer. She'd present all of her evidence and insist it was their journalistic duty to report her findings to their viewers.

While the stewardess rambled on about all of the flight's deplaning instructions, Dominique whispered a prayer. *Lord, please give me the courage to present this story. Help Stew to see its merit.* She pulled out her phone and opened the Bible app she'd downloaded while waiting for the plane. Maybe a Psalm would provide a verse or two that would calm her anxieties.

The flight breezed by with little turbulence, and by the time they landed, she'd read several of the Psalms. Since she had brought only carry-on luggage, she forged her way off the plane and into the long line of travelers waiting for a taxi.

On the ride to the station, she rehearsed her presentation in her head. She wrapped her fingers around the flash drive in a side pocket of her purse and let out a slight sigh. Stew was a stickler for details. He would never listen to her pitch without evidence to back up her claims.

When the taxi pulled up to the curb, she handed the cabbie the fare plus a generous tip, strode through the studio doors, and marched to the elevator.

"Not so fast there, missy." The guard came up behind her. "You have to sign in."

She jumped at his sudden appearance. "It's okay, I work here."

"Where's your ID badge?"

She fished around in her purse. *Where is it? Rats! I think I left it in Ohio.* "I don't have it with me. I'm Dominique Sherwood. I'm a news reporter for WCRW."

"I've never seen you. You're going to have to sign in. Call the party you're meeting and ask them to come down and escort you up."

Grumbling underneath her breath, she grabbed her cell phone and called Stew.

A few minutes later, the elevator doors parted to reveal her boss and Channing, looking perfectly groomed, as always. Why had he come along? His blond hair had been gelled to perfection, and a five o'clock shadow would never dare appear on his face. Next to Channing, Stew's resemblance to middle-aged Lou Grant from the Mary Tyler Moore Show became even more pronounced.

Stew shook her hand. "Hi, Dominique. We're going out to lunch. You can bring me up to speed on the results of your investigation. Channing has already pitched a few great stories. Can't wait to hear what you've come up with."

Channing's gaze scanned her up and down, and she hadn't had a chance to freshen up after her flight. This wasn't going as expected.

"You're looking well." The side of Channing's mouth tilted up in a mocking smile. He could be so charming at times, but clearly this wasn't one of them.

She'd ignore his sarcasm—just this once.

They settled for a local diner known for its fish sandwiches. Her stomach roiled at all of the greasy selections. Both men ordered the daily special, but she closed the menu. "I'll have an iced tea and a house salad with Italian on the side, please."

Stew cleared his throat. "Channing has put together quite a story about big manufacturers dumping pollutants into rivers and streams. The toxins are saturating the water sources up and down the coast of California." He leaned forward.

"What's really fascinating is that many of the chemicals are rumored to cause infertility. While his research and water samples are being verified, we're putting together a short documentary on his findings. With the competition so tight, we have to be fast and accurate." He laid his crumpled napkin on the table. "What do you have for me?"

Her heart thumped inside her chest. "I took a different approach entirely." She took a small sip of her tea. "You sent me to an area that has a high pregnancy rate in comparison with other parts of the nation. What I discovered was not only fascinating, but I can pretty much guarantee we'll have the lead; no other station will beat us to it."

Stew looked like a cat ready to pounce on a poor, unsuspecting mouse. "Don't leave me hanging. Spill it."

She licked her lips. "Please understand that we need to look at the whole picture. That's why I took a different approach. I wasn't interested in why women in southern Ohio weren't getting pregnant, I wanted to know how the women *were* getting pregnant."

Channing winked at her. "I should think you'd know what causes that, Dominique."

Her cheeks burned. She bit back her sarcastic reply. Why had she ever allowed herself to become romantically involved with this man?

Trying to maintain some semblance of professionalism, Dominique took a deep breath and tuned out Channing. "What I'm getting at is this. What is the common denominator among the women able to conceive?" She pulled the flash drive out of her purse and held it up. "That question became the cornerstone of my investigation. The answer is beyond anything I ever thought I'd see in my lifetime."

"What is it?" Stew and Channing's voices questioned in perfect unity.

Dominique sent up a quick prayer for courage. "Faith." She put the flash drive down in front of Stew.

Stew ignored it and reached for his Diet Coke. "Faith? What do you mean?"

Dominique leaned forward. "More specifically, they are all Christians."

Stew choked on the large sip of drink he'd just inhaled. "You have got to be kidding me. I specifically ordered you to stop that foolish line of investigation. I thought you were a professional."

"I didn't want to believe it at first either. The proof is overwhelming." She grabbed the flash drive off the table. "But this flash drive contains the personal and medical information of over one hundred women. All of them are pregnant or have recently given birth. All of them are Christians. Aren't you even the slightest bit interested in seeing the statistics?"

Stew slammed his hand on the table. "That is not proof. It's just some kind of hocus pocus. Some religious fanatic has somehow gotten you to believe it as fact." He signaled the waiter for the bill. "Frankly, I'm disappointed."

She chose to remain silent. Channing looked as if he was choking on a remark. She slid the flash drive across the table to Stew again. "All of my findings are recorded on this. How can you ignore a story like this? It's the answer to the question everyone's asking … and we're the only ones with the answer."

Her boss ignored the flash drive. "Okay, I'll play along. Enlighten me." He looked at Channing and rolled his eyes. His sarcastic laugh chipped away at her confidence.

After a few moments of awkward silence, she relayed the whole story, minus her brief romantic encounter; it would only lower her credibility. She finished with her heroic escape from the hospital.

Stew sat back. "That's a very interesting story. It's a shame I can't use it."

Her shoulders slumped. "Why not?"

"Because, Dominique, it's not only offensive to all other faiths, it's just a little--shall we say—preposterous?"

The waiter arrived with the bill and rushed off with Stew's credit card.

"But it's the truth. Read my reports. It's the same no matter which city you check. Let's go to a hospital right now. I'll bet you my job. If there's a baby in the nursery, both parents are Christians."

"You can't make that bet."

"And why not?"

"Because you're fired!"

She grabbed the flash drive. "Fired? You can't fire me for reporting the truth."

"Watch me. We'll escort you back to the station. Pack up your things, and make it quick. I expect you to be out of the building by the six o'clock news."

Stew and Channing left with their lunches only half eaten. Dominique didn't bother following. It wouldn't be worth the humiliation. Nothing in her little cubicle at the station was worth facing ridicule from her coworkers.

Her ears rang. What a turn of events. She'd actually been fired for trying to report the truth. A small smile turned her lips upward when she remembered that

Penelope had fired her earlier that morning as well. *I've never been fired from two jobs in the same day.*

Exhausted, she hailed the first cab in sight and gave him her mother's address. After the day she'd already had, maybe a visit with her mother wouldn't be the hardest part of her trip after all.

Chapter Twenty-Six

When Houston walked into the hospital lounge, the television in the corner played without sound, and the waiting area still smelled of stale coffee. Cindy and Becky were the lone occupants of the room. Houston joined them on the couch and gave Becky a soft kiss. "I was hoping you'd still be here."

She returned the kiss and added a quick hug. "What a coincidence. We were just talking about you."

"Were you, now? I hope it was all good things, like how incredibly attractive you find me." He pulled her in for another embrace.

She laughed. "Well, we haven't talked about that particular subject yet. Are you off for the rest of the day?"

"Yeah. I was hoping to talk with Travis. Is he around?"

"He's at the office," Cindy said.

"Unbelievable!" Houston huffed. "He's still working?"

"Something came up at work." Cindy took a sip from her water bottle. "Lately, he always has some type of emergency or business that needs his attention."

Becky flashed Houston a concerned look before responding to her sister-in-law. "Have things improved any since we last talked?"

Cindy wiped away a stray tear. "I thought they were. We had a good conversation earlier, then *she* called and ruined everything."

"Who?" Houston asked. What was Travis up to now? Becky had indicated that Travis and Cindy were having problems. Was another woman the source of the trouble?

Cindy rolled her eyes. "Angelica. His new accountant. She's some young, sexy, intriguing woman. She says jump, and Travis asks how high." She walked to the window. "I'm sorry, I didn't mean to burden you both with our problems."

"It's no burden, sis. That's what family is for. Becky and I are happy to help any way we can." His words sounded normal, but inside, all he could think about was knocking some sense into his brother-in-law.

"You two have already done so much." She rubbed her arms. "It's such a relief not to have to worry about the kids."

"We've had help from several women at church," Becky said.

Cindy sat back down. "I miss them. It seems like weeks since I've changed a diaper. I would give anything to have a little normal back in my life."

Becky squeezed her hand. "I know the kids miss you too. I would love to bring them all here or take them to the park, but I can't fit everyone in my car."

"Let's switch vehicles." Cindy leaned forward. "I don't know why I didn't think of this sooner. You take my Land Rover, and I'll drive your car. I'm not leaving until Audrey wakes up, but if I need to go anywhere, your car will be fine."

"That will work," Becky said. "I'll bring everyone back later tonight, if that's okay."

The conversation stopped as the doctor strolled into the room. "Good news, Mrs. Montgomery. Audrey has regained consciousness."

The room erupted with laughter, tears, and hugs. Houston hugged Becky, then jumped up and swept Cindy into the air.

Once her feet hit the firm ground, Cindy asked, "Can I see her?"

"They're finishing up some tests. A nurse will come down to get you as soon as they're completed."

"Is she breathing on her own?" Cindy wrung her hands. "Has there been any brain damage?"

"Her breathing is fine, but we have a few more tests we need to run before we'll know about anything conclusive. I'd say, overall, she's out of the woods."

"Thank you, Doctor. Please tell her I'm here, and I can't wait to hug her."

The moment the doctor left, Cindy retrieved her cell phone from her purse. "Rats. My battery is dead. Can I borrow your phone?"

Before either of them could answer, a nurse walked into the room. "Are you Mrs. Montgomery?"

"I am."

"You can come on up. Audrey's asking for you."

Becky gave Cindy a bright smile. "You go on up, we'll get hold of Travis." As Cindy rushed out of the room, Becky intertwined her fingers with Houston's. "Do you want to call him, or do you want me to try?"

Houston squeezed her hand. "Can you stay here with Cindy? I'll stop by his office and tell him the good news. Hopefully, we'll have a chance to talk on the way back to the hospital." Was the source of Travis's trouble Vinnie Fernandez or another woman? "I hope he hasn't gotten himself into some kind of trouble I can't help him out of."

Why did things have to be so complicated? Travis had been avoiding him. A face-to-face conversation would give Houston the chance to find out what was eating at him. Hopefully, it didn't involve Vinnie Fernandez, because people who got in too deep with that crook ended up in one of two places—prison or the morgue.

Chapter Twenty-Seven

Clutching the foreclosure notice in hand, Travis entered his office and sat down behind his desk. Cindy and Audrey needed him, but if he lost the house and business, what good would he be to them?

The only way to get the money to save them was through Vinnie. He wadded the notice up and tossed it into the trash can. How could he have been so foolish? Getting involved with Vinnie had only increased his troubles.

He retrieved the foreclosure notice and smoothed it out. No. The only way to save anything out of this mess would be to get Vinnie off his back. And to do that, he needed solid evidence proving Fernandez was laundering money. Once he obtained proof, he would make a deal with the police. If he was lucky, maybe he could avoid going to prison.

Everyone involved with Vinnie ends up dead or in prison. Houston's words haunted Travis. Why hadn't he listened to him? *Pride.* He was in deep with a slim chance of coming out unscathed. How could he admit that to anyone, especially someone who could put him behind bars if he discovered what he was involved in?

Travis picked up the picture on his desk. He ran his finger over Audrey's face. When either of the girls smiled, it never failed to melt his heart. The family photo had been taken six months after the boys were born. Cindy's eyes held a sparkle he hadn't seen in a long time. Why didn't he appreciate what he had? He missed those simpler days.

He studied the bulletin board on the far wall, where he pinned notes from clients thanking him for building their homes. Helping people build their family's homes had been satisfying. What had been the appeal of expanding his business?

Money. Now he stood on the brink of losing it all. He swallowed the lump in his throat.

His bruised ribs and sore face screamed at him. He made his way to the restroom next to his office. He touched the red puffy area around his eye. No doubt a whopper of a shiner would make its appearance soon. He ran a washcloth under cool water and patted away the dried blood on the corner of his mouth.

His sore ribs ached with every move, but he returned to his desk and eased himself back into the chair. An x-ray would surely show several broken ribs. The doctors would probably recommend taking it easy, but he didn't have time to rest.

He fired up the computer and surfed the web. What could he use to trap Vinnie in his own game? He keyed in "surveillance tools + private investigators." A few websites popped up. He typed in "hidden surveillance equipment" and scrolled through the results: civil and criminal investigations, domestic relations, surveillance of all kinds. He clicked on the first choice and read in detail a page dedicated to video surveillance. Taped evidence would be sufficient proof to use against Vinnie. Being free from the contract would be well worth the expense of the equipment.

It also could cost you your life.

The disturbing thought had kept him company since he'd gone into business with Vinnie. He should have listened to his gut instinct and never returned after walking away from their first meeting. Ignoring the heaviness in his chest, he pushed up his sleeves. He had work to do if he didn't want his family and friends to know the full extent of his failings.

An image on the website's list of products caught his eye. A voice-activated recording pen. That might work. He could keep the pen tucked in his shirt pocket, and every conversation with Vinnie and Angelica would be recorded. It might take some time, but eventually he could put together enough to bring the big boss down.

His shoulders relaxed, and he smiled. This would work—it had to!

He paid for his order and requested next-day shipping. The cursor blinked in the 'Ship to' box. Travis typed in his home address, then deleted it. Better to play it safe and have the pen shipped to Houston's house. If Cindy saw the package, even the name of the company would make her start asking questions. And if she opened the package … No, it would be better to send it to Houston's house. He'd have to get him involved at some point anyway.

Travis looked at the clock. Mid-afternoon already! He hadn't intended to be away from the hospital for so long.

His glanced at his shirt, rumpled and covered with blood. He couldn't go anywhere dressed like this. He grabbed one of the extra shirts he kept on hand in the closet. Tossing off his dirty shirt and undershirt, he returned to the bathroom. The dark bruises on his ribs evidenced the beating he'd taken earlier. He ran a soapy, wet rag over himself lightly, but winced as it rubbed over his ribs.

He returned to his office but stopped short at the sight of Angelica sitting on the edge of his desk. Her arms were crossed over her chest, and she wore a frown, but when she caught sight of him, she jumped up. "What happened, Travis?" Her gaze locked on the bruises across his bare chest as she closed the distance between them.

"Vinnie happened. That's what."

Her eyes flashed as she lightly touched his side just beyond the bruised area. "Vinnie did this to you?"

"One of his thugs did. I'm still trying to figure out why." If Vinnie found out about his outside deals, either his phone was bugged or Angelica had been on his computer. Or maybe one of the people he was trying to work a deal with was also involved with Vinnie. His couldn't be the only business in trouble.

Her touch caused heat to travel up his neck. He sidestepped her and reached for the clean shirt he'd draped over the back of his chair.

She followed him and set a hand on his shoulder. "It looks so painful. Is there anything I can do for you?" When her eyes met his, the look in them changed from concern to desire. "Travis, I ..."

Warning bells clanged in his head, but he ignored them. He brushed her cheek with the back of his hand. The temptation to kiss her overwhelmed him. He didn't have the strength to resist. Just one kiss. His lips met hers. She tasted like sweet wine. At first the kiss was tentative, a surrendering to forbidden fruit, but it quickly became more passionate.

Angelica seemed to welcome his desire, but suddenly pulled away.

He opened his eyes just as Houston's fist connected with his left eye. Travis stumbled back a few feet.

"I'm not going to apologize for that, Travis. You deserve it." Houston rubbed his fist on his leg and took a step forward.

Travis held his hands up. "It's not what it looks like. Well, it's what you saw, but it's not what you think ..." He fumbled for an excuse.

Angelica touched a hand to her lips. "I'd better leave. We'll talk later, Travis." She slithered out of the room, leaving him to face Houston alone.

"Look, Houston, I know you're not going to believe me, no matter what I tell you, but nothing is going on."

"You call kissing a woman who isn't your wife 'nothing?'" Houston shook his head. "You're a real piece of work."

Travis pulled on his undershirt and tucked it into his pants. "I'm not saying it was right; I'm just saying you don't know the whole story."

"Well, why don't you enlighten me."

"I'm not having an affair." Travis slipped on the clean button-down shirt. "That was the first time I ever kissed her. And I wish I never had." He hissed at the pain as he eased into the shirt.

Houston's eyes remained on Travis like a hawk eyeing its prey. "Where'd you get those bruises?"

Travis finished buttoning his shirt and returned to his seat behind the desk, wincing as he bent. Looked like he'd have to confess to Houston a little earlier than anticipated.

"I fell on a job site. Took quite a tumble." He held a finger up to his lips and mouthed a shush, then motioned toward the front door. He couldn't risk having this discussion in his office if his suspicions about the office being bugged were true.

Houston's eyes narrowed, and he said, "I've got to get back to the hospital, but we'll finish this conversation later."

Travis followed Houston outside. When they reached the driveway, Houston said, "Out with it. What are you involved in?"

Travis couldn't look him in the eyes, but he managed to say, "I'm in something deep. Much more dangerous than I ever imagined."

Houston stood silent for several minutes. "Vinnie Fernandez did this to you, didn't he?"

At Travis's nod, he added, "How involved are you?" Houston asked.

Travis touched his bruised eye. "Way over my head."

"That man's nothing but a criminal. I thought I'd made that clear to you. One day we're going to arrest him; it's only a matter of time."

"You'll never get him." Travis leaned against the porch railing. "He has too many connections." He let out a sarcastic laugh. "As a matter of fact, you probably work with some of them."

Houston's eyes narrowed and a scowl marked his face. "This isn't about me. You need help, Travis, and I need to know how much."

Travis stared at the ground. "I have it under control." He thought about his statement. Was it really under control? If he let Houston know his plan to record Vinnie, his brother-in-law would point out a thousand reasons why it wouldn't work. His plan might be sketchy, but it was his only hope to free himself without putting anyone else in danger. "If you want to help me, don't tell Cindy what you saw today. It was a huge mistake. I never should have let it happen, and it will never happen again. I don't want to hurt Cindy."

"You're putting me in a very uncomfortable position." Houston rocked back on his heels. "She deserves to know the truth."

He took in a deep breath of air. "I know. But the timing has to be better."

They stared at each other in silence for several minutes until Houston cleared his throat. "The reason I stopped by was to let you know Audrey is awake."

Travis stood up straight. "Why did you wait so long to tell me? Is she okay? Is there any brain damage?" He peppered Houston with questions as he pulled out his keys.

"The doctor will know more after he gets the results from the tests they just ran. Cindy's phone was out of juice, so I told her I'd come get you." Houston's gaze held Travis's. "You're going to have to tell her—and soon."

"I know. There's a lot I need to tell Cindy … and you. I just need a little more time."

"Why don't you let me help you?"

"Vinnie has made it clear. If I go to the police, there will be consequences—much worse than I suffered today. I don't want to find out what they are."

"I can't help if you don't trust me."

"I trust you, Houston." He held his head high. "But I don't have any idea what Vinnie might do to you if he finds out you're involved."

Houston's eyes flashed. "I've been after Vinnie for a long time. I'll do whatever it takes to protect you from him."

The ring of Travis's phone interrupted their conversation. He pressed the button and accepted the call.

"I told you not to talk to the police, Travis." Vinnie's icy voice came through the receiver loud and clear. Travis's heart slammed in his chest. How could Vinnie possibly know? He took a long, slow breath. What should he do now?

Houston whispered, "Who is it?"

Travis mouthed, *"It's him."* He spoke into the receiver. "I haven't gone to the police. You've got bad information."

"My sources are usually dead on. Watch your step."

"I'm telling you the truth, Vinnie. I learned my lesson this afternoon." He hoped his tone sounded sincere.

"That's good, Travis. I'd hate for anything to happen to you … or your beautiful wife."

A click followed the threat as Vinnie ended the conversation.

The fire of hatred circulated throughout his entire body. Desperation overwhelmed him. "We've got to get to the hospital." He returned his phone to a pocket with a shaking hand. "Vinnie just threatened Cindy."

Houston shot up and strode to his truck. "Let's go."

Travis followed, no longer concerned about his aching ribs or bruised face. It was one thing for Vinnie to mess with his business and personal finances, but if he thought Travis would let him threaten his family, he was dead wrong.

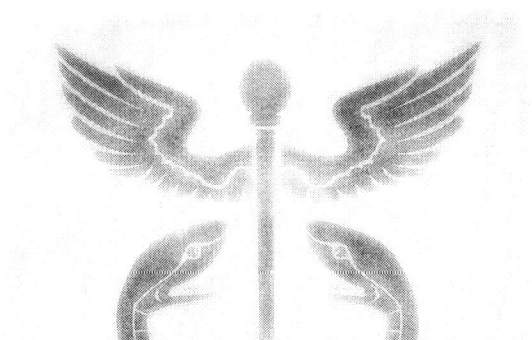

Chapter Twenty-Eight

As usual, her mother's house was in perfect order. "I have something important to tell you." Dominique carefully set the fine china cup on the polished cherry coffee table.

Her mother sat in the mauve wingback chair opposite the sofa. "I hope you're not pregnant. That would be so embarrassing."

What should I do, Lord? In the past she would have flung some dirt right back and left in a huff. This time she'd take the high road. "No, I'm not pregnant. In fact, I think you'll be quite happy with my news."

"We'll see about that."

Okay. You can get through this. Ignore the droll tone and sour expression. Buoyed by her mental pep talk, she forged ahead. "I've become a Christian, Mom. After all those years of running away, I've given my life to Christ."

Her mother rolled her eyes and tipped her head to the right. "Are you sure this isn't another one of your passing fancies? The Lord will not be trifled with." She waggled a finger.

Dominique should have known better. She shouldn't have bothered coming. "You've been praying for me for years. Now it's finally happened, and you just attribute it to a passing fancy?" She bit her tongue before any of the rest of her thoughts could slip out.

A small smile appeared on her mother's face. "Now that's the daughter I'm more accustomed to."

"I don't get it." Dominique reached for her teacup.

"What's there to get?"

"You claim to be Christian, yet you're so different from the others." She replaced the teacup on the table.

"What do you mean, I *claim* to be a Christian? I haven't missed a Sunday service in over twenty years." She placed her hand over her heart. "I've always given my ten percent, and I've taught more Sunday-school lessons than I can count." She pointed a perfectly manicured nail at Dominique. "How can *you* sit there in your rumpled clothing and accuse *me* of not being a Christian? I see you haven't learned the part about honoring your mother yet."

"It's all about rules to you, isn't it, Mom?"

"Without rules, society would run amok."

"What about grace?" Dominique brushed her hand over her mother's. "Is there room for grace in your brand of Christianity?"

Her mother rose stiffly and retrieved the teapot from the silver tray on the formal table. She lifted the teapot from the silver tray. "More tea?"

"No thanks. Are you going to answer my question?"

"I don't think your question deserves an answer." She returned to her seat. "*If* your conversion was authentic, I think you'd be showing me more respect."

The truth hit Dominique square in the face. Her mom didn't have an answer about grace because the concept was completely foreign to her. *She wasn't a Christian.*

All these years she'd been playing church but never connected the dots. "Mom, I *am* a Christian. Just because I ask you a question about grace doesn't mean I'm being disrespectful."

Her mother picked at a piece of lint on the wingback chair she'd taken a seat in. "I really should have this reupholstered."

"Mom?"

Her mother's expression held disdain, but beyond the coldness, Dominique saw something she had never seen before in her mother's eyes: fear.

Her mother stared at the floor. "I think you should leave."

Unbelievable. Her own mother was kicking her out. In their many arguments, Dominique had always been the one to storm out of the room or hang up the phone. "I don't think I understand what happened here, Mom. I stop in to visit you, tell you about the best decision I've ever made in my life, and you ask me to leave? I thought you'd be ecstatic that I'm finally in the fold."

"You see? There. You have no respect for me. You haven't learned a thing, and I doubt highly your *conversion* is authentic. But at least it's a start … albeit a slow one."

There would be no point in arguing. Once her mother made up her mind, little could change it. If what she suspected was true, her mother would need her prayers more than her criticism.

Dominique checked her watch. "I'll see you soon. I didn't mean to hurt you. I honestly thought you'd be happy. I don't leave until Monday, so I promise we'll talk before I leave."

"More traveling? No man would ever want to settle down with a woman who's more committed to her job than she is to him."

There it was again. If her mother couldn't get to her spiritually, she would criticize her personal life. She didn't dare tell her about Joe. That would have to wait. Instead, she left a little nugget of information to chew on. "Well, that's not the case anymore. I was fired today. Now any man I choose to date will have my fully devoted attention."

She stood and gently kissed her mother on the cheek. "I'll let myself out." She couldn't resist a glance back at her mother's slack-jaw expression. Maybe she hadn't handled the situation exactly as the Lord would have had her do, but she was new to this Christianity thing.

Not only had Stew refused to air her story on the declining birthrate, he'd fired her. She mulled over her options. Social media was an excellent vehicle for getting a hot story out. Dominique pulled out her cell phone and dialed the station's cameraman, Calvin Baldwin. She'd heard him talking about his faith on more than one occasion. Maybe he would help her. The call went directly to his voicemail. "Calvin, it's Dominique. You've probably heard I've been let go. I have a story I'd like some help with. Meet me at the Starbucks on the north end at four o'clock. I'll fill you in on the details." Hopefully, he would show up.

The cab dropped her off in the Starbucks parking lot with ten minutes to spare. After ordering a double latte, she chose a booth in the back. She opened the pregnancy crisis file and scanned the material. *Lord, please help me. I know this is a story you want broadcasted, but I can't do it on my own.*

What a comfort. She didn't have to rely on her own strength anymore. Even though her world was falling apart before her eyes, the peace she had could only be attributed to the Lord. She checked her watch. Calvin was fifteen minutes late. Would he show? Stew had probably done a good job of warning others away from her.

After another fifteen minutes, Calvin entered and placed an order at the counter. He joined her and folded his tall lanky form into the seat across from her.

He ran his free hand over his balding head. "Sorry I'm late. I got held up at the station."

"I suppose everyone's tongues are still wagging."

The sympathetic look on Calvin's face gave her hope that he might at least hear her out.

"It's okay, you can tell me the truth."

"Well … let's just say you made an impression."

"What, exactly, did you hear?"

He shifted in his chair and took a sip of coffee. "Word at the station is that you've joined some kind of cult and lost all ability to report any news without a religious bias."

She slammed a hand on the table. "What? If anyone is biased it's them!"

Calvin sat back. "It's always been a challenge being a believer in a field that's predominantly filled with non-believers."

"I'm sorry, Calvin. I'm new at this." How could they completely ignore all of her findings? "What do you think? Do you think I've lost my mind?"

"I think if we're going to get this story fired up on YouTube, we'd better get started."

Chapter Twenty-Nine

Dominique tossed her keys on the kitchen dinette in her small apartment. Amazing how her temporary housing felt more like home than her place in Florida. At least she'd just paid for the month, so she could stay for another few weeks.

The light flashing on the phone sitting on the counter drew her attention. A voice mail. More than a week had passed since Dominique had last seen Joe, but she prayed the message was from him. She pushed the button.

"Dominique, I got your message. I was beginning to wonder if you'd ever return one of my calls." Joe's voice seemed to fill the small room.

Her heart slammed in her chest when he paused. Would he break up with her over the phone?

"We need to talk. I can stop by after rounds."

He was coming over. That could be good or bad. The past week had been torturous. Her mind had played all kinds of tricks on her: *He'll never forgive you. How could you hide the truth for so long?* Maybe she should call and cancel. If he broke up with her face-to-face, she'd be a mess.

No. When he showed up tonight, she would tell him everything and leave the results to the Lord.

The afternoon dragged. After a shower, she passed the time cleaning the apartment, then rearranged the floral decorations in the living room several times. A short walk would help settle her nerves, but she didn't want to take the chance that Joe would come while she was gone.

Before she could make up her mind, two knocks sounded. She held her breath as she peered through the eyehole.

Joe twisted a single, long-stemmed red rose in his hands.

He'd brought her a flower—things were looking up. She opened the door but immediately felt like the wind had been knocked out of her. Words stuck in her mouth. "Hi, Joe. It's good to see you." The heat climbed up her face.

"You too. You look—you look good." He stammered like a teen on his first date.

"Want to come in?"

"Yes. Here … this is for you." He held out the rose.

She smiled and accepted the rose. "Can I get you something to drink?"

"Do you have any iced tea?"

"Coming right up." She returned shortly and set a tall glass on the coffee table in front of the studio couch, where he'd made himself comfortable. His cologne hung in the air and tantalized her senses as she took the seat next to him.

She couldn't keep her mind from flashing back to the kiss they'd shared. She'd recalled their passionate kiss thousands of times in her dreams. *Lord help me keep focused.* Wanting to fill the silence, she blurted out, "I owe you an apology." She cleared her throat. "And an explanation."

His soft brown eyes held no condemnation or anger. "I've talked a little with Dad. He filled me in on some of the details, but said he wasn't at liberty to share your whole story." His words were a statement, but she heard the question in them.

"Your dad is one special man." Dominique moved her thumb through the condensation on her glass. "How much did he tell you about my past?"

"He confirmed Penelope's claims that you're an investigative reporter, and he shared your conversion story." He adjusted the collar on his shirt. "I'm not going to lie, Dominique. I'm more than a little confused. I wish you would have trusted me and told me the truth from the beginning." He took a sip of his tea. "Things were crazy at the hospital when you left. However, I think you should know you missed the best part." The smile he offered warmed her heart and gave her hope.

"What did I miss?" She returned the smile.

"The look on Penelope's face when you grabbed the flash drive and took off running. It was priceless." He chuckled. "I had no idea you could run so fast."

Dominique laughed. "I was one of the top sprinters on my high school track team." She sobered and cleared her throat. "I'm also sorry I didn't return any of your phone calls. I had a lot of thinking and praying to do. It took me a while to work up the courage to face some ugly things about myself. I don't know if you'll be so willing to forgive me once you know the truth."

His eyebrows raised. "The truth about what?"

She twisted a loose strand on the worn sofa. "My past. I've made a lot of mistakes." She turned away from his gaze. He would hate her when he found out about the baby.

He ran a finger down her cheek. The gentle touch sent a shiver down her back. "I've made a lot of mistakes too. Everyone has." His eyes were filled with understanding and compassion.

Lord, help me tell him the truth.

Joe cleared his throat. "Why don't we pray first. Prayer is always a great way to start any difficult conversation."

As they bowed their heads, Dominique wiped away a tear. The urge to tell him the truth swelled. After several minutes of silence, she summoned the courage to speak. "I had an abortion." Her words hung in the air like a balloon filled with air waiting for someone to bat at it.

Joe slid from the sofa and knelt in front of her. He gently lifted her chin until her eyes met his. "Dominique, when you asked Jesus to forgive you and come into your life, He forgave you. You don't have to carry the guilt of the abortion anymore. You're forgiven."

She bit the inside of her lip to try to hold back the tears. When she thought she could speak without triggering a waterfall, she only managed to speak just above a whisper. "I knew when I met you that you were out of my league. You're like this super Christian." She took in a shuddering breath. "I was so scared to tell you. I worried that you'd think I was a horrible person. How could you not? I've thought it for years." She looked away and blinked back more tears.

"I could never think that. I'm the furthest thing from a perfect Christian. "

She let out a long sigh. "You have no idea what a relief it is to have all this out in the open. So many times I wanted to tell you the truth, but I was afraid you wouldn't forgive me for taking an innocent life or for the many lies I told to protect my cover."

"We're both new to this relationship. From here on out, I want you to know you can trust me." He snapped his fingers. "I hate to change the subject, but did my brother ever get a hold of you?"

"Houston? No. Why?"

"While you were gone there was another murder. I know this sounds crazy, but Houston thinks you may know something about it, or have information that could help with the investigation."

She sat up straight. "Why would I know anything? Who was the victim?"

"Houston said he found your business card at the scene. He tried calling you several times, but said you hadn't returned his calls either. He said her name was Sheri or Sharon or something. Why would the victim have your card?"

Dominique gasped. "Sharon? No, that can't be. You must be mistaken." Sharon's face flashed in her mind. Her poor husband … and the baby. Unthinkable. What else could she have done to prevent this senseless act?

Joe stood and pulled her into his arms. "I'm afraid not." He retrieved one of Houston's business cards from a pocket. "Give him a call. He'll be able to answer your questions."

She placed the card on the table. "Things keep getting worse. Someone has to stop him."

"Who?"

She chewed on her bottom lip. "I wish I could tell you, but I have a little more research to do before I can report my findings. I promise I'll fill you in as soon as I can."

"Dominique, no. Please promise me you'll speak to Houston before you do any more investigating. I don't want anything to happen to you."

His kiss on her cheek was so soft. She turned her head until his lips touched hers. Such a sweet, soft kiss. Oh, how she'd missed him while she was gone.

He pulled away and offered her a smile. "As much as I'd love to stay, I'd better take off. I have early rounds tomorrow."

Dominique walked him to the door. He turned and kissed her again. Heat traveled up her neck.

"I'd better leave now."

She ran her fingers along his chin. "See you soon?"

"I'll call you later." He kissed the top of her head. "Please call Houston, and stay safe."

She closed the door behind him and let out a long breath. *Thank you, Lord!*

She picked up Houston's card. *Sharon's dead.* She leaned her head against the wall. How could this have happened?

Her hands balled into fists. Vinnie Fernandez was responsible. She was an investigative reporter. She should be able to dig up something that would connect him with Sharon's murder. She would do everything within her power to make sure he paid for his crimes.

Chapter Thirty

In the quiet office, Travis scrolled through the entries in his accounting software from the last six months. What a nightmare. With a sigh, he clicked through each of the categories. How could that be? He ran his fingers through his hair. He hadn't made any progress on the loan from Vinnie. He switched screens to his personal finances, pulled out a calculator, and ran some numbers. Even without double-checking them, the truth was evident. They were going to lose their house. He dropped his head into his hands. He'd failed his family.

He paced the length of the room. How would he tell Cindy and the kids? They had less than a month to vacate the premises. Not much time to find a place and pack up a house as large as theirs, even if he didn't pour so much time into trying to solve his financial woes and Cindy didn't spend almost every waking moment at the hospital.

The thought of all the accumulating bills, even though Audrey's doctor talked of releasing her soon, made him sink back into the seat behind his desk. He checked his phone to see if he had possibly missed a call or text from Angelica about the medical bills. Did Vinnie have enough pull to get their insurance policy reinstated? But even if he did, the co-pays would still be significant.

The front door squeaked opened. He could have sworn he'd locked it. The hair on his arms stood on end. He opened the top drawer on his desk and searched for something to use to defend himself. He grabbed the letter opener. *I'm going to need more than this to defend myself against Vinnie's thugs.*

Footsteps came closer.

Travis took a deep breath and lowered the opener to his side.

The office door opened. Houston strolled in and tossed a small brown package onto Travis's desk. "This arrived at my house. It's addressed to you."

"Thanks. I've been waiting for it." He dropped the letter opener on the floor and ran his fingers over the package, anxious to open it. Would it meet his needs?

"Mind if I ask what's in there?"

Travis leaned over and turned up the volume on the CD player. The noise would block out their conversation if Vinnie was listening. "It's a pen of sorts."

Houston leaned on the desk. "What kind of pen?" His focused stare and tense shoulders told Travis he was in his detective mode. Maybe it was time to trust him. "It's a recording pen."

"Please tell me you're not planning to use that thing on Fernandez."

Of course Houston wouldn't understand. The pen was his best choice ... his only choice. "I know it's not much, but it's all I could think of." He ripped open the package and plucked the contents out. "It seems like he's always one step ahead of me. I thought if I could lead him into a damaging conversation, I could use the recording against him and get out of my contract."

Houston's eyebrows shot up. "How deep in are you?"

"Pretty deep."

"Can you be more specific?"

He swept his arm over the length of his desk. "He owns it all, Houston." Travis rubbed the back of his neck. "My business, my house, all of my personal accounts. It's only a matter of time before he calls in all of my loans. I have no way of paying him off." He slumped back in his chair.

Houston paced in front of the desk. "How'd you get in this mess? Does Cindy know?"

"Are you talking about our finances, or the other matter?"

"Both." He planted his hands on the desktop. "It's time to own up to your bad choices. You need to talk with your wife."

Travis drummed his fingers on the desk. "I'm going to. It's not like this is some easy conversation." He looked away. "I doubt she'll ever forgive me."

"She'll forgive you, Travis. Do you even know her?"

"Of course I know her; we've been married for almost eight years."

"That's not what I'm talking about. You have to trust your wife. She's your life partner, not some business associate you're trying to hide secrets from. If you want your marriage to survive, you have to be honest with her."

Travis's cell phone beeped. An incoming text. He read the message from Angelica. *Vinnie is on his way to your office ... get the cop out!* His heart rate doubled and he shot out of his seat. "You've got to leave. Now!"

"What's going on? Who's the text from?"

"Angelica. Vinnie's on his way. Somehow they know you're here. He always knows."

"I think you have a mole."

"A mole?"

"How well do you know Angelica?"

"Vinnie assigned her to me after I signed the contract. I've suspected her a few times, but she's helped me with so many other things that I thought I was just being paranoid."

"What kind of things?"

Travis twirled the pen between his fingers. "My health insurance mess for one. I don't know what I would have done if Audrey's medical bills weren't covered. She also helped me with a few side business deals that could help me get out of my contract sooner." Travis let out a long breath. "I don't think she'd put her own neck on the line like that if she was reporting back to Vinnie."

"That's how Vinnie works. He'll plant one of his more dedicated employees in your office to work with you. They build a relationship, get you to trust them. Before you know what hit you, he has complete access to all your information, whether you like it or not."

"Can we talk about this later?" Travis rearranged the files on his desk. "Right now I'm more concerned with you getting out of here alive." Travis lowered the volume on the CD player.

"Okay, I'll leave." Houston signaled for a notepad.

Travis handed him the paper and tapped his fingers on the desk while Houston scribbled a note. *Don't record him now. It's too dangerous. I'll think of a plan.*

Travis motioned to Houston to leave from the back end of the subdivision.

Houston held his gaze for a moment, then made a quick exit.

Travis looked over the recorder pen on the desk and quickly scanned over the directions. *This isn't too hard to figure out.* Thankfully, the manufacturer included a battery with the recorder. He shoved the contents and directions in a drawer and slammed it shut.

He didn't want the device to stand out, and after assembling it, was impressed with how compact and inconspicuous the pen looked. The device was nearly identical to a Montblanc pen.

He glanced around the room. Where could he hide it?

Should he heed Houston's advice and forget about the pen for now? No. He'd thought this through already. He didn't have time to wait for Houston to come up with a plan.

Travis pressed the record button, then hummed a little tune. He pressed the play button and smiled when he heard his attempt at music. Should do just fine.

He tucked the pen in his shirt pocket. Now he'd just have to steer the conversation in a direction that would offer incriminating evidence against Vinnie.

Chapter Thirty-One

You have a mole. Travis couldn't get Houston's words out of his mind. How else could Vinnie continually stay one step ahead of him? Angelica had been feeding information to Vinnie all along. He'd let his attraction to her blind him to the truth. How could he have been so stupid as to trust someone employed by a crime boss?

Vinnie was still about ten minutes away, not really enough time to search Angelica's office. She probably wouldn't be careless enough to leave any telling evidence around. But if Vinnie caught him looking, he would be more likely to say something incriminating. At the least, it would be easier to maneuver the conversation in that direction.

Muscles that still ached reminded him of Vinnie's last warning, but Travis pushed the thoughts aside. If he could get evidence against Vinnie, it would be worth another beating.

He hiked the stairs two at a time to Angelica's second-floor office. He grasped the cold brass knob, but it refused to turn. *She put a lock on the door?* His fingers swept across the top of the doorframe, seeking an extra key.

Nothing!

A curse escaped under his breath. *Enough is enough!* Whose office was it anyway? He took two steps back and kicked the door open, ignoring the pain that radiated through his body from his still-bruised ribs.

Inside, everything was in perfect place. The unobtrusive cherry desk sat in the center of the room, the top completely cleared of clutter. Not even a speck of dust would dare to rest on top of it.

Books sat neatly organized on the shelves along the side of the wall, and the file cabinets lined up one next to the other like obedient soldiers standing in formation.

If I were Angelica, where would I hide something?

He opened each drawer in the first filing cabinet and rifled through the files. All appeared in order, with the names of his clients and vendors all alphabetized and their statements up-to-date.

He slammed the last drawer closed. *There has to be something here.* The desk seemed too obvious, but the most convenient, and Angelica was nothing if not efficient. Travis slid into the chair behind her desk and pulled open the top right drawer.

The sensual aroma of Angelica's perfume filled the air as he sifted through the items in the drawer. A memory of the kiss they'd shared lingered in his mind. He shook aside the memory. How could he have kissed another woman? *I've got to tell Cindy. I can't keep putting off this conversation.*

Travis closed the drawer on the personal items and tugged on the drawer beneath it.

Locked.

His heart beat wildly, and his palms became clammy. This must be it. He fished the letter opener from the top drawer, jammed it in the lock and wriggled it around.

The wood split and the lock gave way.

The files bore the names of clients he didn't recognize. He pulled out one with nothing on the label, and several photographs spilled onto the floor. All were of women in various stages of pregnancy. He pulled out the rest and flipped through them. Three quarters through the pile his heart stopped.

Cindy.

She sat on a bench at the hospital with her hand resting on her expanded belly. Since she was wearing the outfit he'd brought her from home, it must have been taken within the past week.

Fear sliced through him. Why did Angelica have a picture of his wife in her desk?

"I'll take those." Vinnie grabbed the pictures and dropped them back into the folder.

Travis shot out of his chair. "What are you doing with a picture of my wife? And who are these other women?"

Vinnie turned to the tall, muscled associate who stood at the door. "I need to have a private conversation." After the man closed the door behind him, Vinnie leaned against the desk, crossed his arms, and looked down his nose at Travis. "You've put me in an uncomfortable position. How much did you see?"

"I'm not answering any of your questions until you tell me what a picture of my wife is doing in Angelica's drawer."

"You're not the one calling the shots here. Now tell me what you saw."

Travis clenched fists. "A few spreadsheets and those pictures." He looked Vinnie in the eyes. "You and I both know this business arrangement isn't working. I want out."

"You just may get your wish." Vinnie reached in his pocket.

Travis held his breath. Was this what his death would look like—taking a bullet from a criminal? Who was he kidding. He'd become a criminal too.

Vinnie pulled out a cigar and a lighter. "I have another business proposition for you. Listen carefully; I don't like to repeat myself." He took a long drag from the cigar. "I'll give you two million dollars." He walked toward the door. "You can pay me back what you owe me, get your business back in the black, and even keep your house."

Why was Vinnie caving so easily? There had to be a catch. "Two million for my silence?"

Vinnie turned to face him. "No. The two million is for the baby."

Travis fell back into the chair. "You want me to sell my child? You're insane." Were there no limits to this man's greed? "Who were all those other women in the pictures? Did you buy their babies too?"

"Babies are a hot commodity. It's a simple matter of supply and demand. You have twenty-four hours to give me your answer." Vinnie waved the file folder. "If you even think about telling anyone what you've seen, I'll make your death look like a suicide. Do I make myself clear?"

At a complete loss for words, Travis simply nodded.

"Twenty-four hours, Travis." Vinnie strutted from the room, file folder in hand.

Travis waited until he heard the front door close before he pulled the recorder pen from his shirt pocket. He pressed the rewind button for a moment, then the button to play the recording.

Vinnie's distinctive voice boomed from the tiny speaker.

A smile spread across Travis's face. The device had taped the entire conversation.

Chapter Thirty-Two

Dominique pulled her rented Taurus into the half-full parking lot of Castalgia's restaurant. She circled around the restaurant. A white cargo van was parked in the alley. *That's the same van that followed Sharon, I just know it.* She swallowed past the lump in her throat. Concentrating on the job at hand would be the best way to assure Sharon and her baby hadn't died in vain.

Choosing a space at the back of the lot, she positioned herself so she could see who entered and exited the restaurant. After ten minutes, with only two people entering and one exiting, she drummed her fingers on the steering wheel. This wasn't working. It wouldn't provide her with all of the information she needed to move her investigation forward. She pulled into a parking space but didn't get out of the car. It was as though some part of her brain recognized the danger she was about to put herself into and refused to make her body move. But getting inside Vinnie's world was the best way to move her investigation forward.

She blew out a long breath, closed her eyes, and whispered a prayer. Strength seemed to return to her body, so she straightened her cameo necklace and freshened up her make-up. Then before she could think about the danger again, she walked into the restaurant.

An elderly hostess looked her over but said nothing.

Dominique cleared her throat. "I'd like to apply for a job."

"We're not hiring."

"May I put in an application in case an opening does occur?"

"That isn't necessary. Check back in six months."

Not quite ready to be dismissed, Dominique stepped up the risk factor. "Is Vinnie here?"

The hostess raised an eyebrow. "I didn't realize you knew Mr. Fernandez. I'm afraid he's not in. Try back later."

"I'll do that. Thank you for your time. Here's my card." Dominique managed to hold her composure together as she left the restaurant. Once back at her car, she was surprised to see Houston leaning against it.

"You're a hard person to track down." He stood to full height. "I saw your car in the lot when I drove past."

"Joe told me you were trying to reach me. I'm sorry I haven't called."

Houston pulled his keys from his front pocket. "We need to talk, but not here. It's not safe. Let's go to the hospital—we can talk over a cup of coffee."

"I'm not exactly welcome there, but they can't keep me from visiting a patient can they? Give me half an hour."

Houston nodded, then got in his truck and pulled out of the parking lot.

I have a little more business to attend to here. A feature story would require solid evidence, regardless of who she pitched the idea to. She tossed her purse on the front seat and pulled a tracking device out of the glove box—one of the leftover items she needed to get back to Stew. But not until it served its purpose. She pushed the power button and flipped the little black device over to ensure the battery was at full capacity.

A black town car, followed by an SUV, pulled into the parking lot.

Dominique's heart doubled its pace. She ducked low in the vehicle.

Two car doors slammed shut.

Dominique peered out just in time to see Vinnie and his hired help walking into the restaurant.

It would have been easier to plant the device without Vinnie there—and his extra security team. Now the staff would be more vigilant She stared at the small device in the palm of her hand. Should she wait?

Thoughts of Sharon and her baby stiffened her resolve. The sooner she found information to help put Vinnie in jail, the sooner the murders and baby snatchings would stop. *Give me courage, Lord.*

It's now or never. She dashed out of the car and scurried to the alley at the back of the restaurant. The white cargo van was parked almost in the same spot where she saw it before. *This is it. I'll find out exactly where you're going, and I'll have a record of it.*

She slipped between the building and the van and knelt by the back bumper. Her hands shook as she fastened the transmitter to the vehicle. She ducked her head low to make sure the transmitter couldn't be seen, then brushed the dirt and gravel off her pants as she stood and headed back to her car.

When she came around the corner, she ran straight into two rough-looking young men. One was tall and slender, and the other bore a striking resemblance to Vinnie Fernandez. The hair on her arms stood up. Dominique felt like a mouse trapped between two cats.

"What are you doing back here?" the taller one called out.

"I made a wrong turn." Dominique attempted to step around the other boy. "I think I'm at the wrong address."

They both blocked her path. "We don't believe you. You're coming with us." The young man even sounded like Vinnie.

She winced when they grabbed her arms. "Let go of me! This is all a misunderstanding. You don't even know who I am."

"We're about to find out," the taller one spouted.

They dragged her back down the alley alongside a building and pushed her through a door she hadn't even realized was there. As they herded her down the hallway, she scrambled to think up an excuse.

They stopped in front of a solid wood door. Vinnie's look-alike tightened his grip on her arm and knocked twice.

"Come in."

The boy opened the door and shoved Dominique into the room. "Look what we found snooping around out back."

The man before her looked like an iron statue—no emotions on his face and every hair precisely in place. Vinnie leaned forward. "Who are you?"

Dominique pulled against her captor's grip, but he squeezed tighter. "My name's Dominique. This is all a big mistake. I would appreciate it if your associate would remove his hands from me."

"Let her go." He waved at them. "You can leave us alone."

After they left, Dominique adjusted her blouse and took a deep breath, hoping to slow her pounding heart. Her eyes met Vinnie's lustful glance, and a chill ran up her spine. She'd seen similar expressions during her stint as a news reporter, but she'd always had a crew of people with her. *Lord, please protect me ... help me to get out of here alive.*

"What were you doing nosing around behind my restaurant?"

She licked her lips. "As I told your men, this is all a big misunderstanding, Mr. Fernandez."

"How do you know my name? We haven't been introduced."

Dominique wiped her sweaty palms on her pants. Things were going from bad to worse. She needed to think fast. "I know we haven't been formally introduced, but I know who you are. I think most people in this town do."

Vinnie's eyes narrowed.

Just play it cool. Dominique glanced around the room for another exit or way out.

Vinnie slammed a hand on the desk. "Answer my question. What were you doing out in the alley?"

Dominique jumped. "I'm a reporter, Mr. Fernandez, I was conducting research for a story I'm working on."

"I'm sure you are." He mocked. "Exactly what kind of story are you working on?"

"On the restaurant business and how much food is wasted. Food that could be used to feed the underprivileged." *Why did she give that explanation? He'd see right through it.* She swallowed the lump in her throat. The lie tugged at her conscience, even if it was told to a despicable man.

Someone knocked.

"Come in," Vinnie ordered.

The hostess Dominique had spoken with earlier stepped into the room. "Here's this afternoon's receipts." She glanced at Dominique. "I'm sorry, I didn't realize you had company."

Dominique's heart dropped into her stomach.

The hostess raised her eyebrows. "I see you finally caught up with Mr. Fernandez."

"What are you talking about?" Vinnie leaned forward.

The hostess pointed at Dominique. "That young woman—was here earlier looking for a job. When I told her we weren't hiring, she asked to speak with you. I was under the impression she knew you."

"Thank you. You can leave now." After the hostess left the room, Vinnie's gaze bored into Dominique. "Well now. If there's one thing I can't stand, it's a liar. Now tell me the truth. What were you doing snooping around behind my restaurant?"

She remained silent. She should have left with Houston when she had the chance.

He leaned forward. "Are you with the police?"

"No. I told you, I'm a reporter." She shifted back and forth. "I'm working on a story."

"Problem is, I don't believe you." He walked around the desk, stopped in front of her, and leaned close. "And I don't like loose ends." He stalked to the door and called the two young men into the room. "Your next job is scheduled for this evening," Vinnie said to the men. "Take her with you and leave her there."

Hands grabbed her from behind. Rope cut into her arms as it drew her hands behind her back. She wriggled her wrists to loosen the rope. "You're going to kill me?" How had things gotten out of control so quickly? This couldn't be it. Joe's face flashed in her mind. She never got to tell him she loved him. "Please don't do this. I promise not to do the story."

Vinnie didn't respond.

The taller youth shoved her into the hallway, then toward the back door.

Should she resist and run out into the restaurant? No, they'd overpower her before she made it a few feet. "You don't have to do this! I swear I won't tell anyone."

The first man stepped out into the back alley, then called back, "All clear. Bring her out."

Pain radiated up her arms when the second man grabbed her and shoved her out into the alley. *Lord, please send someone to help me. Don't let me die at their hands.*

The man pushed her toward the van as his partner opened the back doors. "Get in."

She looked around frantically. If she got in the van, she'd be dead. With all of the strength she could muster, Dominique slammed a high heel down on the man's toes, then twisted and kicked her leg back as hard as she could.

He lost his grip on her arm, but only for a moment. Before she could take two steps away, he caught her wrist and pulled her close. Their noses only inches away from each other, he said, "So you want to play rough? I can do that." He pushed her away from him.

She stumbled backwards, but before she hit the ground, his fist bored into the side of her face. Pain ricocheted throughout her head.

"I said get in!" The man pulled her up and practically threw her into the back of the van.

"We're going to have trouble with this one."

The taller one threw the rest of the rope in the back. "No we won't. Get me the kit. I'll give her something to make her a little more agreeable."

The smaller man rummaged underneath a seat, retrieved a small box, and threw it to his partner.

Dominique's heart raced. They were going to kill her. No one knew where she was. A small glimmer of hope lit as she remembered that Houston was expecting her. When she didn't show up, he'd come look for her. Just as quickly, the light faded. He might know where to start looking, but he wouldn't know where they took her. Even if he did, he would most likely just find her dead body. *Lord, please help me!*

The man who threw her into the van took a syringe from the box. She scrambled away from him, but only ran into the back of a seat. She kicked at the man's arm, but he dodged her. His arm darted toward her neck.

A sharp pain pierced her below her left ear. She tried to reach the needle, but her hands were still tied. He said something, but his voice only echoed in her ears. Her vision blurred. She blinked slowly and took in several deep breaths. What had they injected her with?

Her whole body seemed to relax at once. In spite of her effort to keep her eyes open, everything faded into complete darkness.

Chapter Thirty-Three

Houston took the stairs up to the fifth floor of the hospital. Joe and Cindy sat on the couch in the waiting room, deep in conversation. Cindy wore a smile—the first Houston had seen in over two weeks.

"I take it Audrey's doing better."

Cindy nodded. "The doctors say she may be released as early as next week."

"That is good news." Houston glanced around the room. "Where's Dominique?"

Joe gave him a confused look. "I thought you said you were going to meet with her. Didn't that work out?"

Houston took a seat on the couch. "I caught up with her at Castalgia's, but since that's not exactly the safest place to have a conversation, we agreed to meet here. I had to stop at the station, so I thought she'd be waiting for me."

Joe grabbed his cell phone. "We haven't seen her. I'll give her a call." He shook his head and mouthed that he'd gotten her voicemail. "Call me as soon as you get this, Dominique." He placed the phone on the table. "I don't like this, Houston. Last time I saw Dominique, she had that expression on her face."

"What expression?"

"A determined look. Like no matter what happened, she was going to get the story. I think she's planning to go after Vinnie herself."

Houston cursed under his breath. He should have insisted she come with him. What had he been thinking? "I'll see if there's a black and white nearby. Vinnie's accustomed to police dropping in, so we'll send a few his way."

After twenty minutes and no word from headquarters he dialed the sergeant on duty again. "Any updates on that drive by at Castalgia's?"

The officer replied, "We were just getting ready to call you. It's not good, Houston. Her car's there, but we don't have eyes on her. It's like she's disappeared."

His heart stopped. If Dominique was alive, she wouldn't be for long. How would he tell his brother? He ended the phone call and turned to Joe. "Her car's there, but she's not on the premises. I'm heading back over there. I'll call you when I have more information."

Joe met Houston's glare. "I'm going, too. Question is, do you want to go together?"

Houston nodded. "Let's go."

As Houston reached the door, Travis rounded the corner into the room and nearly plowed him over. Travis stepped to the side. "I'm glad I ran into you, Houston. I thought about calling you, but I wanted to deliver the news in person."

"What news?" Cindy rose from the couch.

Travis eyed Houston and shook his head the tiniest bit. He must not have talked to Cindy yet.

"Can you give us a few minutes alone? I really need to speak to Houston privately. I promise I'll fill you in as soon as I can."

She crossed her arms over her chest, and her smile disappeared. "I think whatever you say to Houston, you can say to me."

Travis's face turned beet red. He rubbed the back of his neck. "I'm asking you to please trust me on this."

She gathered her purse and stalked to the door. "I guess I'll see you boys in a little bit."

Joe pulled out his keys. "I'll leave you two alone. I'm heading over to Castalgia's to see if I can find Dominique."

"Give me two minutes, Joe. I'm coming with you," Houston said. He waited until Joe disappeared around the corner before speaking. "Okay, what do you have for me? I hope it's good, cause I know my sister, and she was more than a little mad at you."

Travis pulled out the recorder pen and placed it on the table. "It's turned up as high as it can go. You can hear it much better when it's uploaded on a computer, but you'll get the meat of the conversation."

Houston bent his head toward the device. As the conversation unfolded, the full impact of what the recording contained sank in. His emotions volleyed between fear for his family and the excitement of finally having solid evidence to put Vinnie Fernandez away for a long time. "You have to get Cindy out of town. He'll kill her and take your baby."

"Those were my thoughts exactly. I've made arrangements for someone from church to stay with Audrey while we're out of town. Would Becky mind watching Megan and the boys until you have Vinnie behind bars?"

Houston nodded. "That's not a problem. We love having them." He pocketed the pen and the cable trailing from it. "I'll get this to the station as soon as possible. Is this the only copy you have?"

"No. There's a copy on my desktop at the office and on my laptop. I also e-mailed you a copy."

"Do you have a plan? I need to be able to get in touch with you."

Travis rubbed the back of his neck. "I'll take her to a hotel or something."

Houston held up his hand. "A hotel won't work; he'll find you. I have a friend who owns a private cabin down in Hocking Hills. We've used it in the past to house witnesses. It's pretty secluded. You should be safe there." Houston gave him the details. "I'll meet you out in the garage. I have an emergency travel pack I can give you with a few essentials."

Houston tossed Travis some keys. "Take Becky's car. It's parked on the second floor in the garage. Don't go back to your house or do anything else that would tip someone off that you're leaving town. Buy whatever you need when you get there." He pulled out his wallet, took out the bills, and handed them to Travis. "This is all I have on me. Don't use any of your credit cards, or he'll know where to start looking. Leave your cell phone here at the hospital. I'm sure Vinnie has a tracking device on it."

"Thanks, Houston. I'll get in touch with you in a couple days." As he headed towards the door, his cell phone rang. He checked the caller ID and paled. "It's Vinnie. What should I do?" He held the phone as if it were a hot potato.

"Answer it."

"This is Travis." His eyes narrowed and a scowl formed on his lips. "I can't talk right now. I'll call you back in half an hour." He jabbed at the button to end the phone call.

"What did he want?"

"He wanted to know if we have a deal. I've got to get Cindy out of here. How soon can you have him behind bars?" Panic filled his tone.

"Give me forty-eight hours. Then call my cell and see if it's safe to come home."

"I don't know if it'll ever be safe. Not after I've betrayed Vinnie. He's made it more than clear what happens to people who betray him." His hands trembled as he slid his phone in his pocket. "But I won't let him have my child. That's unthinkable!"

The door to the waiting room squeaked, and Cindy walked in. "What's unthinkable?"

Chapter Thirty-Four

Houston drove up next to Dominique's Taurus in the far corner of Castalgia's parking lot. Where was the patrol car he had requested earlier? Unless they sent an unmarked car, the officers must have already headed back to the station.

Joe frowned as he hit redial on his cell phone. "She's still not picking up."

Houston got out and peered in the windows of Dominique's car. Everything appeared normal. He motioned to Joe to follow him. "Let's go inside and check things out."

The smell of garlic and bread baking greeted them. No one stood at the hostess station, so Houston walked farther into the restaurant. The only customers were a family of four enjoying a late lunch.

They approached the table and Houston flashed a picture of Dominique. "I'm sorry to disturb your meal, but have you seen this woman?" Anyone eating in Castalgia's might be on Fernandez's payroll, and their answers suspect, but at the least, his questioning would annoy Vinnie.

The man took the picture and adjusted his dark-rimmed glasses. "No, I don't think we have. She missing or something?"

"We were supposed to meet her here. She never showed up, but her car's in the parking lot. So we're a little concerned."

The man returned the picture. "She may be in the back, but I haven't seen her. Good luck."

"Thanks anyway," Joe said, then headed for a table where two waitresses rolled silverware into perfectly pressed white napkins.

Only a few feet from the table, an elderly woman slid between Joe and Houston and the table. "I apologize. I left my station for just a minute. Let me get you a table. I'll grab a couple of menus."

"That won't be necessary," Houston answered. "We were hoping someone could help us." He held up Dominique's picture. "We're looking for this woman. Have you seen her?" He handed the picture to the hostess, and her eyes flashed. Adrenaline coursed through his body. *She recognizes her!*

She looked at the floor. "I'm sorry. I can't help you."

"You didn't answer my question. Have you seen her?"

The hostess walked toward the front of the restaurant. "I shouldn't leave my station unattended."

Houston followed her. "We think she may be in some kind of trouble. Please help us."

"If you know something—anything—please tell us," Joe added. "We're desperate."

The woman peered over her shoulder, walked to the front door, and held it open. "I'm going to have to ask you to leave."

Houston nodded to Joe. A spark of anger flashed in his eyes before he stalked out of the restaurant.

The hostess caught up with them in the parking lot. "Your friend was in here a few hours ago. She was speaking with Mr. Fernandez in his office." She looked at the ground. "I haven't seen her since. Now please leave, before you get me in trouble."

"Let's go." Joe rushed back into the restaurant. Houston followed only a few steps behind.

"You're not allowed back in there," the hostess called after him.

"We don't have much time before she calls for help," Houston said, "and I don't think it'll be the police."

Joe slammed the door open and they both rushed past the empty tables to the hallway in the back.

Joe opened the first door, stuck his head in, and flicked on the light. "Some type of storage closet. Canned goods and paper products, but no place to hide a person."

The hostess appeared at the end of the hallway. "Please, I'm asking you to leave. I don't want to have to call someone."

"Then don't." Houston tried the next door. "We're not leaving until we're certain she's not here." The next didn't open. "Is this Vinnie's office?"

"Absolutely nobody goes in there without his permission." The older woman's face paled.

"Do you have a key?" He stared her down as he held out his hand. "Look, you know as well as I do time is running out for her."

"Please help us," Joe begged

"She's not in there."

"How do you know?" Houston asked.

"I saw them put her in the back of the van and leave with her. I don't know where they went."

Houston's heart slammed in his chest. "What does the van look like?"

"A big white van."

Houston mumbled under his breath, "She could be dead by now."

"I know what happens to people who have loose lips. Now please leave." Her lips pressed into a tight line and she looked Houston in the eyes.

After a long moment, Houston gave a short nod and motioned Joe toward the back door. They could start the search with the information they had and get someone at the station to run a trace on vehicles registered to Vinnie for the rest. Before he followed Joe, he handed his business card to the hostess. "If you see her or hear any more information about her, please call me."

After calling the station to give them the information about the vehicle carrying Dominique, Houston walked up and down the alley. He scanned every inch of the pavement in case Dominique left some type of trail for them to follow.

He bent down to pick up a tattered piece of paper laying against the building, glanced at it, then wadded it up and threw it against the wall. Just a worn receipt from several weeks ago. "Let's get to the station. There's nothing here."

Before leaving, Houston peered through the windows of Dominique's Taurus again.

"You would think they'd move her car," Joe said. "Maybe that's a good sign."

The desperation in his brother's voice haunted Houston. He had to make sure he covered all the bases. He didn't have time to wait for a search warrant.

He rushed to his car and retrieved a crowbar from the trunk. He hefted it high and swung into the passenger's side window.

The glass shattered and pieces dropped on the pavement and passenger seat.

Joe held his arms up in front of his face. "Are you allowed to do that?"

Houston shook glass fragments from his hand. "I don't have time to ask permission." He reached inside and unlocked the door, wiped aside the fragments of the safety glass, then slid in. He reached underneath the driver's seat and touched something soft and smooth.

He pulled on the object and saw that it was Dominique's purse.

Joe leaned against the car. "Is that Dominique's purse?"

Houston started digging through the contents. It contained all of the usual items—wallet, checkbook, cell phone, a few pens, and a tin of mints. Stuffed beside the wallet was a cardboard box.

He flipped it over and read the label.

MYPLAR TRACKING DEVICE – INSTRUCTIONS FOR UPLOADING LIVE TRACKING INFORMATION

A tracking device? "We need to get to the station, Joe." He quickly repacked Dominique's belongings and got in his car.

Joe climbed into the passenger's seat. "What did you find?"

"The packaging for a tracking device. We can only hope Dominique attached it to the vehicle she's traveling in."

If they were going to find her alive, they didn't have a second to waste.

Chapter Thirty-Five

Travis pressed the gas and maneuvered Becky's car around the corner. They hadn't passed another car in over a half an hour. Maybe they'd really made it without being noticed.

"I think I'm going to be sick." Cindy pushed the button to unroll the window. "I don't mean to sound like one of the kids, but are we almost there yet?"

He let out a nervous laugh. "It's about another hour or so." Gravel crunched under the tires as he steered the car to the side of the road. "I picked up some saltines and ginger ale when we stopped at the grocery. Would that help?"

"Sounds great." She rubbed a hand on her expanded belly.

He checked the rear view mirror to make sure no one was approaching before he popped the trunk and hurried to the back of the car. He unzipped the gym bag Houston had passed to him at the hospital. The sight of the .35 caliber pistol and emergency cell phone brought both a sense of security and a jolt of fear. Hopefully, he wouldn't need either. He quickly gathered the saltines and some ginger ale, plus a diet coke for himself, and slid back into the driver's seat.

Cindy reached in her purse and retrieved a tissue. "I can't believe you made me leave my phone at the hospital. What if one of the kids needs us? I assume there's a phone where we're headed?"

Travis placed the sodas in the drink holder and set the crackers between them. Anything to keep from looking her in the eyes.

"Travis? Did you hear me? There *is* a phone where we're going, isn't there? If something happens with Audrey, the hospital has to have a way to contact us."

He stared out the windshield and put the car in gear. "Houston knows how to contact us if there's an emergency. We'll probably only be there for a few days, a week at the most."

"A week?" Her voice elevated. "I never would have agreed to come if you'd told me that."

"We can't come back until it's safe."

Her eyebrows formed a peak. "What does that mean, Travis? Safe from what?"

"Not what. Who." Better to wait until they were safe at the cabin to tell her everything.

"What is going on?" She grabbed Travis's arm.

"Please be patient with me for a little longer. Once we're at the cabin, I promise I'll tell you everything." He prayed she would forgive him.

Silence filled the car again as Cindy closed her window.

* * *

Houston dumped the contents of his mug into the break room sink. The police station coffee was thicker than usual—any thicker and he'd have to chew it. He checked his watch again.

Thirty minutes! What was taking Kenny so long to see him? He told him it was urgent.

He clenched his fits. Dominique was out there somewhere, and every minute counted.

All he needed to do was present the taped evidence to Kenny and accompany him to the courthouse to obtain a bench warrant for Vinnie's arrest ... if Kenny would see him.

He dialed Joe. "Any update from the computer expert?"

"Not yet, but Dan says we're getting close."

"Keep me posted." He plopped down on the worn leather chair and pulled the recorder pen from his pocket. *This time you're going down, Vinnie.*

The dispatcher popped her head in the room. "He'll see you now, Houston."

Despite laws prohibiting smoking in public buildings, the aroma of cigarette smoke permeated Kenny's office. His boss tossed a file on his desk and took a seat. "What can I do for you, Houston? Isn't this your day off?"

"Yes, sir, but something came up. I knew you'd want to know about it right away."

"You working a case on the side?"

"Same one I'm always working."

Kenny frowned. "We agreed you were to leave Fernandez alone. The city can't afford a harassment lawsuit."

"There's not going to be a lawsuit. Not this time." Houston held the prized evidence up. "I've got him. There's no way the man will escape this."

"What is that?" Kenny reached for it. His voice held a slight edge to it.

"It's a recorder pen."

"Probably not admissible in court. You have anything else?"

What was his problem? He'd dismissed the evidence before he even listened to it. Suspicions he hadn't wanted to contemplate returned. The nagging question sounded warning bells. How much should he reveal? If Kenny was on Vinnie's payroll, disclosing Travis's name could put him in even more danger.

Beyond the windows of Kenny's office, Travis's accountant Angelica strutted through the main doors and into the station.

"What's she doing here?" Houston pointed.

Kenny stood and put his suit coat on. "I didn't realize you two knew each other."

"Yeah, she works for Vinnie."

Before Kenny could explain further, Angelica stepped into the office and closed the door behind her like she owned the place. She looked Houston in the eye. "Do you have the file?"

"What file?" Not that he was about to hand any information over to her. "We haven't been formally introduced, but I know she's Travis's accountant. And she works for Vinnie Fernandez."

Kenny scratched the top of his head. "Angelica is a special agent with the FBI."

Houston's eyebrows shot up.

Angelica crossed her arms. "I've been working on this case for a little over two years. I've finally collected enough evidence to put our friend away for quite a while. Problem is, when I went to retrieve my information, the door had been forced open and one of the files was missing. You wouldn't happen to know where it is, would you?"

He and Angelica were on the same side of the law? He rubbed the stubble on his chin and sank into the chair across from Kenny. He held fast to the recording device. Could he trust her enough to share the evidence?

Kenny pounded his fist on the desk. "Do you have the file or not, Houston? Before Angelica arrived, you were all fired up about some new evidence you had against Vinnie. Let's hear it!"

"Vinnie has the file you're looking for." He explained what Travis shared with him.

She let out a frustrated sigh and threw her arms up in the air. "That's just great!"

Houston placed the recording device on the desk. "But I'm willing to bet what's on this is more valuable than anything that file contained."

Angelica stared at the pen. "Is that one of those recorder pens?"

"It is."

"Well, I hope it contains something good, because if Vinnie has that file, my cover is blown."

Houston connected the device to the desktop computer on the chief's desk and turned up the volume so they could hear the conversation clearly.

"That puts a new spin on this case." Angelica tapped a finger against her lips. "I have to call my boss and apprise him of this latest development." She pulled her cell phone from her purse and stalked from the room.

The hair on Houston's arms raised. His years of experience told him something wasn't right. He cocked his head towards the door. "Have you checked her credentials?"

Kenny stepped around his desk. "What are you getting at, Houston?"

"I'm simply asking how much you know about her."

Joe burst into the room, followed by a thin young man with glasses Houston recognized as one of the computer techs.

The young man placed the GPS device from Dominique's purse on the desk. "We got a signal. Upload the information on this device to your phone, and you'll get the exact location of the device Dominique planted."

"Fantastic! Let's fire it up." Houston connected the GPS to his phone. "Let's see if there's any active movement."

While it loaded, he looked out into the station. Angelica stood isolated in the corner, still on her cell phone. What was she hiding?

His cell phone beeped.

"Looks like the vehicle is on the move. Let's see where it's headed." The map popped up on his screen. His heart lurched. "They're headed toward my house. Becky and the kids are in danger!"

Chapter Thirty-Six

Becky bounded down the stairs, picking up trucks, dolls, and several mismatched socks. She breathed out a long sigh. She'd miss it when the kids left. Would she be able to handle going back to a home without all the hustle and bustle?

At a snore from the living room, she glanced through the railing to Samuel's lanky form stretched out on the couch. And how much longer would he live with them? If only Houston would at least entertain the idea of having Samuel live with them permanently.

Her cell phone chimed from the bedroom. She glanced up the flight of stairs. Probably not worth the dash up the stairs to try to answer it in time. Whoever it was would call back or leave a message. She picked up another stray sock and continued down the stairs.

Only seconds after the cell phone quit ringing, the house phone rang. Odd.

She put down the items she'd gathered and picked up the receiver on the coffee table. "Hello?"

"Becky, get out of the house!"

"Houston? What? Why?"

"Please trust me! We don't have time to talk. Just get everyone out of the house!"

She tightened her grip on the phone. "Where are you? Should I go to the station?"

"No! Don't take Cindy's Land Rover. Please hurry."

The line went dead.

Fear rippled through her body. Houston had always been very cautious, but never panicked. "Samuel, wake up," she called as she gave him a nudge. "We've got to get out of here." She gave him a firm shake. "Samuel, did you hear me? Houston said we need to get out of the house."

Samuel struggled to get up. He gripped his cane, but couldn't pull himself up. It was of little use to him. "Go get the kids; I'll take care of myself."

She took the stairs two at a time and ran to the guest room, where the twins were engrossed in building a Duplo city and Megan lay on the plush rug, immersed in a picture book. She took a slow, deep breath so her voice wouldn't shake. "Come on, kiddos, we're going out for a little bit."

"Can I finish my book, Aunt Becky?"

"Sorry, honey we don't have time. Let's go."

The twins cried out as she scooped up one in each arm. With Megan close behind, they trotted down the stairs. Becky rushed over to Samuel. "Grab my arm, Samuel. I'll pull you up."

Samuel held up a hand. "I don't know what's going on, but if Houston told us to leave immediately, he means it. I'll just slow you down.

"I'm not leaving without you, Dad."

Tires crunched on the gravel driveway.

The sound echoed through the living room and propelled Becky to the kitchen. Her heart slammed in her chest. Houston couldn't have arrived so quickly.

At least Houston always insisted on keeping the house locked, so whoever it was couldn't just waltz in.

"Houston's on his way. Hold tight, Samuel!" Tears streamed down her face. She wiped them away so she could see clearly.

"Megan, Aunt Becky needs you to open the back door for me, then close it and run as fast as you can to the barn."

Becky sidled through the door as fast as she could. Both of the boys clutched her like leeches. Megan followed behind her and closed the door. Adrenaline and physical exertion pumped Becky's heart, but fear drove her beyond her limits. Just a little further. Just over the hill, where they wouldn't be seen from the house. But her legs seemed to move in slow motion.

Becky looked over her shoulder. Megan trailed several yards behind. Not wanting to draw attention, she remained quiet, even though everything in her wanted to scream *Hurry up! Run, Megan, run!*

Becky topped the top of the hill and slowed, but held onto the twins until they entered the barn.

Seconds later Megan joined her. "Why are we running, Aunt Becky?"

"We're going to play a little game of hide-and-seek." Better safe than sorry … just in case whoever had arrived came looking for them.

"Where should we hide?"

Becky thought for a moment. They would be easily discovered in one of the four stalls. "The loft. It'll be the best place."

"No! No loft!" Megan cried. "The loft hurt Audrey."

"It'll be okay. You're going to have to trust me." She quieted Megan's crying. She craned her neck to look up. She'd forgotten how high up it was. "You first, Megan. I'm right here. You'll be okay. Once you're up there, scoot all the way to the back."

Megan started crying again and turned away from the ladder. "I can't. I'll fall. I know I will. And Mommy and Daddy will be sad again."

Becky sent up a quick prayer for patience. "I'll climb right behind you. Okay?"

Megan nodded.

Becky sat the boys down. "It's very important to listen to Aunt Becky. I need both of you to sit still. See who can stay frozen the longest." They would tire of the game quickly, but it might just give her enough time to help Megan up the ladder.

Becky kept a hand on Megan's back as she took the first four steps up and positioned herself behind her. "That's it, honey. Keep moving. I'm right behind you." Becky stepped on the ladder and followed Megan up two more steps.

The knuckles on Megan's hands were white. She took several more steps, then stopped. "I can't do it. Please don't make me."

"Come on honey, just a little further."

One slow step at a time, Becky followed Megan up the ladder. At the top, Megan scuttled away from the edge. Becky gave her a quick hug. "I knew you could do it. Stay put; I'll be right back."

After two more trips that seemed to take hours instead of minutes, Becky sat on a hay bale. She held Megan's hand while Max climbed into her lap. "We have to be very quiet until Uncle Houston tells us we can come down."

Her moment of calm was shattered by the blast of a gun firing.

Chapter Thirty-Seven

Racing down the familiar country road in his car, Houston glanced at Joe. His brother's head was down, and his lips moved.

He's praying? Somehow that both irritated and comforted Houston. Maybe it would work for Joe, although it had never worked for him. Growing up, his mom had repeatedly told him to give his troubles over to the Lord, but every time he tried, he ended up disappointed. He'd leave praying and spiritual things to Joe, and Becky … and his father.

"We're almost there," he interrupted Joe's prayer time. "You've seen a lot as a doctor, but I have to warn you about what we might face. Dominique's been missing for several hours, and Vinnie is a despicable man with no regard for human life. It could be brutal." He glanced at his brother.

"I know, Houston." Joe's response was barely a whisper. "That's why I've been praying. I'm praying for Becky, the kids, and Dad too."

The thought of harm coming to Becky sent a wave of fear coursing through Houston. For the first time in a long time, he wished he possessed a small measure of Joe's faith. Although Dominique's situation was precarious, somehow Joe remained peaceful. Houston envied him.

The police radio squawked. "We're less than a mile out, Houston," his boss said. "We'll come in with sirens blaring, to try and scare them off as quickly as possible."

What was Kenny thinking? He knew it would also warn the attackers, who might then take drastic measures to keep from being apprehended. He picked up his radio and responded. "I'd rather the sirens be off so we have the element of surprise on our side."

The thought of Vinnie's men harming Becky or the kids—or using them as hostages—sent a shudder through him.

"Houston." Kenny's voice practically growled through the radio. "You need to step back. You're too close to this."

Houston gripped the steering wheel tight as he turned the truck onto his road. The same warning bells that had just gone off about Angelica now sounded the alarm against Kenny. Could his boss really be on Vinnie's payroll?

The sight of the white utility van parked in his driveway stiffened his resolve. He would protect his family against Vinnie's men, no matter what, even if that included his own boss.

An ambulance and an unmarked police car were parked along the side of the road, and two men were positioned at the corners of the house. Houston pulled his car across the driveway behind the van, at an angle to block any possible escape.

Joe reached for the door handle, but Houston grabbed his arm. "Wait here until we're sure it's safe. If shots are fired, keep low."

Joe hesitated, then let go of the handle and nodded.

Houston walked to the police cruiser, and the officer unrolled the window. Everything in him screamed that they should storm the house and rescue his wife and family immediately, but his professionalism ruled over his protective instincts. "Any word on what's going on in the house?"

The officer shook his head. "No contact's been made."

Houston ran his hand over his service revolver. At the sound of sirens in the distance, he gripped the revolver with a tight grasp but left it in its holster.

The sirens became louder. Several black and whites turned onto the road. Houston eyed the house, searching for any signs of the enemy's actions, but saw nothing.

Kenny pulled his car to a screeching stop in the road at the end of the driveway. He hopped out, nodded to Houston, and started barking orders. "Let's clear the van first, then we'll head into the house."

"Let's go," the officer in the car radioed.

Officers popped out of their vehicles and filed down the driveway. Houston joined them at the end of the line.

Kenny took the lead in front of them, approached the back end of the van, and motioned for two others to approach the front doors.

When the all-clear sign came from the officers at the corners of the house, Kenny yanked open the back doors.

Houston's heart sank at the sight that greeted them. *Joe will be devastated.*

Dominique's lifeless body lay sprawled on the floor of the van, face down.

At a nod from his boss, Houston crawled inside. He gently turned Dominique onto her back. He checked for a pulse and let out a sigh of relief at the slight beat. "She's still alive."

Houston rushed back to his car, pounded on the window, and motioned for Joe to follow him.

Joe grabbed his bag, flew out of the car, and raced around Houston to the van. He crawled in the back, grabbed his stethoscope and listened to Dominique's heartbeat. Next, he opened each eye and flashed a penlight over them. "I think she's been drugged. I'll know more once I can get a blood workup. Right now, I'm thankful her vitals are strong."

Houston waved for the officer waiting outside the van to come in. "Bring a gurney and help him transfer her to the ambulance." He eyed Kenny as he led the remaining men toward the house. Could he trust him to secure the house properly?

He rushed toward the house as Kenny entered the front door. His men followed and entered one by one, weapons in front of them.

Houston pulled out his revolver and leaped up the porch stairs. He eyed the splintered wood near the doorknob, evidence that Vinnie's men had shot their way into the house.

The last man to enter the house before Houston glanced back. He pointed to the door and whispered, "You shouldn't be in here. You're too close to this."

Houston ignored the warning. He didn't care about protocol; Becky needed him. As men charged up the stairs and others entered the kitchen, Houston positioned himself against the armoire next to the curtains and scanned the room. All appeared in order, yet the hair raised on his arms.

Shuffling came from the spare bedroom off the dining room. He aimed his Glock and approached the door.

One of Vinnie's men jumped out from behind the bedroom door. He targeted Houston's chest.

Houston shifted his aim, but before he could shoot, Samuel stepped out from behind the curtains on the other side of the armoire. Two faltering steps put him between Houston and the gunman as a gunshot echoed throughout the room.

Samuel dropped to the ground in front of Houston.

Dear, God! What had just happened? Houston dropped to one knee and returned fire.

Vinnie's men darted from the bedroom and ducked low as they ran behind the dining room table and toward the back of the house.

Houston lurched after them, but an officer appeared from the kitchen and cut him off. "We've got'em! Hold your fire!"

Houston holstered his gun and grabbed the radio from his belt as he returned to his dad's side. "Shots fired! My dad's down. Get my brother and the ambulance up here fast."

His dad stared up at him, his face pale. His mouth moved, but no sound came out. Pain rippled across his face as he tried to suck in a breath.

Houston ripped open his dad's shirt. Blood flowed from a hole the size of a quarter only inches above the heart. He grabbed a panel of the curtains a few feet away and pulled until it ripped from the rod. He wadded up one end and pressed it gently against his dad's chest. "Take it easy, Dad. Help is on the way."

The realization of what his father had done seeped through the shock. He hadn't even hesitated to step into the line of fire.

Joe rushed into the room, followed by two paramedics carrying a gurney. He grabbed Houston's shoulder. "What happened?" He knelt next to Houston

Fighting emotions long buried, Houston explained. "Vinnie's man came out of the spare bedroom, and Dad jumped in front of me and took a bullet."

"We've got it from here." The paramedics knelt next to Samuel.

Houston stood and allowed Joe to take his place. Joe's brow furrowed, and the paramedics wouldn't make eye contact. He'd seen it before … usually when someone was dead or about to die.

Static from his radio diverted his attention. "This is Houston, go ahead."

"We found your wife and the kids. They're fine, just a little shaken up. We'll bring them to the front of the house."

"I'm going outside to check on Becky and the kids," he told Joe. "Let me know when Dad's ready to transport. I'll follow behind the ambulance."

Joe stood as he gave a few instructions to the paramedics, seemingly oblivious to the fact that his shirt and pants were covered in their father's blood. He placed a hand on Houston's arm. "I don't know if he's going to make it, Houston. We need to notify Cindy and Travis."

"Let's get him to the hospital. Then I'll call Travis."

As Houston walked outside, Becky led the boys by the hand down the ridge from the barn, and Megan walked alongside. He rushed to greet them. He wrapped Becky in his arms. "Thank God you're okay." The kids circled around them. Houston smiled at them and tousled their hair.

At the scream of an ambulance siren in the distance, Houston sobered. "I have to go."

Becky squeezed his hand. "What happened?"

Houston pulled her to the side and filled her in on the details.

"We'll be fine, Houston. Go!"

* * *

Houston sat in the surgical waiting room, surrounded by friends from church. How many times had they had he spent his day off helping them with a project, while keeping an emotional distance from them? Now they were here for him and Becky, cramped in the small waiting room, praying and supporting his family.

He looked up when Joe walked in, dressed in his scrubs. His presence drew everyone's attention, but he headed straight for Houston. "Let's go out into the hall and talk."

Houston followed him, but before they even came to a stop, he asked, "How's Dad?"

"Well, he made it through surgery, but he's lost a lot of blood. He's also had some damage to his chest cavity. He's very weak, Houston." He paused and looked down. "I noticed Cindy and Travis aren't here yet. Have you contacted them?"

"I left them a message."

Joe nodded. "I don't think he's going make it through the night. I hope they make it in time."

Kenny came up beside them. "Don't worry about contacting your brother, Houston. I've already got that taken care of."

His eyebrows shot up. "I don't understand."

Kenny glanced at Joe, but said nothing.

Joe cleared his throat. "I ... uh ... I'll just pass on the news to the others.

"You left in such a hurry, I didn't have a chance to speak with you." Kenny lowered his voice. "The Feds want to move on this. Angelica wants to know how many copies of the recording there are." Kenny averted his gaze. "She's called several times, and it sounded urgent, so I gave her the address of the cabin. I'll call her and have her tell Travis about your dad."

Houston took a step forward. "How did you know about the cabin?"

Kenny held his hands up. "Take it easy. I'm not the bad guy here. The pen recorded it. I assumed you knew that."

Houston slammed his fist against the wall. "I can't believe you gave out their location. I still don't know if Angelica can be trusted."

"Her credentials checked out, Travis. If it will make you feel better, I'll call the local police and have them send a car by."

"You better have them send more than one." Houston leaned forward. "If there's one thing I've learned in all these years of investigating Vinnie, it's never under-estimate him."

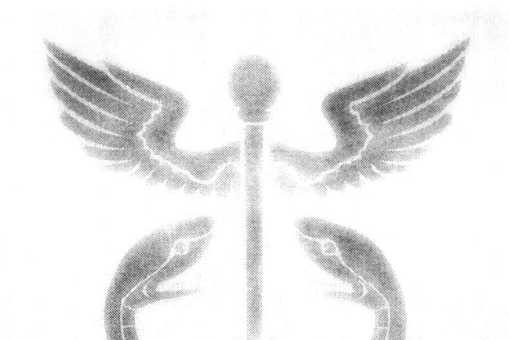

Chapter Thirty-Eight

Travis unlocked the door to the cabin, opened it for Cindy to enter, and retrieved their few belongings. He closed the trunk and stared at the miles of endless woods surrounding them. Just as Houston has promised, the cabin was simple and secluded, perfect for their needs.

Now he had a different hurdle to jump over: telling Cindy the truth. *"I'd rather hear the worst truth than the best lie."* Cindy had repeated the saying to the girls since they were old enough to talk. Would she still feel this way after their afternoon talk? *Doubtful.*

The moment he closed the door behind him, Cindy stood from the wooden sofa with mismatched cushions. "Okay, spill it, Travis. My imagination is running rampant." She rubbed her hand over her belly.

He took her by the hand and drew her back down onto the sofa, but he couldn't look her in the eyes. *Just tell her.* "I'm going to have to file for bankruptcy. My company's finished."

She sucked in a quick breath. "What? How could this have happened?"

If she only knew. "That's not all."

Cindy's hands clenched his.

"The house is in foreclosure. We have thirty days to get out."

She pulled her hands out of his. "Travis—how could I not know? How could you keep this from me?" She rambled off several incoherent questions, then turned away from him. "I feel so stupid."

"Don't."

Suddenly, she placed her hands on either side of her stomach

"What's wrong? Are you having contractions?"

"They're just Braxton Hicks contractions. If I lay down on my left side, they'll go away."

Travis jumped to his feet to allow Cindy to lie down.

During the forty-five minutes the contractions continued, Travis alternated between pacing in front of the window, putting their belongings away, and dashing to Cindy's side whenever the pain made her gasp.

Between contractions, she tried to question Travis more, but he convinced her to wait until after she had a nap. She tried to argue, but her heavy eyelids betrayed her. He walked her to the bedroom and tucked her in.

Before he turned out the light, he hoped the nap would refresh her enough. The rest of his news would change her world again.

Travis scrounged through the kitchen cabinets, found some coffee and put on a fresh pot of decaf. When the aroma filled the cabin, he poured himself a cup and sat on the couch.

A Bible sat unopened on the coffee table. When was the last time he'd spent time in God's Word? The Lord had been so distant for so long. No, it was he who stepped away. The enormity of his situation hit him like a train. He'd walked away from God and led himself and his family into grave danger. He fell to his knees and wept. *God forgive me!*

Circumstances had not changed, but now he could breathe easy for the first time in a long time. *Don't leave me, Lord.* A selfish prayer, but at least progress in his communication with God.

He glanced at the bedroom where Cindy rested. *What happened to us, God?* How had they moved from newlyweds who could hardly keep their hands off of each other to living more like roommates than man and wife? But he already knew the answer: kids, work, life, busy-ness. All had taken precedence over his relationships with both the Lord and Cindy.

Cindy walked into the living room. She'd let her hair down, and her eyes were red and puffy.

"You feeling better?"

She placed her hand on her belly. "Yes. The pains have stopped."

He closed the distance between them. "Can I get you anything? I made a pot of decaf."

She stepped away from him and eased herself onto the sofa. "I'm fine for now, thanks."

He sat down beside her and placed a hand on the baby.

She placed her hand on his, and his heart soared. Maybe there was hope for their relationship. But they still needed to finish their conversation, no matter how difficult or painful it became. He placed a kiss on her cheek and hoped it wouldn't be the last one she would ever accept.

"Please tell me the truth, Travis. Have you been unfaithful?" The pain in her eyes cut him to the core. She really thought he would cheat on her? He let out a long breath. The silence lasted several minutes.

She leaned back. "I guess I have my answer. It's a yes or no question. It shouldn't be so difficult."

He stared at his cup of coffee, unable to look her in the eyes. "It's more complicated than that."

She crossed her arms and struggled to get to her feet "What's so complicated? Either you're cheating on me or you're not." She moved toward the window and paced.

"Are you having more labor pains?"

"No. And please don't change the subject. Tell me the truth. I deserve to know."

The truth would break her heart. "I kissed another woman. That's as far as it got. I regretted it the moment it happened."

She looked him in the eyes. "It was Angelica, wasn't it?"

"Yes." His finger circled the top of the coffee mug.

"Do you have feelings for her?"

He placed the mug down on the coffee table. "No."

"But you do find her attractive."

"Yes … no … that's a difficult question. Was I attracted to her? Yes. Am I still? No. I wish I'd never kissed her. Thank God, Houston walked in when he did."

"Houston knows?" Her eyebrows shot up and her mouth hung open. "I can't believe he didn't tell me."

Travis ran his fingers through his hair. "I begged him to let me tell you. I thought it would be best coming from me."

"Is that why you're losing your business? Because you're spending time with Angelica instead of taking care of business?"

"No. It's two separate issues."

"I don't understand." She returned to her spot on the couch.

Travis took her hands in his. "There are many reasons why I lost the business, Cindy. The main one is that I made a lot of poor business choices."

"How does that lead to us being here?" She waved an arm to indicate the cabin.

"Angelica works for Vinnie Fernandez."

Cindy's brow furrowed. "Do you mean that thug they mention on the news, someone involved in organized crime?

Travis nodded.

She shook her head. "I still don't understand, Travis. How can she work for Vinnie when she works for you? And why would you have anything to do with someone who works for a man who—"

He held up a hand. "If you'll hear me out, I'll explain everything." He poured it all out, from his first inklings that trouble was on the horizon to accepting Vinnie's help to the decision to get evidence that would put Vinnie behind bars. The expressions that rippled across Cindy's face tore his heart apart, but he held back nothing—except about the baby.

"So we're in danger because you decided to play detective?"

"No." His voice was barely above a whisper. "It's because of the baby."

"What does the baby have to do with this?"

He let out a slow breath. How do you tell your wife some monster wants her child? *Give me the words, God.* "Vinnie wants the baby."

"He wants to adopt our baby?"

"He wants to *buy* the baby, so he can sell it on the black market."

She wrapped her arms around her belly and shrank away from him. "Dear God!"

"He offered me two million dollars. When I refused, he became very angry. That's why I had to get you out of town. I was afraid he'd take matters into his own hands."

"What makes him think he has the right to our child?" Her eyes flashed.

"It's not just our baby. Think about how many babies have disappeared. Vinnie's a very dangerous man."

Cindy rubbed her arms as though to warm herself. "Vinnie's behind all of the kidnappings?"

"Yes." He leaned forward. "There's one more thing."

She let out a frustrated sigh. "How much more could there be, Travis?"

He knelt in front of her. "I let Vinnie use my business for illegal purposes. We have to face the fact that my actions were illegal. I may have to spend some time in prison."

Cindy shook her head. "He's killing pregnant woman and selling their babies on the black market, and *you* have to go to prison? What kind of justice system do we have?"

He sat next to her. "I'll need a lawyer. Maybe I can ask for leniency in exchange for my testimony, but—"

Pounding on the door made them both jump. Travis shot to his feet. His heart slammed in his chest. No one had followed them. Who could it be?

Cindy gasped. "I thought you said no one knows we're here."

"Go hide in the bedroom."

"Open up, Travis, I know you're in there," a loud male voice called out.

Travis opened the side table drawer and pulled out the handgun and a cell phone. He pressed the cell phone into Cindy's hand. "Call Houston. Tell him Vinnie Fernandez found us!"

"Where did you get those?" Cindy squeaked.

He motioned her toward the back of the cabin. "Houston gave them to me to use in case of an emergency. I can't think of any bigger emergency than this." He tiptoed to the window, but Cindy followed on his heels. He pressed the cell phone into Cindy's hand. "Do it! Call Houston!"

Chapter Thirty-Nine

Dominique felt Joe's presence before she actually saw him. She eased her eyes open and licked her chapped lips. The last time she'd felt like this was when she woke up from having her appendix taken out. In spite of the soft pillow, pain radiated through her head.

"Hi, sleepyhead. How are you feeling?" Joe took her hand in his.

She fumbled with her free hand to find the control for the bed. "That depends."

"On what?"

She opened her eyes a little further. "Are you asking as my boyfriend or as my doctor?"

He helped her adjust the pillows. "Both." He fished the remote out of the tangled sheets and pressed the button to raise the head of the bed.

"What happened?" she asked. "Did the men who abducted me turn Vinnie in? Please tell me he's behind bars?" Her voice trembled.

Joe brought one of her hands to his lips and kissed it. "I was so worried about you, Dominique. I may never let you out of my sight again."

"I take that as a no." She looked around the room. "I need to speak with Houston." She pointed to the water pitcher on the rolling tray. "Can you hand me that?"

Joe poured a glass of water for her and stuck a straw in the glass. "Here. Go slow with this." His eyes narrowed. "Why do you need to talk to Houston?"

She took a small sip. "When I was in the back of the van, I faded in and out of consciousness. When they thought I was out of it, one of the men received a phone call from Vinnie. They were talking about some papers that document where each of the kidnapped babies are."

Joe's eyebrows shot up. "Did he mention where it was hidden?"

"No. But he mentioned Angelica. Please tell Houston. I know he'll want to look into it."

Joe didn't respond.

"Is everything okay? What aren't you telling me?"

He took a deep breath. "I wanted to wait till you were a little stronger. Houston's with Dad."

Peculiar, considering what Joe had told her about Houston and Samuel's relationship. "You still haven't answered my question. Is everything okay?"

He ran his hands over his face. "My dad was shot. He's in the recovery room right now. We don't know if he's going to make it."

Dominique sat up straight. "What! Who shot him?"

Joe rubbed the back of his neck. "Vinnie Fernandez's men. We think they were looking for Cindy."

Her hands fumbled with the bed's railing. When she managed to get it down, she started to ease herself to the side of the bed.

Joe set his hands on her shoulders. "Wait a minute. Where do you think you're going?"

"We have to do something. I won't stand by and let that man harm Cindy and the baby." She pushed against Joe's hands and let her feet slide to the floor. Blood rushed to her head, and she swayed.

Joe grabbed her arm and her eased her back onto the bed. "I don't know what you have in mind, but you have to take it slow and easy."

Tears slipped down her face. "I am so sorry. You should be with your family. They'll need you." She patted his arm.

He kissed the top of her head. "You're my family too."

Warmth radiated from the tips of her toes to the top of her head. "I would never forgive myself if something happened to your dad and you weren't there."

"The staff knows how to contact me, and Houston knows where I am. You worry about getting better."

"I want to see your dad, Joe. As soon as he can have visitors, I want to see him." Her heart broke because she might never have the opportunity to thank Samuel for helping her to understand the Lord's love and forgiveness. Her time with him had been so short, yet she knew him better than her own father.

A sharp rapping on the door pulled her from her melancholy.

"Come in." Still weak from the effects of the drug, her voice came out faint and hoarse.

Penelope Nordstrom barged in the room, sporting her trademark frown and carrying a medical chart. "And how are we feeling, Ms. Sherwood?"

Dominique made the mistake of looking at Joe. The comical expression on his face made her bite the side of her cheek to keep from laughing. "I'm surprised to see you, Penelope. It's nice of you to be concerned."

Her former boss pushed the glasses higher on her nose. "This isn't a social call. Billing was on the way up here, but I told them I'd speak with you. Since you no longer have insurance, the hospital needs to know how you're planning to pay for the services we're providing you."

"That's easy," Joe said.

Penelope's eyes narrowed. "Will *you* be paying for Dominique's medical charges?"

"If I need to I will, but I think the responsible party should pay for them."

"And who's that?"

Joe leaned forward. "Vinnie Fernandez."

Penelope's mouth flew open. She scrawled some notes on the chart and stomped out of the room.

Dominique squeezed Joe's hand. "Well, I guess you told her. If only I really could just send him the bill." She let out a long sigh. "I can't believe how exasperating that woman can be."

Joe's cell phone ring cut off his response. He checked the text. "I have to go. Dad is coding!"

Chapter Forty

The pounding on the cabin door grew louder and more incessant. Cindy stood perfectly still in the middle of the cabin's living room, cell phone in hand.

Her deer-in-the-headlights expression drove a knife of fear through Travis. He turned her toward the bedroom. "Call Houston! We don't have time to waste."

"Travis, my water broke!"

Behind him, the door splintered. Cool night air rushed into the cabin.

Vinnie shoved the broken door open and barged into the room. "Thought you could hide from me, did you? I told you I don't like being deceived."

Travis stepped in front of Cindy. He firmly planted his feet, aimed the gun at Vinnie's chest, and glared at him. *If you have to use it, shoot to kill.* That had been Houston's advice. "You don't have any business here, Vinnie. Get out!"

Vinnie leered at Cindy.

Travis prayed Vinnie didn't notice the small puddle of water at Cindy's feet. He took a step forward to divert Vinnie's gaze.

Vinnie stared at the gun in Travis's hand. "You know the terms of our arrangement. Only I say when our business is concluded. And I'm not quite ready to part ways."

"What unfinished business do you think we have?"

"I'm surprised you don't remember, Travis." Vinnie took a few steps toward him. "We still have a little two-million dollar business deal to resolve."

Travis transferred the gun to his right hand and moved a protective arm in front of Cindy. He immediately regretted the movement. It drew Vinnie's attention to the water on the floor.

"Looks like things are progressing." Vinnie's eyes gleamed. "Let's finish this business. I want that baby! Either you meet your end of the bargain, or I'll handle it my way."

"I never agreed to sell you the baby." Travis tightened his grip on the gun. The pounding of his heartbeat filled his ears.

"I'll give you a choice, Travis. There's a doctor, a *friend* of mine, not far from here. Your wife can deliver the baby, and he'll document it as a stillbirth. I'll deposit the money in whatever account you want." He rubbed his chin. "Or you stand on your ridiculous morals, and I call an associate whose only concern is getting paid to harvest a healthy baby."

Cindy gripped Travis's arm and let out a slight groan. No Braxton Hicks contractions this time. He didn't have much time. "You're in no position to threaten me. I've already spoken with the police. I handed them evidence they've wanted for a long time. If I were you, I'd be plotting my escape, not wasting time trying to make one last heinous deal."

"You're bluffing!" Vinnie's eyes narrowed.

"What did I have to lose? You took everything I owned. But you can't have my wife or my child. Now get out of here!" He waved the gun towards the door.

"You son of a—," Vinnie spat. He closed the distance between them faster than Travis thought a man his size could move. A meaty fist connected with Travis's jaw.

Travis's head snapped back. He pushed Vinnie with both hands, then smacked him on the side of his head with the gun. The force knocked Vinnie to the ground.

He stared at Vinnie sprawled out on the floor. He kicked him in the gut, but Vinnie's groan brought no satisfaction. He aimed the gun at Vinnie's head.

Cindy stepped to his side. "I'll call the police."

"He owns the police." Travis's hands shook. This man had taken everything from him, but he wouldn't become a murderer like him. He tossed the gun to the couch. It missed and thunked to the ground. He grabbed Vinnie by the collar, pulled him several inches off the ground, and pounded him back down.

He drove his right fist into Vinnie's face, then his left into his stomach. Anger seemed to flow through his veins. It fueled punch after punch.

"Travis, that's enough!"

The voice from the doorway made Travis freeze.

Angelica pointed a gun at him. "It's over, Travis. Don't do anything more you'll regret. Let's go."

Cindy's horrified expression broke his heart. He had to protect her.

"We're not going anywhere with you." He spotted Houston's pistol just in front of the sofa. Too far to reach.

"I'm afraid you don't have a choice."

Chapter Forty-One

Houston's large frame felt even larger crammed into one of the two small chairs in the compact ICU room. The steady sound of the ventilator both comforted and disturbed him. He'd seen people on breathing machines before, but this was his dad.

Why did you do it, Dad? The unanswered question stabbed at his conscience. The nurses had told him to talk to him, but other than a host of questions, he didn't know what to say.

"How's he doing?"

Joe's voice triggered a wave of relief. "He's holding his own." He let out a long sigh. "They wanted to know if Dad has a DNR. After he coded, they said they need to know his last wishes." Houston forced the words past the lump in his throat.

Joe studied the monitors and pulled the chart up on the computer. "His numbers have improved. That's encouraging." He pointed to the ventilator. "Did anyone indicate how long he'll be on the machine?"

"The doctor wants to meet with us in the morning. He'll probably let us know more then. How's Dominique doing?"

"They're keeping her overnight as a precaution." Joe squeezed into the chair next to Houston. "How are you handling things?"

Joe's question released a swell of emotions. He focused on his hands, clasped together in his lap. Questions had been burning in his mind since the shooting, but he wasn't sure he was ready to hear the answer.

"Have you heard from Travis and Cindy?"

"Kenny said he's sending word to them. If they're not here in a little while, I'll try the burn phone I gave Travis." He got up and paced back and forth in the small room.

"Why don't you go grab a cup of coffee? You've been here the whole time. I'll take a shift."

"Thanks, I could use a break. You want me to bring you anything?"

"No, I'm good."

The tension left Houston more with each step away from Dad's room. What he really needed was a strong cup of coffee and a little fresh air.

He took the stairs down to the first floor and headed toward the cafeteria, but slowed at the sight of the hospital chapel across from the elevator. Without additional thought, he opened the chapel door and entered the empty room. The smell of cedar and carnations hung in the air. The soft lighting reflected on the wooden pews and the stained glass windows.

His feet felt heavy as he took a few steps in. *What am I doing here?* He left as quickly as he entered, and let the rich smell of fresh coffee draw him down the hallway to the cafeteria. After filling a tall Styrofoam cup with brew and paying the cashier, he returned to his original plan for a little fresh air and headed outdoors.

He took a deep breath of the cool night air and slowly let it out. He circled the hospital gardens twice, then sat on one of the wooden benches. Thousands of bright stars sparkled above in the clear sky. Stunning. He automatically searched for his favorite constellations, but nothing could keep his mind from the questions eating at him. *What if I never have a chance to speak with him? Is this how it's going to end?*

"I thought I might find you out here. Mind if I join you?"

Becky's voice never failed to bring a smile to his face. He stretched his arm along the back of the bench as his answer and brushed her lips with a light kiss when she snuggled next to him. "You sure are a sight for sore eyes." He kissed her neck and pulled her even closer. "How are the kids doing?"

"They're all settled in. Tabitha and Henry from church are watching them tonight."

Her comment nettled him. Was it truly *his* church? He attended, but didn't belong. The lonely, empty feeling that had become so familiar stabbed at him again.

Becky put her hand on Houston's knee. "Are you okay?"

He took her hand in his. "I'm sorry, honey. I have a lot on my mind."

"Want to talk about it?"

"It's my dad." He moved closer to Becky, drawing her in for another hug.

She remained silent.

"I've hated him for so long. I'll never forgive him for the way he treated us when I was growing up. But now—" His throat tightened, but he wasn't sure of what else to say anyway.

"I've never understood what you have against him."

"You don't know what it's like to grow up with an alcoholic for a father. He missed every single little league baseball game I played in. He never saw the winning touchdown I scored my senior year to win the championship. Instead he was in a bar, smashed." He stared out at the few cars remaining in the parking lot and shook his head.

"I can't even count how many times I made excuses for Dad's drunken behavior. In spite of all that, Mom begged me on her deathbed to forgive him. She begged me not to let the hate keep me from knowing Christ as my Savior. But I couldn't do either. I still can't." He voiced the last words in little above a whisper. He finished the last of his coffee and tossed the empty cup into the trash.

Becky took his hand and gave it a squeeze but said nothing.

"I've spent all day trying to figure out why he did it." He tossed his hands in the air. "He knows I wear a bullet-proof vest. Why would he step in front of me and risk his own life? Why did he have to take matters into his own hands? The doctors aren't even sure if he's going to live."

"It was instinct, Houston. Your dad didn't have time to think about whether or not you had a vest on. The only thing he was thinking about is that you're not ready."

"But I was armed and had backup. We were more than prepared."

"I'm not talking about physical preparation, Houston. He knows you're a great cop. Your dad stepped in front of you because you're not *spiritually* prepared. He couldn't chance whether or not you had your vest on. He wouldn't have been able to live with himself if you died without Christ." She paused. "I couldn't bear it either." She rested her head on his shoulder. "I know you find it hard to believe, but your dad loves you. That's why he did what he did." She squeezed his hand and released it.

His throat tightened at the truth she spoke, but this time he was finally ready to listen. He had sat in church with her for too many years, listening to the preacher speak of heaven and hell. Despite all of the warnings, he'd never taken that step of faith.

Becky cleared her throat. "What's holding you back, Houston? What is it you're clinging to that keeps you from the Lord? I used to think it was your unwillingness to forgive your father, but now I think there may be something more."

He focused on her face. She was so beautiful, so loving and kind. Her question was dead on. *What is holding me back?* Rejection? Disappointment? Not having all the answers? Deep down, he knew. He whispered, "I'm afraid."

Her eyes widened. "What are you afraid of?"

He brushed away the hair that had fallen across her eyes. His fingers trailed down across the softness of her cheek. Heat climbed up his face. He'd gunned down criminals, had seen the depravity of man first-hand. How could he fully explain his apprehensions when he barely understood them himself? "I've been doing things on my own for so long. I don't know any other way."

"Are you afraid God will let you down?"

How did she do it? She always asked the best questions, the kind that cut right to the heart of the matter. "Did I ever tell you about my eighth grade science fair project?"

She shook head. "I don't think so."

"It involved training a service dog. As my final project, I wanted to present the dog to a person in need of a trained companion. I found just the right dog at the humane society. His name was Bo. He was half Golden Retriever, half Lab, and 100 percent heart. He took to the training like a duck to water." He stared up at the sky. "My mom was concerned because she knew I was becoming attached to the dog, but I kept on.

"For the first time in my life, I felt I was not only was I helping someone, but I had my dad's attention. As the science fair drew near, I kept pestering him about coming, and he promised me he would.

"The day finally arrived, and I was sick to my stomach." He rubbed the stubble on his chin. "I don't know which worried me more, giving the dog away or wondering if my dad would show. I was so sure he would finally be proud of me."

"Did he show up?"

"No. He never made it. I worked for almost an entire year, gave my best friend away, took first prize at the fair, and my dad was too busy drinking to remember his promise." He spoke past the lump in his throat. "To make matters worse, the next day he asked me where Bo was. I don't think he ever cared. I promised myself

I would never trust him again. My mom tried to make excuses for him, but I didn't want to hear any more lies. To me, my father was dead."

"Did he ever apologize?"

"Yeah, after he was sober. But by then it was too little, too late."

"The Lord's not like that, Houston. He'll never let you down."

On some level he wanted to believe her, to let go and trust God. Like when he'd encouraged Megan and Audrey to jump in the pool. He promised he'd catch them. Could he take that leap with God? He grasped Becky's hand and interlocked his fingers with hers. "I don't know if I'm ready for that yet. But I am thankful to God for blessing me with you."

Tears streamed down Becky's face.

He hated to see her cry. Worse, he hated it when he was the reason for the tears. "I'm sorry, honey, I didn't mean to upset you. It's been a long day. Let's go up and check on him."

She retrieved a tissue from her purse and wiped the tears away. After she cleaned her face, she shifted to fully face him. "Don't wait too long."

"I'm not sure I know what you mean."

"None of us are guaranteed tomorrow. Even bullet-proof vests can fail. Someone might not be there to jump in front of you."

He stared at the ground. Normally, this was the part of the conversation where he would clock out, or change the topic. Today he didn't want to. Becky, Joe, and his father had something he wanted: peace.

"I know how dangerous my job is. I'm always careful." His voice was soft.

"A thousand different things could happen." She wrung her hands. "Where would you be then? Where are you going to spend eternity, Houston? I know your father hurt you, and I know it about killed you to watch your mom go downhill, but don't you remember her dying words?"

He gritted his teeth. His mom had pleaded with him to listen.

"She begged you to forgive your dad and ask Christ into your heart. I've always wondered how you could just dismiss your own mother's dying words."

He flinched at her words, but remained silent.

"I know this sounds harsh—especially with Samuel fighting for his life—but I want you to think about what I've said." She planted a kiss on his cheek. "I'm going to go up and see your dad. Please promise me you'll think about what I've said?"

How could he let her down? He would do just about anything to not disappoint her. His eyes met hers. "I promise."

"That's all I can ask." She stood and kissed him on the lips. "I'll see you upstairs."

Her words bounced around in his mind. *Where are you going to spend eternity, Houston?* The question nagged at his conscience.

He didn't have an answer, but for the first time in his life he wanted one.

Chapter Forty-Two

The cabin walls closed in around Travis as he stared at Angelica. Travis stepped closer to Cindy and wiped away the blood accumulating at the corner of his mouth. "Take Vinnie and get out of here." His heart thumped in his chest as he kept his eyes on her gun.

Angelica's gaze shifted to Cindy. "My instructions are to bring you both in. You're wanted for questioning." She took out a badge and flashed it. "I'm a federal agent. I've been on an undercover assignment. We share the same opinion of Mr. Fernandez."

Something didn't add up. Why was she holding them at gunpoint if she was a federal agent?

Cindy let out a series of short puffs. "She's in labor. We can't go anywhere."

"There's a hospital about thirty miles away." She put her gun back in its waistband holster. "I'll drive you both there."

"If her labor is like her other pregnancies, the baby might be here before we can make it there. If you want to help, I suggest you start boiling some water." He gently nudged Cindy back to the bedroom and helped her settle in on the bed. He tried not to think about the gun Angelica still had in her possession. "I should have never brought you so far from medical care. I'm sorry."

"You did what you had to in order to protect us." She let out a quick gasp. "That was a big one. I'm scared, Travis. I'm not due for almost another month. What if something goes wrong?"

He wanted to assure her they would be fine, but his insides were tying themselves up in knots. She didn't need to add his fears to her own. "Let's leave it in God's hands."

Three quick raps sounded on the door. "I put the water on," Angelica called through the door. "Do you want me to call for help?"

"No, don't call anyone," Travis yelled from his perch next to Cindy. "Vinnie has too many connections. He wants this baby, and he'll stop at nothing to get it."

"Ask her if she can call Houston," Cindy whispered.

"Don't you have the phone I gave you?"

She shook her head. "I left it in the living room."

"I don't know if we can trust her," he whispered. "We'll figure something out. I'll find the phone after I search the place for clean rags and towels." He pulled the comforter up to her chin. "Can I get you anything?"

"An epidural?" She let out a short laugh. "Are you sure you can't trust her? If she called Houston, he'd send help."

"I'm not convinced she's on our side. If anything happened to you or the baby, I'd never forgive myself."

In the bathroom, Travis pulled several large towels and washcloths off the white wicker rack. From the medicine cabinet, he plucked a bottle of peroxide off the shelf from between a pack of matches and an old pair of glasses.

"Everything okay in there?" Cindy called out.

"Just seeing what's in here. There's not much to choose from."

He balanced the bottle of peroxide on the towels, carried the supplies to the bedroom, and set them on the chest of drawers.

Cindy had propped herself up on the bed against a small stack of pillows. If he didn't know better, he'd think she was getting ready to settle in for a relaxing evening ... until she let out a series of controlled breaths.

"I'll get the First Aid kit from the car. I'll be right back." He hustled to the door.

"Hurry!"

In spite of the need to hurry, Travis stopped when he entered the living room.

Everything looked perfectly normal. Had it not been for the streaks of Vinnie's blood on the hardwood floors, he would have been hard pressed to find evidence of a struggle.

Where could she have taken him? He pulled the curtains back and peered through the window. No one appeared to be lurking about, so he stepped outside. His foot sent something flying across the porch. He picked it up and held it to the light. Vinnie's cell phone. *That's odd.* He tucked the phone in his pocket, grabbed his keys, and pressed the fob to unlock the trunk.

Travis lifted the trunk and stared at the darker blackness inside. The light was burned out. He swiped a hand to the left, searching blindly for the First Aid kit. His hands brushed against something moist and sticky.

What in the world?

He fumbled for the key fob, but couldn't see which button unlocked the doors. As he stuck the key in the lock, an unwelcome thought intruded. Prickles of fear spread like spiders crawling across his skin. With quick motions, he popped open the glove compartment and grabbed the flashlight, then ran back to the trunk. The dome light exposed red liquid on his hands. Blood? Where would …?

He grabbed the flashlight from the glove compartment with shaky hands and returned to the trunk.

Darkness seemed to swallow him, even as the flashlight's rays lit up the trunk.

Vinnie's pale eyes, a bullet hole between them, stared up at him. Even as he fought the urge to empty his stomach, relief filled him. He was finally free from Vinnie's clutches … and it hadn't been because of his own death, as Vinnie had threatened.

But the victory faded quickly as the reality of his situation sank in. His instincts had been right. Angelica wasn't who she claimed to be.

He flashed the light around the yard. Only Becky's car and Vinnie's. Angelica had left him at a crime scene with his fingerprints all over the place and Vinnie's body in the trunk. He was still caught in a web of lies.

Sirens screamed in the distance. The sound felt like a slap in the face, but it woke him from his shock. His jaws clenched, and he tightened his grip on the flashlight. *I am not going to prison for a murder I didn't commit.*

He slammed the trunk shut, then ran into the cabin. "We've got to get out of here." He headed into the bathroom. "Get your shoes on, and I'll grab the supplies."

"What? Are you crazy? In case you haven't noticed, I'm a little busy having a baby here."

"Vinnie's dead. Angelica killed him, and she's framing me for the murder."

The sirens in the distance punctuated the urgency of their situation.

Cindy swung her legs over the side of the bed and struggled to put on her shoes. "Let's go."

Travis washed the blood off his hands, grabbed the remaining supplies, took Cindy by the hand, and led her outside. She leaned against him as she shuffled toward the passenger side of their car.

He nudged her toward Vinnie's car. "We can't take Becky's car."

"Why not?"

"Vinnie's body is in the trunk, and I don't want to disturb it more than I already have." He pushed the unlock button on the remote to Vinnie's black Mercedes.

The sirens swelled as he tucked Cindy inside, then ran to the other side.

Travis backed out of the driveway and sped down the dark country road. He pulled Vinnie's cell phone out of his pocket. "Call Houston."

The cell phone rang before Cindy could take it.

His eyebrows shot up. "Who could that be?" Travis turned the phone and read the caller ID.

"Who is it?"

"Angelica."

Cindy rubbed a hand over her stomach and blew out several short puffs. "Do you think you should answer it?"

"I want to hear what she has to say." He scanned the rearview mirror and let out a sigh of relief at the pitch blackness surrounding them. They weren't being followed. "Hello?"

"You're in a lot of trouble, Travis. Give me what I want, and it all goes away."

He swallowed a wave of panic. "What exactly do you want?"

"The baby."

He gripped the steering wheel. "Is that why you killed Vinnie? So you can sell the baby yourself?"

She let out a bitter laugh. "Vinnie broke the rules. That's why he's dead."

"What rules? He *makes* the rules. You should know that. You worked for him—or pretended to."

"You still don't get it do you?"

He remained silent.

"I don't work for the FBI, and I certainly didn't work for Vinnie. In fact, he worked for me. He was too stupid to figure it out in time and double-crossed me on more than one occasion. That's why I killed him."

"I'll tell you the same thing I told Vinnie. My baby isn't for sale."

"How are you going to raise a baby from prison?"

"I didn't kill Vinnie! And I won't go to jail for it."

Angelica laughed. "You really are naïve, aren't you? One word from me, Travis, and the police will drop their investigation."

"I'll take my chances." He glanced at Cindy and wished he could erase the fear in her eyes. "Leave my family alone."

"We'll see how you feel once you're facing a capital murder charge. Ohio is still a death penalty state, Travis. If you're convicted, your children will grow up without a father. They'll know you as a convicted killer. You wouldn't want that, would you?"

He hung up on her and fumbled for the button to unroll the window. For all he knew, Angelica was tracking him with Vinnie's phone. He found the button, pushed it, and revved his arm back to toss the phone out the open window.

"Don't!" Cindy screamed.

Travis held the device up. "She's probably tracking us with the GPS on the phone."

"Then drive faster. Right now, the call log and other information on Vinnie's phone may be the only piece of evidence we have to prove you didn't murder Vinnie."

"We're about thirty minutes from the hospital. You think you can make it?"

"It'll be close. My contractions are five minutes apart." She winced. "Let's see how fast this car can go."

He handed the phone to her and focused on the winding road before him. "I'll get you there!"

Chapter Forty-Three

Dominique sat up in the hospital bed and punched the pillows down, then grabbed the remote and skipped through the stations. At the sound of her cell phone's familiar ring tone, she muted the television and picked up her phone from the tiny drawer on the underside of the table next to her bed. The caller ID displayed an unfamiliar number. "Hello?"

"Is this Dominique Sherwood?" The muffled female voice sounded vaguely familiar.

"Yes, it is. May I ask who's calling?"

"You still investigating Vinnie Fernandez?"

A chill ran up her spine. Who knew that she was investigating Vinnie? Curiosity won out over caution. "I'm interested in any information you might have."

"You ever hear the term Caporegime?"

" I'm not familiar with it."

"It means Lieutenant. Vinnie Fernandez is a Lieutenant."

Her brain still a little fuzzy, Dominique tried to process what the caller meant. "I'm confused. I thought he was in charge. The police have been investigating him for a long time."

"He's a big fish. One of many. But you should be fishing for a shark."

"If Vinnie's not in charge, who is?"

"All I know is that something big just went down. If you want access to any records Vinnie may or may not have, you better get yourself down to Castalgia's before they're destroyed."

Hair raised on Dominique's arm. Leads like this didn't come around that often. Was it legit? "Who is this?"

"If you can get your hands on those records, all of your questions will be answered."

"How do I know this isn't some kind of trap?"

"You don't. I'll leave the keys to Vinnie's private office in the glove box of your car."

"Hello? Hello?" It was no use. The line was dead. Dominique hit the callback button. The phone rang several times before a recorded voice informed her the person she was trying to reach had not set up voice mail.

She grabbed her belongings from the closet and untied the hospital gown. Pain shot up her side as she pulled on her jeans. Once dressed, she glanced in the mirror. The last twenty-four hours had taken a toll, but this was an investigation, not a beauty contest.

Dominique opened the door and walked straight into Joe. Her purse and cell phone spilled onto the floor. "I thought you'd be tied up all night with your dad."

"He's doing much better. They took him off the vent, and he's holding his own. Houston is sitting with him now." He scanned her attire. "Are you going to tell me where you're headed in such a rush? You're not being discharged until tomorrow. It's after ten o'clock."

She chewed on her bottom lip. He was carrying such a heavy load worrying about his dad.

He took her hands in his, and her heart broke in two. "Dominique, please don't go anywhere tonight. You need your rest."

She squeezed his hands and brushed a quick kiss on his lips. He deserved an explanation, but would he understand? "I have to go." She picked up the items from her purse, ignoring the pain shooting up her side.

Joe pulled his keys from his pocket. "You've got that determined look on your face. If I can't convince you to stay, I'm going wherever you're going. Whatever you're up to, I'm not letting you go by yourself."

She swallowed the lump in her throat. "That's really not necessary. I was planning to call a cab." *Tell him the truth? Or let him drive you home, then call a cab?* She remembered the caller's warning. She had to hurry.

"A cab's not a good idea. Vinnie's men are everywhere."

His words snapped her out of her dilemma. *He cares for you. He wants to help.* She hugged him. "I'm not going to my place."

He raised his eyebrows. "Where are we going?" His head cocked to the right.

"Castalgia's."

His eyes narrowed. "I don't think that's a good idea, especially after what you've been through today. We can go get your car in the morning."

"I'm not going to get my car."

He paused and took a deep breath. "Want to fill me in?"

"Someone called and told me to get to Castalgia's. She said something big went down, and if I don't get over there fast, the evidence will be destroyed."

"You can't go. It's a setup." His words were rushed. "They know you know something. They're trying lure you in and finish the job."

She said nothing.

He threw his hands in the air. "Okay, I know I'm not going to be able to talk you out of this, but I'm coming with you."

She let out a breath she hadn't even realized she was holding. "You don't have to come with me. I'll be fine."

He pulled her into an embrace. His hand caressed the side of her neck, and he drew her closer still. His lips met hers like a gentle whisper.

Dominique relaxed into the kiss. Just when she thought he was going to pull away, he intensified the kiss.

"You have no idea how crazy you make me." He ran his hand down her back. "I was out of my mind with worry when you were missing. There's no way I'm letting you walk into the lion's den alone."

Heat traveled up her cheeks. "After that kiss, you think I'm going to say no?"

He pulled his phone out. "Let's have the police meet us there."

She snatched the phone from his hands. "No cops. They'll show up with a hundred cars, sirens blaring. We have a better chance by ourselves."

The drive took less than fifteen minutes. Joe opened her door and put his hand on the small of her back. "Are you sure you're up to this, Dominique? It's not too late to change your mind and call the police."

"I need to see this story through to completion. It may never make the news, but it deserves to be told."

They walked hand-in-hand down the street. The streetlight cast shadows on the pavement, and the red and green lights of Castalgia's glowed up ahead. The closer they came to the restaurant, the louder her heart pounded in her ears. When they reached her car, she immediately noticed the broken window.

"Sorry about your window. We were desperate to find anything that might lead us to you." Joe opened the car door, snapped open the glove compartment, and pulled out a ring of keys and a flashlight. "Do you think we should go in the front or the back?"

She scanned the empty parking lot. "Let's use the front door. It doesn't look like anyone else is here."

At the front door, Joe searched through the ring of keys.

Dominique tested the handle. "It's unlocked."

"Why would someone leave the door unlocked if there's incriminating evidence in there?"

"Only one way to find out." She followed him into the restaurant. The glare from the lights in the parking lot provided a little illumination inside. Dominique surveyed the mess and gasped.

Tables and chairs lay in splintered shambles. Broken glass and garbage were strewn about the floor. "Someone trashed the place."

Joe grabbed her hand and led her through the overturned tables and chairs toward the back hallway. "What's that musty odor? I can't quite place it."

She turned the flashlight on and directed the light to the doorknob of Vinnie's office while Joe tried key after key.

The key finally turned on the fourth try. Dominique crowded behind Joe as he stepped into the office and fumbled for the light switch.

The office was just as she had remembered it. Whoever trashed the rest of the restaurant hadn't made it into the office. She walked around the desk and pulled on each drawer. All locked. "Think we should pry these open?"

"What exactly are we looking for?"

She plopped down in Vinnie's chair. "I think we're looking for files, or ledgers—something like that." She swiveled in the chair to face the back of the office. A set of mahogany bookshelves drew her attention. Her gaze drifted over a vast collection of family photos, leather bound classics, and a few expensive art pieces. "You ever hear the saying that if you want to hide something, put it in plain sight?"

Joe joined her. "You think whatever he's hiding is on one of these shelves?"

"Not on it, behind it." She stood in front of the last bookshelf. After examining it for a few minutes, she took a firm hold on both sides and pulled. Pain shot through her midsection. "This is heavier than I expected."

"Let me help you." Joe took hold of the sides and pulled. The bookcase folded like an accordion, revealing a four-drawer filing cabinet. "How did you know to look behind here?"

She laughed. "I was investigating a story a while ago, and the husband had a secret room behind a row of bookshelves." She pointed to the manufacturer's brass plate. "These shelves are made by the same company."

Dominique opened the first drawer and leafed through the manila folders stuffed inside. The number of local merchants who did business with Vinnie surprised her.

The second drawer contained a vast collection of video surveillance DVDs and other high tech recording equipment. The third drawer held two large ledgers. "I think we're getting warm." She lifted them out and set them on the floor, sure the information contained within them would put Vinnie away for a long time. "I wish we could take all of this stuff, but at least we can tell the police where to look."

She opened the bottom drawer. Only two folders? The first one was labeled *Prospects*. She opened it and gasped at the pictures of pregnant women. The top of each page had the woman's name, address, place of work, attending physician, and due date.

"Joe, look at this." She pointed to a page. Staring up at her was a picture of Cindy outside of a grocery store as she loaded the twins into the Land Rover. The hair on Dominique's arms stood on end. *He was targeting Cindy.*

Joe took the photos from her. "That's Cindy!" He leafed through the remaining pictures. "Lord, please protect these women."

Dominique perused the second folder, which was labeled *Placements*. "I think this is what we're looking for." She opened it and a chill ran up the length of her spine. A list of the names and addresses of the couples who had *adopted* the kidnapped babies. *Lord, please help me get these babies home.*

The shattering of glass from the front of the restaurant broke the silence.

Joe rushed to the door and placed his ear near the frame. "Grab what we need. I think we have company."

Her heart raced. Whoever was out there wasn't going to get their hands on this evidence. She scooped up the ledgers and file folders and darted to the door. "I'm right behind you."

He opened the door and smoke blew into the room. "Now I know what that smell was—lighter fluid. Someone wants this place completely destroyed." He stepped out into the roiling smoke that filled the hallway. "We have to go out the back." Taking hold of her free hand, he ran to the right. "This way! I see an exit sign."

Dominique tightened her grip on his hand. A charred taste filled her mouth, and her eyes burned. She tried to cover her mouth and nose with the ledgers, but her lungs burned as they filled with smoke. A cough racked her body, and one of the folders slipped from her grip. "Joe—" Her parched throat would not allow her to get out any more. She released his hand and kneeled as another coughing fit overtook her.

Where was that folder? She had to have it.

Heat surged down the hallway, warming her like a bonfire. Her head began to swim, and her eyes watered, blurring her sight.

Joe suddenly appeared beside her. "Duck your head lower to the floor and breathe. The air is fresher there."

She stared at him. For some reason, his words did not make sense.

Joe took her head in his hands and pulled her down. "Breathe, Dominique, breathe." He lowered his own head and sucked the cleaner air close to the floor.

"The folder—"

He snatched it from the floor, then pulled her up. "Hold your breath; we're almost out."

Several steps later, she found herself in the alley. Sweet air cleansed her lungs. She stopped and took in several deep breaths. Her coughing eased and she spit out the bitter taste in her mouth.

"Are you okay?" Joe leaned against the building and coughed several times.

"Joe Armstrong, you're an amazing man." She kissed him soundly on the lips.

His eyes met hers. "Let's get this evidence to Houston."

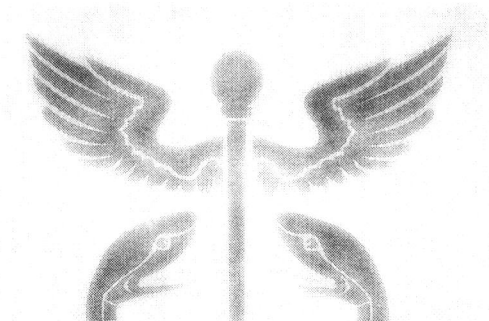

Chapter Forty-Four

Houston stood near the hospital bed and let out a sigh of relief. Despite the beeping of the monitors and the oxygen tubes, his dad slept peacefully. Even in the dim light, his father's face looked relaxed. His hands, though studded with small bandages from multiple attempts to start an IV, rested on his stomach. How could he look so tranquil after what he'd just been through? Houston longed for just a sliver of that peace.

His cell phone rang. A call this late? *I hope Travis isn't in trouble.* "This is Houston," he responded in a low voice.

"It's Joe. Where are you?"

"I'm still with Dad. Everything okay?"

"Yes and no. We're at Castalgia's, or what used to be Castalgia's. It's burning to the ground."

"What?" His voice rose, so he turned away from the bed.

"It's a long story. You'll be interested in what we found."

"What do you mean? You didn't break in there, did you?" His voice grew louder.

"It's complicated."

"Okay, now you have my curiosity up. What did you find?"

"I'll show you when we get there."

"Joe?"

"Yeah?"

"Be careful." He ended the call. The past twenty-four hours had proven to him that an entire life could change in a second.

"He depends on you. You know that, don't you?" His father's voice was so soft, Houston almost thought he'd imagined it.

"Hey, Dad. How are you feeling?"

Dad shifted slightly in the bed. "I've been better. How's Joe doing?"

"Things are all coming to a head. He and Dominique are on their way here with something important."

A shaky hand touched Houston's. "Good. That'll give us a few minutes to talk."

Why was it so difficult to listen to him? True to his word, Dad hadn't had a drink in years. Said he was sorry so many times. Hadn't he paid enough penance?

Pain filled his eyes. "I'm sorry, Houston. When you were growing up, I was a lousy father. My drinking destroyed everything I loved. It killed your mother and any relationship you and I had. Your mother forgave me. I can't expect you to do the same, but I do want you to know not a day goes by that I don't regret my drinking."

Houston grabbed his dad's hand. Images of his father standing in the line of fire remained fresh in his mind. The chains of unforgiveness dropped away. "I forgive you, Dad." Four little words. That's all it took for years of anger and resentment to dissolve.

His father swiped at the tears coursing down his cheeks. "Praise God. I can't tell you how much your forgiveness means to me. I have prayed for this moment for years. The Lord is so good."

First thing he mentions is God's goodness. For the first time, Houston felt free to speak with his dad about his faith. Since the day his father had come banging through the front door, Bible in hand, spouting that he'd been *saved*, Houston had resented his dad's newfound faith more than the drinking. At least drunken behavior was something familiar. But he hadn't slipped back into his old habits like Houston expected. "How did you get saved?"

His father reached a shaky hand for the cup of ice on the tray next to his bed. He spooned a few ice chips into his mouth, then was quiet for a moment. "You know those three crosses up on Mountview Hill? One day when Mike and I drove by them, he asked me point blank if I knew where I was going to spend eternity. I told him I didn't think anyone could know. Mike told me I was wrong. He said *we all choose our cross*."

Houston shifted in the chair. "What did he mean by that?"

"He said it's from the Bible. You ever hear the account of the two thieves next to Jesus? The thief on the right chose to believe, and Jesus told him he would be with Him that day in paradise. The thief on the left didn't believe and is spending eternity without the Lord."

"Just a choice? That seems too simple."

Dad nodded. "It is that simple. We all choose our cross. I choose to believe in Jesus's perfect sacrifice. I still make mistakes, but I'm so thankful I finally understood the truth."

How could he have missed it? Houston's heart quickened. Years of struggle melted away. He was through running. It was time to ask the Lord for forgiveness "You know, if anyone would have told me I'd be discussing spiritual things with my father, I would have told them they were crazy." He rubbed the back of his neck. "I'm still confused about some things and have a lot of questions."

"Ask me anything you'd like."

"If you're right about what is God doing with the pregnancy rates, why would He allow only Christians to conceive? I've seen nothing but destruction come from this. What could be His reason?"

"Would it help to know I'm as mystified as you? Maybe it's judgment for our attitude towards taking a pre-born life. Maybe it's so we'll value life. Or maybe he's building a generation of people to do His will." He coughed. "No matter His reason, we can trust Him. He sees the whole picture and orchestrates it all for the good of His kingdom. We may not understand it, but he promises that all things work to the good of those who love Him and are called according to His purposes."

Houston stared out the window. Red lights from an incoming ambulance flashed in the night. "I've struggled for months trying to make sense of the crazy things that have been happening."

"I noticed the problem four years ago when I was in the nursing home recovering from my stroke. Two nurses' aides came in my room. While they were working on me, one mentioned she was pregnant. When the other one asked what she was going to do, she said get rid of it." He snapped his fingers. "Just like that. No regret, no remorse. The baby was an inconvenience to her.

"She explained that she thought a baby would make her boyfriend commit to the relationship. When that didn't pan out, the baby had to go." He tugged at the oxygen tubes protruding from his nostrils. "It broke my heart. Several months later the news started reporting that pregnancies were down. But I noticed a lot of pregnant women at church. I started praying—and reading my Bible.

"I've spent a lot of time reading Scriptures. What stands out to me is the fact that God's ways are not our ways. He knows the value of life. He's the author of life." He wiped away a stray tear. "I'm worried about this generation. God doesn't make mistakes. What does the future hold for these children—this generation the Lord is bringing forth?"

Houston shook his head. He certainly had no answer. He just knew that if God wanted a group of people to love and serve Him, he wanted to be one of them.

Chapter Forty-Five

Travis maneuvered Vinnie's car along the winding country roads. He checked the rearview mirror again. Still no headlights. Cindy let out a cry, followed by a series of short, controlled breaths.

He placed a hand on her expanded belly. It felt hard and tight. "How far apart are the contractions?"

She groaned. "I've lost … track, but they're … pretty close." She continued her patterned breathing. "I think we … have a little over … an hour. Maybe less … since there's only … one baby."

He looked at the clock on the dashboard. "The highway entrance is about twenty miles away. After that, it's easy going."

"Travis?" Her tone held such a vulnerability it almost crushed him. "I forgive you. For everything. I don't know how we got … to this place. But I know you've done your best to protect your family from a horrible situation. And I know this … I still love you." She cried out again. "I think we should … take this chance … the Lord is offering us."

For the first time in a long time, he felt a small glimmer of hope. Travis squeezed her hand and released it. "I don't deserve you, Cindy." *I'm overwhelmed! Thank you, Lord.* "I don't know what to say." He smiled. "Thank you doesn't seem to quite cover it."

She reached for his hand. "Do you realize … how blessed we are?"

He let out a stilted laugh. "Well, that puts a different spin on it. I'm rushing my wife—who's in labor—to the hospital in a criminal's car. For all I know, the police are minutes behind us, waiting to arrest me for his murder."

"We're still blessed. Think about it. The Lord chose to bless us with another child while couples everywhere are trying everything and anything to conceive. He has a plan for us, Travis. I trust Him."

He checked the rearview mirror again. Was that a flash of movement behind them? If it was, the car didn't have its headlights on.

He squinted and took another look. Surely the police would have their headlights on and lights flashing.

Had Angelica found them?

Travis focused on the road. Only ten miles to the highway, where there would be more traffic. He checked his mirrors again.

The vehicle was gaining on them. A big car, maybe a Crown Victoria. He pressed on the accelerator.

"Everything okay?" Cindy asked as she shifted in her seat.

"We're being followed." His eyes were trained on the rearview mirror. "Better start praying." He looked forward in time to take a sharp curve.

Just on the other side of the bend, his headlights lit up a white cargo van blocking the road in front of them.

He slammed on the brakes.

The car's back end swung wide. It just barely missed a row of pines lining the roadside.

Travis jerked the wheel the other direction, but it did no good. The car spun out of control.

Cindy screamed.

Shattering glass was the last sound he heard.

Chapter Forty-Six

Houston eyed the two officers standing in front of him through narrowed eyes. Was he dreaming, or had it been their presence that woke him?

Sunlight peeked into the hospital waiting room from behind the curtain-clad windows. Curled up in a small recliner, Becky didn't even seem to notice the sliver of brightness that crossed her shoulders. Beyond her, Joe and Dominique sat on a couch, with her head resting on his shoulder.

Houston rose from the vinyl chair, stretching his sore muscles. "What can I do for you, gentlemen?"

The way they glanced at each other and the expression on their faces told Houston something was dreadfully wrong. The hairs on the back of Houston's neck stood up.

The first officer took his hat off. "I'm sorry to have to tell you this, Houston, but your brother-in-law Travis and his wife have been involved in an accident."

Houston's stomach clenched as he gently nudged Becky on the shoulder.

She sat up immediately. Her eyes widened when she noticed the police officers behind him. "What's wrong?"

Joe and Dominique stirred.

The taller officer repeated his words.

Becky stood beside Houston. "Are they all right?"

"I'm sorry, ma'am. They both were killed."

Houston's hands numbed and his ears rang. *This can't be.* It was as if he were watching some horrible scene play out in front of him. If only someone would shake him and wake him up.

Becky fell back into the recliner. "What happened?"

Joe rose next to Dominique. "There has to be some kind of mistake." He ran a rand through his hair. "Are you certain?"

Houston took several deep breaths. "What about the baby? Were they able to save the baby?"

The two officers looked at each other, then shook their heads. "We weren't aware there was a baby," the shorter officer said. He pulled a cell phone from a plastic evidence bag and handed it to Houston.

"What's this?" Houston didn't recognize the phone.

"I was first on the scene," he explained. "Right before he passed, Travis gave this to me. His last words were, *Please give this to Houston*. I have to tell you, he was driving Vinnie Fernandez's car. If this phone contains some type of evidence, I have to impound it."

"Why was Travis driving Vinnie's car?"

The policeman cleared his throat. "There's one more thing you need to know. Vinnie Fernandez was found dead in the trunk of the car Travis had at the cabin. Right now, Travis is the main suspect."

Becky shot out of her seat again. "Travis would never kill anyone!"

Houston took a step toward the officers. "The only thing Travis is guilty of—was guilty of ... " The admission made his stomach churn. "Travis was trying to protect his family. My brother-in-law was no murderer. He—"

Becky's sobbing cut short the rest of his words. "Find the baby, Houston. You have to find the baby." Wiping away the tears, she wrapped her arms around herself. "How are we going to tell the kids? What about Samuel?"

Dominique put her arms around Becky.

Houston struggled to shift his mind from the tragedy playing out in his personal life to his calm, logical, police mode. "Let's see what's on this phone."

He punched the buttons to bring up recent calls. He scrolled through the menu. "The last person to call was Angelica. She was just at the station, claiming to be an FBI agent. My guess is she's a fraud. Let's have headquarters run her phone number and see if we can get a location on it. If we're going to find the baby, we have to move fast."

"You can have a few minutes of privacy," Officer Dannon said. "We'll be waiting for you in the hall. We're going to need that phone." Both officers left the room.

Houston joined Becky, Dominique, and Joe in a huddled circle. Finally, he broke the silence. "I don't know how, but somehow the Lord will get us through this."

Becky looked up at him through eyes swollen with tears. "The Lord is already helping us. You don't know how long I've waited to hear you speak those words." She wrapped her arms tightly around his waist. "Please be careful. I don't want you to be her next victim."

* * *

Two hours later, Houston stared outside the passenger-side window of an unmarked police car parked outside the Hilton Hotel in downtown Cincinnati. He noted all the entrances and exits. *We don't have enough backup here.* If something went wrong, Angelica would get away and they might never find the baby.

Patience ... you have to be patient.

Ten minutes later, two unmarked cars and two black and whites pulled up next to the police cruiser Houston sat in. He got out of the car, secured the police-issued Glock on his belt, and checked the backup weapon in a leg holster on his left calf.

The officers gathered between the cars. The officer in charge asked, "You sure you're not too close on this one?"

Houston stuffed aside his mounting grief and fear. "I'm good. Let's do it."

The four officers pushed through the front doors of the hotel, with Houston the last man in. Eight more closed off the back exit.

Please let us have the element of surprise.

The light on the GPS one of the officers clutched in his hand blinked rapidly. Angelica was close by. He turned the unit off and stuffed it in his front pocket.

Thick carpet ran the length of the long hall, with more than twenty doors dotting the walls. Which one did Angelica hide behind?

He stepped softly down the hall, keeping close to the wall.

Muffled voices came from the behind the seventh door on the right. The officer in charge pressed his ear up to the oak door. After a moment he nodded to the rest of the men. This was it. Angelica was behind that door.

Houston and the others surrounded the door. In one fluent move, the officer in charge twisted the doorknob and pushed the door open. He took several steps in and circled to the right. His team filed in behind him.

Two large gentlemen stood against the wall behind Angelica, who sat with a smiling, middle-aged couple at a conference table. The woman across from Angelica clutched a tiny baby in her arms.

Houston charged towards the woman. "That baby needs medical attention."

Angelica's guards stepped in front of him. In tandem, they reached into their jackets.

"Keep your hands where we can see them," the officer in charge called out.

Both men raised their hands.

Houston stood over the woman clutching the baby to her chest and held his arms out.

Her glare drifted from Angelica to Houston. "You'll find our paperwork is in order. You can't do this."

He kept his arms extended. "I don't care what paperwork you have. This transaction is illegal."

With trembling hands, she handed the baby to him.

Houston pushed the blanket away from the newborn's face. The baby was perfectly formed. A tiny nose and lips, and the same birthmark Cindy had on her left cheek. He sucked in his breath. The baby's eyes were identical to Travis's.

He swallowed the salty taste in his mouth. "I think this little baby wants to go home." Houston drew the little one to his chest and breathed in the fresh scent.

* * *

The hospital room in the cardiac care unit was twice as large as the ICU rooms. Samuel held a worn Bible in his hands. "Psalm 46:1. The Lord is a stronghold, an ever-present help in times of trouble."

The words soothed Dominique's aching soul. How did Samuel do it? His faith was rock-solid. He'd just lost a daughter, a son-in-law, and possibly a grandchild. Yet he clung to the Lord. What a privilege to be included in their private family grief.

Joe draped his arm around her shoulders, and warmth spread up her back and down her arms. She leaned closer to him and kissed his cheek. "Any word from Houston?"

"Not yet—"

Houston burst into the room, carrying a tiny bundle in his arms. "Everyone, I'd like you to meet the newest member of our family. She doesn't have a name yet, but I know she wants to meet everyone."

Becky and Joe crowded Houston, anxious to get a look at the precious baby girl. Dominique joined the circle.

She was tiny, but perfect!

Houston let them look for a few moments, then approached the bed and lowered the newborn. Samuel peered at the bundle.

The baby cooed and wriggled in the blanket.

Dominique sucked in a breath and bit her bottom lip. Travis and Cindy would have fallen in love with this beautiful little baby. But she'd never know her mother's voice or have the chance for her dad to walk her down the aisle.

Becky wiped at her tears, and Houston made no effort to stem the flow down his cheeks. Joe stood next to his dad, hand on Samuel's shoulder.

Samuel broke the silence. "What a miracle. Life is such a miracle. Every life is a gift from the Lord."

Becky held out her arms, and Houston placed the little girl in them. Their eyes met. Becky kissed the baby. "She's beautiful!"

After several minutes, Joe stepped in. "Hey, don't hog her."

Becky laughed and handed him the baby. He pulled her close to his chest. "Hey baby girl, I'm your Uncle Joe. All the kids like me the best."

"Hey!" Houston spouted.

The laughter helped. When it was Dominique's turn, Joe placed the baby in her outstretched arms. She held her up and kissed the baby's cheek. Soft, like velvet. "What should we name you? We can't keep calling you baby girl."

Samuel cleared his throat. "May I hold her?"

She looked to Joe.

He nodded. "Just be careful to keep her away from his incision."

Dominique placed the baby in Samuel's arms, and the family gathered around the bed. Samuel's gentle caress trailed from the top of the baby's head to her tiny fingers.

"You look just like your mommy did at this age." Samuel held her closer still. "I'm sorry you'll never know your parents this side of heaven, but don't you worry. You have two brothers, two sisters, and a whole room full of people to love you." His glance encompassed everyone gathered around his bed.

"Does anyone know what names Travis and Cindy were considering?" Samuel asked.

"I don't think they had a chance to think that far, or if they did, they didn't tell anyone." Houston paused for a few seconds. "I think I know the perfect name. Grace. God's gift."

Samuel brought the baby's hand to his lips and kissed her tiny fist. "Well, Grace, it's an honor to meet you." He remained silent for several minutes, his gaze beaming down at the newborn. Then he held the newborn girl up. "I don't know what God has in store for her, but of this I am sure—every life is a precious gift, but this one, I will especially treasure."

Epilogue

Eighteen Months Later

Candles lit the altar. Friends and family filled the pews on both sides of the aisle, and the smell of lavender permeated the air.

"I now pronounce you man and wife. What God has joined together, let no man put asunder. You may kiss the bride."

Dominique leaned into Joe's embrace. She only pulled away from his kiss when their guests started laughing. "I think they're ready for the reception, Mr. Armstrong."

"Is that so, Mrs. Armstrong? Well, maybe I'm not ready." He went in for another kiss.

Houston cleared his throat. "Okay, little brother, save the honeymoon for later."

Dominique and Joe laughed. Were her feet even touching the floor? They turned and faced their friends and family. John and Emily Sanderson sat in the front row, their son sitting quietly between them. Dominique's throat swelled. Reuniting them with their infant son had been one of the highlights of her life.

Calvin smiled at her from the third row. He'd traveled all the way from Florida. He'd lost his job after helping her upload her story on the pregnancy crisis to YouTube. The video had received millions of hits, and she still received comments both positive and negative. *Use it for your glory, Lord.*

On the other side of the aisle, Samuel sat in the front row, tears streaming down his face. Dominique guessed the tears were a mixture of happiness for her and Joe and grief knowing two family members would never celebrate with them again. *We'll celebrate in heaven, Samuel. What a glorious reunion that will be.*

She smiled when Becky waved a fan in front of her face and rubbed her expanded belly. One more month and they all would meet the newest family member. Houston and Becky had willingly accepted their role as guardians when they discovered Cindy and Travis had listed them in their will. They were somehow making the adjustment from zero kids to five.

Joe grabbed Dominique's hand. "You ready?"

She smiled back at him. "To live the rest of my life with you? You bet!"

He escorted her down the aisle and out into the waiting car.

* * *

Several guests had left, but many had remained to enjoy the music and dancing. The kids were out on the dance floor, twirling and swaying to the country tune. Houston sat next to Becky. "Would you like to dance?"

She laughed. "I think you're going to have to ask one of the girls. I'm pooped."

He ran a hand over her belly. "Have I told you I love you today?" He brushed her cheek with a kiss. "You're beautiful."

"I certainly don't feel beautiful."

Houston straightened as Robert and Monica Davenport approached. Even from a distance they looked like some polished politician and his wife—the kind you see on a television commercial begging for your vote. "Did you know they were coming?" he asked Becky.

"Who?"

"Travis's sister and her husband. I didn't know they were going to be here." A chill traveled up his spine, even as he stood to greet them. "Robert, Monica. Thanks for coming." *Their smiles are plastic too.*

Robert handed Houston an envelope.

"What's this?"

Monica clicked her nails on the table. "Read it and get back to us."

As soon as they walked away, Houston ripped open the envelope and read the paper.

Becky touched his arm. "I don't have a good feeling about this."

He clenched the paper in his fist. "Dear, Lord." He sat down. "We need a lawyer. They're suing us for custody of the kids."

The End

Dear Reader,

I hope you enjoyed my story. If you want to help spread the word about it, please leave a review at Amazon, Goodreads, or other site of your choice. And be sure to recommend it to your friends!

If you want to hear when the next book comes out, sign up for my newsletter at ColleenScottFiction.com

Let's keep in touch!

Colleen Scott

Acknowledgements

There are so many people who have helped me in my journey to publication, I don't know where to start. Dave, thank you so much for all of your love and support. You never stopped believing my dream could come true. I love how when we are on our dates and perusing the bookshelves at the bookstore, you always make a space where "Scott, Colleen" would go and say to me, "This is where they'll put your books." I am so blessed to be your wife.

Jeremy, Curtis, Joy and Colby … I love writing, but my greatest blessing is being your mom. Thank you so much for believing in me. For helping with things around the house so I could write. It's a lot of fun strategizing plots with you, and coming up with opening lines. I love each of you so much!

Mom, thank you for believing in this day, and for reading all of my first drafts. (I know they needed work, but you encouraged me anyway.) You've passed on your love of reading to me, and that blossomed into a love of writing. Thank you for being such an example of a godly woman. I love you.

My family: We've lost a lot, but we are so blessed. The Lord has blessed us with so much love and laughter. I love each of you so much.

Greg, my first editor. It wasn't an easy job, but you did a great job!

Beth Loughner, thank you for reading my very first manuscript and encouraging me to keep on writing.

Dawn Kinzer, thank you for your help in getting this manuscript ready for publication.

Suzanne & Phyllis, thank you for taking a chance on this debut novelist. You're both a lot of fun to work with.

Linda Glaz, thank you for believing in my story. I am blessed to have you as my agent.

Ladies of the Light Brigade, thank you for praying for me, and for sharing the writing journey. You're each so special to me, and I'm thankful to be part of this group.

FictionFlurry members – thank you for all of your help in critiquing the first draft. Keep writing!

Michele Buchholz, I enjoy our writing/brain storming meetings. Thank you for all of your help.

ACFW Scribes Critique group. Thank you for helping shape this manuscript. I so appreciate your insight.

Thank you also to the many friends who I've met along the way, and who have encouraged me.

Thank you, Lord, for giving me the love of writing, and a story to tell. Praying that my readers will come to know you.

Made in the USA
Charleston, SC
22 October 2015